It Was a Riot

Daniel Hall

Copyright © [2024] by [Daniel Hall]

All rights reserved.

No portion of this book may be reproduced in any form without written permission from the publisher or author, except as permitted by U.K. copyright law.

Dedication

To my dear boys, Albie and Archie,
Whilst I strive to avoid embodying the character Lenny in this book, I acknowledge that I share some of his negative traits as a father, and for that, I apologise. I have always tried to be the best dad I can be, even though I know I fall short at times.

And to anyone who reads this book, I offer my heartfelt thanks. There are millions of books out there, so for you to choose mine to read means a lot. And it's not just words; I really am grateful.

Author's Note On Language

Please note that as the book is set in England, it is written in British English and uses British words. For example, whilst in North America you may call it an Emergency Room, in the United Kingdom we call it Accident and Emergency or A&E. In terms of spelling, this means words such as *mum* are used instead of *mom*. The author acknowledges that certain readers from across the pond might find this rather unsettling. Although the author wants to please all readers as he really desires 5-star reviews, he did learn English in the very land that birthed the language and thus holds the linguistic high ground. Nevertheless, as a gesture of goodwill, here are a few words spelled in a non-standard English style to provide this book with a touch of familiarity:

mom

garbage

color

soccer

apologize

Contents

1. Chapter One   1
2. Chapter Two   4
3. Chapter Three   12
4. Chapter Four   19
5. Chapter Five   29
6. Chapter Six   38
7. Chapter Seven   47
8. Chapter Eight   56
9. Chapter Nine   63
10. Chapter Ten   70
11. Chapter Eleven   79
12. Chapter Twelve   89
13. Chapter Thirteen   99
14. Chapter Fourteen   107

15. Chapter Fifteen — 114
16. Chapter Sixteen — 123
17. Chapter Seventeen — 134
18. Chapter Eighteen — 141
19. Chapter Nineteen — 150
20. Chapter Twenty — 158
21. Chapter Twenty-One — 167
22. Chapter Twenty-Two — 173
23. Chapter Twenty-Three — 182
24. Chapter Twenty-Four — 192
25. Chapter Twenty-Five — 200
26. Chapter Twenty-Six — 206
27. Chapter Twenty-Seven — 218
28. Chapter Twenty-Eight — 228
29. Chapter Twenty-Nine — 238
30. Chapter Thirty — 245
31. Chapter Thirty-One — 253
32. Chapter Thirty-Two — 263
33. Chapter Thirty-Three — 269
34. Epilogue — 278
35. Reviews — 280

Chapter One

London, 1990

I drag my weary feet up to the courtroom dock, feeling my heart thudding like a sledgehammer in my chest. The room is dim, the air thick with the incessant humming of speculation. With every step, I can feel eyes on me, heavy with expectation, and hear the low buzz of murmurs and whispers. These onlookers know what this means for me better than I do, and it weighs on them as heavily as it does on me.

As I peer up towards the judge, my gut wrenches at the sight of her. She's raised high above us all on a towering platform, and her steely glare rains down upon us with an unyielding command. Her eyes express a powerful warning—she is not one to be toyed with or swayed by flowery language or lies.

"Order in the court!" The bailiff's booming voice echoes through the courtroom, commanding everyone's attention. I tremble as I attempt to stand and face the judge. She stares at me intently from beneath her stern brows.

"You wanted to read a statement to the jury, Mr Turner?" she inquires.

"Yes, Your Honour," I say, my voice hoarse and strangely unfamiliar. Sweat drips from my hands, and the papers I hold in them are becoming damp from the moisture. Some words smudge from the sweat.

My gaze wanders the room, looking for a familiar face. I spot my mother, Linda, sitting in the front row. Her brown eyes sparkle as they meet mine, and she nods in approval. Her expression is stoic yet calm, her grey hair pulled back into a tight bun, and her hands gracefully folded together in her lap.

I look down at the papers, the words going in and out of focus. It's like I'm trying to read from the reflection of a puddle. I blink, attempting to bring the words into focus. Even without looking, I can feel the disapproving stares of the onlookers burning into my skin. The judgement. Each of them, I am sure, has already condemned me.

At last, I turn to face the jury. Twelve impassive faces stare back at me from the jury box. It's impossible to know what they are feeling or thinking, if they are leaning towards acquittal or conviction. But this is my chance to show them another side to my story: to convince them that even if I am not innocent, I am not guilty.

I take a deep breath to steady myself, and eventually, the words become clear. Whispers in the room cease as I begin to read.

My voice ricochets off the walls of the hushed courtroom, reverberating with a thunderous intensity. "Ladies and gentlemen of the jury! I stand before you today as a man accused but also as a person who wishes to make things right: to the victim and his family, to these witnesses, to you as my judges, and to the world at large."

I look up, my gaze darting from face to face. The jurors are like motionless wax figures, their eyes pinned unblinkingly on me. It feels like the air has been sucked out of the room, and even the walls are breathing down my neck.

"There has been much misunderstanding and prejudice in this courtroom," I continue. "The prosecution has resorted to cheap stereotypes and fear-mongering vitriol to convince you of my guilt. This, I'm sure, has led many of you to make incorrect assumptions about me. And while those assumptions might be irrelevant to the case at hand, I do not wish them to define me."

I want to look at Mum, to see her reassuring gaze again, but I force myself to remain facing the jury.

"I don't deny my actions on that fateful night, but I do want to explain myself and correct some of the misinterpretations about me. I have made many poor decisions in life. Most of them were the result of chasing the approval of the wrong person, the person who should have been helping me make the right decisions—my father."

I take a deep breath and begin to tell my story.

Chapter Two

I was born in Dagenham in 1958, a deprived area in East London famous for its large Ford factory. My father, Leonard "Lenny" Turner, was one cog in this industrial beast, working long hours at the assembly line with the rough hands and gruff manners of a man who had known nothing but hardship.

Our home, a modest three-bedroom terraced house on Rogers Road, stood about a mile and a half from the factory. My parents had bought the house during the craze of new development during the postwar years when a house was easy to afford on a modest working-class salary. My mum, Linda, was a nurse before Lenny swept her off her feet. But when I arrived, she hung up her scrubs to become a devoted housewife—until our family started to struggle again. That's when she donned her old blue overalls once more, this time stitching car seat cushions in the Ford factory.

One of my earliest memories is from when I was four or five. It was late at night, and I was at home, playing with the toy fire engine my dad had given me for Christmas. I was in the small living room, the fire engine bumping over the thick, frayed carpeting, when I heard a commotion outside. It sounded like someone shouting, and then there was a loud banging on the front door. Being a curious kid, I went to investigate what the noise was.

Mum, who had been waiting for my dad to get home, was smoking at the kitchen table. She stared straight ahead past the clock as if she couldn't hear anything. The banging started again, and she jolted as if just hearing it. Quickly, she rose from the table and went to the door.

My father stumbled at the moment the door was opened. His eyes were red. There were bruises on his face, a cut over his right eyebrow that was bleeding into his beard. My heart skipped a beat as I watched him stumble inside and roar something about how he'd misplaced his keys.

"Lenny! What happened?" Mum gasped, seizing his arm and leading him to the kitchen table. He leaned heavily on her, half-laughing, half-shouting, his words slurred. It was clear he was very drunk.

"Fuckin' Chelsea cunts," he spat, wiping blood from his face as he sat down on the chair she had just vacated. "Coming over West Ham thinking they are the boys in London. We had to show them who the real top dogs are."

My father's swearing had not yet ceased, but my mother paid little attention. Instead, she flew to the cabinet beneath the sink, returning with a first-aid kit. Unseen in the doorway, I watched her sit by his side while he muttered under his breath, "Fuckin' Chelsea rent boys." She dabbed at the cut above his eyebrow and plastered it cleanly.

With her lips pursed, she said, "There's nothing you can do about the bruising except for cold presses. I think we have some peas in the freezer."

She rose again, and that's when she saw me. Immediately, her expression became a scowl.

"You should be asleep, Eddy," she said sharply. My father looked up at her words, his eyes fastening on me. I took an instinctive step back. Up close and backlit by the kitchen light, his bruised skin and bloodied beard were even more frightening. The smell was strong and metallic, and it made my stomach curl. I wanted to run, to get as far away from him as possible, but before I could, he called out to me.

"Come over here, son," he barked, and I didn't dare to resist him. Coming to stand before him, I stared up into the black-and-blue face, the eyes watery and unfocused, the nose broken from too many fights and the sinister smile. I shrank back, and he grabbed my arm. "Do you know what happened to me today?" he demanded.

"Don't scare him," my mum warned as she slid back into her seat, holding the bag of peas.

"Fear is good for him," my old man insisted. "Teaches him how to be brave."

My mother frowned but didn't argue.

"Answer me," Dad said, shaking me slightly. "Do you know what happened to me?"

Wordlessly, I shook my head.

"West Ham might be shit on the pitch, but we're the best off it," he explained, and his voice gentled just a little. "We're West Ham, and don't you ever forget it, son. That means when anyone ever gives it about West Ham or East London at all, we don't take it. That's true of anyone, but especially those Millwall, Chelsea or Tottenham cunts."

"Leonard! Don't cuss in front of him!" Mum interjected, but Dad ignored her.

"You understand?" he said, his eyes not leaving mine. "Your old man was defending the club today, and we done 'em like we do 'em all." Then he burst into song. "Fuck 'em all, fuck 'em all, fuck the Chelsea, the Tottenham, and the Millwall, we are the West Ham, and we are the best, we are the West Ham, so fuck all the rest!"

My father took the bag of peas from my old dear and slapped it over the right side of his face. As he did, his left eye closed, and he leaned back in the chair, letting out a sigh of contentment.

My gaze was transfixed by the kit before my mother. The usual paraphernalia—plasters and antiseptic wipes—stared familiarly back at me. But there was one object, which I would later learn was a stethoscope, that seemed out of place between the other mundane items. It fascinated me, but I dared not touch it. Somehow, I felt that if I kept staring at it and not at my father, his shouting and swearing would stop. That I'd be safe.

My father, Lenny, meanwhile, was still talking.

"You should be proud of your old man," he said. Wrenching my gaze away from the object in the first-aid kit, I nodded. "Someday, you'll be a man, too, and you'll follow in my footsteps."

He slapped me hard on the back, buckling my knees, and shook his head. "Now off to bed, son. Let your mother clean me up."

That night, I lay awake for a long time, thinking about his words. Someday, you'll be a man too. Each time the word man floated through my head, it was accompanied by the sight of his twisted, bruised, bloodied face.

It wasn't the last time I saw my father return bloodied from a football match, far from it. Whenever West Ham was playing, my father was out late with the other hooligans, drinking and getting into fights. If they were playing Millwall, he was bound to come home looking close to death's door.

The worst came only a year later. I must have been six and nearing the end of reception because Sharon and I were thick as thieves by then, and she was over at my house. We met on the playground—me with a chunk of chalk in hand, drawing outnumbered triangles to play hopscotch while the other boys were busy being naughty.

The evening my old man came home drunk and cut up, Sharon was over, and he was angrier than usual. More often than not, my dad returned in a good mood, even if he'd received a beating. He took out his anger on fans from opposing teams, so by the time he got home, any frustration that was pent up inside of him during the week had gone.

That evening, however, he was furious, and when he collapsed through the front door, my mother screamed.

Sharon and I were playing outside when we heard the scream. We looked at each other, alarmed. "What happened?" Sharon whispered, her eyes wide. "Did your mummy see a spider?"

But I knew it was my dad. It was always my dad.

As we came in the back door, I almost screamed as well. Down Dad's face, from above his left eyebrow to his cheek, was a long, deep gash. Not just a cut from being punched in the face, but a gashing, gaping wound, as if someone had slashed him open with a knife.

By now, my mother's stalwart calmness had returned. She no longer looked like someone who had screamed bloody murder at the sight of her husband bleeding from a knife wound. She was sitting at the kitchen table, her usual spot, while my father sat in front of her. The only sign of her distress was her shaking hands. Otherwise, her face was placid. In years to come, I would come to recognise that look on the faces of all the doctors and nurses I worked with: the look of someone who has to shut down all emotion to treat their patient calmly and carefully.

Dad, meanwhile, was still muttering insults under his breath. Every so often, he would flinch as another jolt of pain went through him.

Unusually, it wasn't just Mum's first-aid kit in front of her; she also had her sewing kit out. As Sharon and I watched, our mouths open and our eyes wide, my mother threaded a needle, then turned to Lenny.

"This is going to hurt," she said. He grimaced but nodded. She raised the needle, her hands no longer shaking.

That's when I knew what was about to happen. If I'd been older, I might have told Sharon to look away. My mother brought the needle to Father's face, and then she began to sew his skin closed.

The sight should have made me sick. It should have made both of us sick. We were six years old, gaping in awe as my mother stitched my father up like she would a hem on a pair of trousers. To his credit, my dad didn't scream or moan about it. His jaw was clenched, his eyes were closed, and his face was red, but he didn't complain.

Someday, you'll be a man, too. Those words would plague me for the rest of my life.

Mum finished stitching the wound. She then cleaned the skin again with an antiseptic wipe. "You really should go to hospital," she said, frowning with anger and worry. "I did the best I could, but their stitches would be better…"

"I'm not going to hospital over a little knife wound," my father scoffed. Only when a tear ran down my mum's face did his posture soften.

"It'll be okay," he said, reaching across the table and taking her hand. "It's only superficial."

"One of these days, you're going to get yourself killed," she snapped, pulling her hand away.

Dad shook his head. "Don't be stupid. I won't get killed. It's just a bit of fun with the boys."

"You don't know that, Lenny! What kind of example are you setting for our son?"

"I'm showing him what it means to be a man," he said, his voice rising. For a long moment, they just looked at each other, saying nothing. Then my old man stood up. He stretched and yawned as if attempting to prove he was fine.

"Now, why don't you get me a beer?" he asked. Mum didn't answer. She stood and stormed out of the kitchen, leaving my dad staring after her, expressionless. After several moments, he got a beer out of the fridge, went to the front room, and began watching TV as if nothing had happened.

Slowly, Sharon and I crept into the kitchen. I'm not sure what we hoped to find there. I think we both felt a morbid curiosity to see the sewing instrument that had been turned into a brutal torture device to stitch up skin.

At the table, we stopped and stared down at the needle. Blood still glistened on its tip. Funny how, in those days, blood wasn't something to fear. I can't remember if we touched it, but it's possible we did.

The black stethoscope I'd seen in my mother's first-aid kit was also there, tucked under some plasters and gauze. I fished it out, and Sharon and I took turns examining it.

"What is it, do you think?" I asked quietly. I didn't want my old man to hear us and come back into the kitchen.

"Doctor Aggarwal uses one of these," she whispered back. Then her eyes lit up. "Let's play doctor!" Sharon took the stethoscope, and her eyes centred on mine as she slowly positioned the wishbone-like end towards me. I felt her soft fingers brush against my skin, carefully manoeuvring the two knobs so that they fit snugly in my ears. In an instant, the world grew distant, and the sound dulled to a muffled whisper. With her free hand, she pressed the silver knob against her chest, her gaze unwavering. "Listen," she said calmly.

Sharon's voice was strange and mysterious through the stethoscope, deeper and louder than it usually was and seeming to emanate through her chest. It made me giggle, and she moved the silver knob around as if searching for the right place.

And that's when I heard something even more mysterious. It was the steady, arrhythmic pounding of something... inside... of Sharon. I looked up, astonished, and she grinned.

"Can you hear it?"

"Yes," I breathed. I didn't want her to speak. All I wanted to hear was the *ba-bump ba-bump ba-dump* sound of the unseen organ buried deep in her chest.

The thunderous beat of the human heart pounded in my ears as I hovered close. Its rhythm was so powerful and raw that it left an imprint on my mind that would forever remain. Even after listening to thousands of hearts in the years to come, I will never forget this very first one.

Chapter Three

"Doctor" quickly became Sharon's and my favourite pastime. Usually, only girls wanted to indulge in our imaginative medical games; most of the time, the lads found it too tame for their liking. Only if we concocted a particularly gory injury or fake blood would some wander over to join in on the fun. Every game went the same way: Sharon or one of her friends would come to me with an imaginary affliction that I, as the doctor, would need to "treat" by examining them on one of the park benches within our school grounds. This always brought shrieks of laughter from those involved.

"My mummy says that boys aren't supposed to touch you," my friend Lucy said one time as I checked her stomach for the "pains" she'd been having there. "Except doctors, she says. They're allowed to touch your body."

"Lay still, please," I said, frowning with feigned concentration. "If you move, the wound could tear, and then all your guts will spill out."

"Ewwwwwww!" Lucy exclaimed in delight, wriggling around. I tried to hold her still, but she looked at me with a suspicious glare. "Boyfriends can touch your body too, Mummy says," she said. "But only when I'm eighteen… Are you my boyfriend, or are you my doctor?"

I was unsure how to reply, so I simply replied, "I'm your doctor, so it's alright." She seemed unsatisfied with this answer and suggested I be her boyfriend instead.

"You need stitches," I stated, ignoring her comment. "Let's sew you up." I opened up my backpack and fished out a hair clip stolen from my mum that I liked to pretend was a needle. The moment Lucy saw the hair clip, she screamed.

"Nooooo, Eddy, you aren't actually going to sew me up, are you?" she shrieked.

"Remain still if you want to keep that wound from getting infected!" I bluffed, not sure if her cries were of genuine fear or part of our game. Boys close by playing with a football stopped their game and looked over at us curiously.

Some instinct told me I had to get Lucy to stop screaming. Placing one hand on her stomach, I used my other to turn her head towards me. "If I say I'm your boyfriend, will you lie still?"

Slowly, her eyes wide, Lucy nodded.

"Alright then, I'm your boyfriend."

Lucy broke into a wide smile. "Ohhh, Eddy, I've always wanted a boyfriend! Mummy will be so happy!"

I pretended to sew her up, declared she was all better, and watched her scamper away, crowing loudly that she had been saved from the brink of death. Twenty minutes later, the entire school seemed to have discovered that we were now boyfriend and girlfriend.

I had thought little about having Lucy as a girlfriend until later that week when Sharon was at my house, and we were playing doctor. Sharon had "broken her leg" falling from a tree, and I had to make a splint. My mum, Linda, had shown me how to do this the last time

Sharon pretended to injure her arm. Sharon loved exaggerating her pain, while I relished the skill of creating the perfect splint for her injury. We would search around the estate for sticks, then steal tea towels out of the kitchen to wrap around the areas of her body that were supposedly broken.

After wrapping her injured leg in a bandage, Sharon and I sat in the grass together. I asked if she was still in pain, and when she didn't answer immediately, I looked up to see why. Her face was pink, and her eyes were red. In a panic, I asked if the bandage was too tight.

"I thought I was your girlfriend," Sharon said, squirming slightly.

"What do you mean?" I asked quickly.

"Lucy says she's your girlfriend. But I thought I was? I come over to play every day after school. Lucy never comes over. We barely even play with her!"

At a loss for what to say to this, I said nothing, staring at the ground and holding still. Sharon leaned towards me. "Don't you like me?"

The question made my stomach curl with nerves. It felt like when our teacher asked me a question and I didn't know the answer. "Of course I like you," I said finally. And it was true. I did like Sharon. She was my best friend. And yet, I had a feeling I had misunderstood her question.

Sharon flushed, then smiled triumphantly. "Good," she said, settling back on the grass. "I'm your girlfriend. You'll also have to sit next to me at lunch and hold my hand." Sharon beamed. "That's what Mummy says boyfriends do."

I wasn't sure how I was supposed to be Sharon's and Lucy's boyfriends, but I supposed I could just sit between them at lunch. I wanted to ask if that was allowed, but since Sharon was much more knowledgeable on the subject than I was, and my ignorance embarrassed me, I kept quiet.

We continued to play until the chill of sunset descended, and Sharon said her mum was expecting her back home. By this time, my own parents were home. I could hear my mother's frantic singing as she rushed to prepare dinner. My dad, meanwhile, had dragged a lawn chair outside and was baking in the sun while gripping a beer can tightly in his hand. He seemed to ignore Sharon and me playing and never showed any interest in us—until I went to the toilet. I'd left the door slightly open, and as I finished drying my hands with a scratchy towel, I heard my father ask my mum in an accusing tone, "Does Eddy always play with girls?"

If anyone else had mentioned it, I wouldn't have minded much. But when it came from my father, I could tell he thought something was wrong with me playing with girls. I stood still, paralysed by fear from my father's question that echoed through my house. The two of them were in the kitchen, just around the corner from the toilet, but my father wasn't trying to keep his voice down.

"Most of his little friends are girls, yes," my mum replied more quietly.

Dad didn't answer her for a long moment, and then he said, "And do they always play those girly games?"

"What girly games?"

"Nurse or whatever."

My mum laughed. "Is that girly? I thought they were playing doctor, and doctors are always men."

My old man replied with something I couldn't hear, but it wasn't hard to hear the raised voice through which my mum responded. "I've never seen you complain about the role of a doctor when you've needed one!"

"I just don't like him playing just with girls," my father continued bullishly. "Why doesn't he have any mates that are boys like a normal kid would?"

"He's only seven," Mum protested. Plates and glasses clinked against each other as she pulled them down from the press. "They don't differentiate between boys and girls at that age. I'd be worried if he were only playing with girls at ten, but it's just the age he's at..."

"It better be." The darkness in my father's voice sent a chill up my spine, and I decided to make my presence known before he could say anything else.

Pushing the door open roughly, I ran down the hallway, letting my feet slap against the lino to announce my presence. When I arrived in the kitchen doorway, my dad didn't look surprised to see me.

"Eddy, be a dear and put these on the table for me, will you?" Mum said, smiling at me as she handed me several glasses.

Once we were seated at the table, Mum dished up the food. I sat still, staring at the plate in front of me, trying to think of something to reassure my father. Even then, I knew that playing with girls, or "girly" games, was wrong; that I had to earn his respect by proving... something. What it was I had to prove, I wasn't exactly sure.

Then, the look on Sharon's face when she asked if I was her boyfriend floated through my mind, and an idea occurred to me.

Looking up at my father, who was chewing methodically, I blurted out, "I have a girlfriend."

Dad looked up, surprised. "What was that, son?"

"I have a girlfriend," I repeated. My face flushed, but I held eye contact. "Her name is Sharon."

My old man watched me for a moment, his eyes narrowed. "Is that the girl who was here today?" he asked finally.

I nodded. "Yes. Actually..." I hesitated, unsure of whether this helped prove I wasn't girly. "I have two girlfriends."

"Two?" Dad's eyebrows shot up into his forehead. He glanced at my mother, who was watching this exchange with a tight expression. "Two girlfriends?"

"Yes. Lucy and Sharon."

Dad's face broke into a wide grin. "Well, well... I must say, I wasn't expecting that. My boy already a lady's man. Can't say I'm too shocked you take after me, but well... I wasn't sure you had it in you." He reached across the table and ruffled my hair. "Just be careful, son. It can be hard balancing two birds." He laughed as if he'd said something very clever, although when I looked at my mum, she wasn't smiling.

Lenny was still chuckling as he returned to his food. Then he looked back up. "Is that what this 'playing doctor' is all about? Getting to touch girls?"

His look was so expectant that even though I wasn't sure what he meant, I still nodded.

My old man laughed again. "Good boy! It's never too early to learn how to seduce a woman..."

"Lenny..." my mum began. "Isn't he a bit young for all that?"

"He's not too young," Dad said, waving a hand dismissively. "Anyway, what else can you expect from a Turner? Takes after his old man, that's for sure..."

He locked his gaze on me. With a slight tremble of emotion in his voice, he said, "I'm proud of you, son." It was the first time my father had ever used those words. I could barely contain my joy and noticed my mum smiling too. I grinned from ear to ear for the rest of dinner. Dad even let me have two helpings of dessert as if it was a celebration.

My voice shook with nerves as I informed them of the situation. Both stared at me, and Sharon began to cry. Lucy started as well, and soon enough, we had landed in the headmistress's office. Our parents were called, and as Mum walked me home later, she seemed relieved.

"Lucy's and Sharon's mums and I have decided you're too young to be dating," she said. "Your father will just have to accept it." I kept quiet, but secretly, I was relieved as well. Balancing two girlfriends seemed more trouble than it was worth.

Despite the disastrous ending to my first romance, Dad was still proud of me. And at the end of the week, he stepped through our door later than usual, clasping a box wrapped in brown paper. When my mother inquired what it contained, he smiled and set it in front of me.

"It's for the lad."

Gifts seldom came my way aside from Christmas and my birthday. We weren't poor yet could scarcely manage indulgences. As I undid the twine and unfurled the covering, my fingertips shook with anticipation.

Inside was a small black bag with a red cross on the outside.

"Go on, open it," my father said, giving me an encouraging nudge. With still trembling fingers, I opened the bag. Inside was a complete set of plastic doctor's toys.

"So you can operate on your next little girlfriend," Dad said, chuckling.

My fingers smoothed over the plastic, and I felt a joy I had seldom felt.

"Thanks," I whispered, glancing up at my father's flushed cheeks and joyful expression.

"Anything for my little Casanova," he said, patting me gently on the back. "Anything at all."

Chapter Four

Much to my dad's disappointment, I was still playing exclusively with girls by the time I was ten. This might have been fine if they were my girlfriends, but after my failed relationships with Lucy and Sharon, I never had another romantic entanglement with any of the girls I played with. Even worse, I was getting picked on at school. It was always the same, and eerily similar to the things my dad said: that there was something wrong with me because I preferred playing with girls, that I was weak, that I was feminine.

It never made sense to me because I didn't feel feminine. At that age, I was short and overweight but not girly. I assume the supposed feminine nature came from my preference for the company of girls. Boys were just too loud, always getting up to mischief and into fights. They were too much like my dad. Meanwhile, the girls I spent time with were sweet and gentle, and they never scared me.

By the second year it was 1970, and while the world may have been becoming more open-minded, it was still the Dark Ages in Dagenham. So, instead of fizzling out, my bullying only intensified. It was also becoming physical as well as verbal.

There was a group of boys, spearheaded by Tommy Burke, who would hang out together after school, smoking cigarettes and trying to look tough. Tommy's older brother sometimes bought them booze, so even though they were only twelve, the same age I was, they would occasionally drink beer after school in Pondfield Park like they were already in the fourth or fifth year. From where they sat on the graffitied benches, they would hassle girls who walked by and shout abuse at anyone who looked their way.

Unfortunately for me, I walked past them regularly. I couldn't count the number of times I was called "poof", "bender", and "shirt lifter". I was now in a senior school called Eastbrook, and there were only two ways to get there from my house. There was a way where I was safe from abuse on my way home from school, or there was a way I had to walk if I wanted to walk with Lucy, as her house was by the park.

Occasionally, Tommy would push me to get a laugh from his friends. Then he'd shout "bundle", and all his friends would jump on me, punching and kicking. Things escalated one night near the beginning of the second year when I was walking through Pondfield Park and glimpsed the boys from a distance—the cherries of their cigarettes a smudge of light against the grey skies.

"Oi, Eddy!" The first voice came, sneering and slithery, from a boy named Shaun. He was sitting on the bench with his ripped jeans spread wide, leaning back and pulling on his cigarette. "Been off fucking a bloke, have ya?"

The words echoed around my head, but I didn't respond. This much I had learned: any response was a provocation to keep heckling me. Anyway, I didn't understand what Shaun meant by fucking a bloke. While boys at school made jokes about being gay, I'd never actually met or seen a gay person. They seemed more like a mythical species—or a demonic one—than something real. And I had no clue about the mechanics of sex between men. Heterosexual sex was a complete mystery to me at that point, let alone gay sex. All I knew was that it was wrong—very wrong—to be gay.

"You been off playing with girls again?" Shaun asked, leaping up from the bench and sauntering towards me. "Or did they finally realise you're weird and tell you to do one?"

"Yeah, Eddy," another boy chimed in, "sad you can't play dollies anymore?"

"Lads, lads," Tommy said. He was the tallest and meanest looking of the bunch, with hollow eyes and gaunt cheekbones but a broad, muscled chest. "Leave little Eddy alone." At this, the other boys' faces fell, disappointed that Tommy was defending me. Then he grinned. "Not when he's come to provide us with some entertainment. After all…" He reached out a single finger and pressed it hard against my chest. "We could use a good laugh."

"Don't touch me." I heard the words like a whisper from my chest. I'd said nothing like this to Tommy, or any of the boys, before, and his response was immediate. His hand curled into my jacket, grabbing the denim, and then he thrust backwards, hard, throwing me to the ground. He advanced towards me, his eyes gleaming, and I struggled to crawl backwards out of his reach.

"Now, let's see what kind of boy you really are, eh?" he shouted.

The other boys let out a cheer, and Tommy grabbed my arm, yanking me to my feet. Then he pushed me towards the boys. They laughed and jostled me, pushing me from one to the next, their cackling voices echoing in my ears.

"Come on, Eddy," taunted one of them, shoving me hard in the chest. "Show us how strong you are!"

"Hit me," demanded another, smirking as he loomed over me.

"Please," I whispered, fear constricting my throat. "I don't want any trouble."

"Trouble?" scoffed Tommy, his eyes narrowing with contempt. "You ain't seen trouble yet, mate."

In a swift motion, he unleashed a ferocious punch directly at my face. A searing burst of pain erupted, propelling me backwards, and I slid across the unyielding tarmac. Desperately attempting to halt my descent, my hands grappled with the unforgiving surface, tearing through skin and inflicting an agonising ache in my arms. The world blurred into an array of stars, and a pulsating agony engulfed my head.

"Pathetic," spat Tommy. I blinked up to see him standing over me. Behind him, I could dimly make out the faces of the other boys, who were all laughing wildly. "Bet your old man's real proud of you now, eh?"

They left me there like that, lying flat on my back. I could hear them howling with laughter as they retreated into the night, their voices screeching with malicious delight through the mist. Once I was sure they were gone, I pulled myself to my feet and ran the rest of the way home, not stopping until I was through the front door.

Inside, Mum was making dinner. The moment she saw me, she gasped.

"Eddy! Again?" She dropped the ladle she was holding and hurried over, then tilted my head up so she could examine me closer. "Don't tell me it was Tommy and his mates..."

She grabbed me by the shoulders and steered me towards the kitchen table, then went to fetch her first-aid kit. When she returned, she began to clean me up. I still had said nothing. Embarrassment was paralysing my brain, and I couldn't formulate words.

It was embarrassing enough to be such an easy target for the boys, but the more pressing sense of shame came from having returned to our home covered in bruises, just like Dad always did. I hated that I was forcing my mother to be a nurse for me like she was for my father.

As she mopped up a scrape on my cheek, I finally found my words. "I'm sorry, Mum."

She smiled gently as she continued to clean at the scrape. "You don't have to be sorry, love. I'm just worried."

"That's why I'm sorry." I forced myself to meet her gaze. "I don't want you to worry."

Her expression clouded, but she bit her lip and said nothing for several minutes. Finally, she sat back to survey her handiwork. "That's better," she murmured, caressing my cheek. "Good as new."

"You won't tell Dad, will you?" I asked hopefully.

"No, love, of course I won't." She hesitated. "Your father knows how to fight. Even when he comes home with scrapes, he gives as good as he gets. You're different, love. You're... gentle. I've always known it. Maybe it's my fault. I protected you too much. Maybe I should have let your father teach you how to fight. You don't need to be like him... well, you'll never be like him, and for that, I'm eternally grateful, but you need to fight back. The bullies will never stop until you do."

Her expression was earnest, and I felt a lump rising in the back of my throat. "But, Mum..." I began slowly. "I don't want to fight. I just want them to leave me alone."

"I know, love. I know." She pulled me into a brief, tight cuddle, then released me, turning away and brushing at her eyes. I'd never seen her cry, and I averted my gaze to give her privacy.

When she returned to the kitchen table with a bowl of stew for me, she looked calmer. I began to eat, and she lit a cigarette.

After smoking in silence for a minute, she said, "Do you remember the strikes at the Ford factory in sixty-eight?"

I looked up and nodded. "You and the other sewing machinists went on strike for equal wages as men."

"That's right. Our jobs were classified as Category C or less skilled labour than our male counterparts, whose jobs were classified as Category B. That meant we made fifteen percent less than them, despite being mothers and having mouths to feed." She shook her head and took another long drag on her cigarette. "Well, as you know, we went on strike for three weeks, and in the end, they increased our pay by seven percent and last year, they bumped us up to Category B workers." She smiled, a faraway look in her eyes. "This year, the government passed the Equal Pay Act. The entire country changed because me and my mates made a stand at the factory."

I frowned. "But... the sewing machinists never resorted to violence, did they?"

"That's true, we didn't. Our power came from the trade union, not violence."

"Maybe... maybe there is a way for me to have power without violence, too," I said.

My mum thought about this for a moment, ashing her cigarette in the small tuna tin she used as an ashtray, then smiled. "Maybe there is. And I hope you find it, Eddy. If anyone can, it's you."

But whatever I tried in the ensuing year, nothing worked. As each of my attempts to stop Tommy's bullying failed, I felt more and more like a failure. Each night, I lay awake, dreading the next morning and wondering why I was so pathetic. Why was it that some boys were born tough, able to throw a punch, while others couldn't defend themselves? And why was I, the son of a hooligan and the toughest man I knew, one of the latter?

Tommy Burke and his friends seemed to have a vendetta against me, and no amount of rationalising, bargaining, or pleading worked on them. After the incident in Pondfield Park, I never walked through the park again. But it didn't matter. Tommy Burke and his gang found me, anyway. Sometimes, they would wait for me right after school, rough me up a bit, call me names, and then leave me to walk home shaking with fear and anger. Their favourite form of torture was to taunt me, saying that if Hitler had won the war, poofs like me would have been eradicated.

The idea of fighting back always made my stomach turn. Even the thought of it was enough to conjure the sickening memory of my dad arriving home, drunk and angry, blood dripping into his beard.

I'd rather endure the boys' name-calling and relatively tame violence than cause them to increase their attacks and do me a real injury.

But near the end of the second year, things were getting worse. Tommy, clearly bored by my lack of response and frustrated with his inability to elicit my violence, was stepping up his attacks. One day, on my way from the corner shop, I heard the telltale sounds of bicycles behind me, and I knew that Tommy and the others had found me. I stayed staring ahead, but I increased my pace. Not that it mattered. They were on bicycles, and I was on foot, weighed down by shopping.

"Oi, Eddy!" I heard Tommy shout. Seconds later, his bike skidded to a stop in front of me, cutting off my path. Tommy seemed to have grown several inches in the past six months alone, and on his bike, he towered over me.

He eyed my bags. "Carrying the shopping home for Mummy like the good little daughter you are?"

The other boys circled me, laughing, until they surrounded me. I turned slowly, fear making the blood pound in my head. All the boys were leering at me, their eyes maniacal with the thirst for pain that I have seen so many times in the eyes of men spurred to violence.

Tommy got off his bike, letting it fall to the ground, and approached me. "Why do you never fight back, you little mug?" he growled. "Are you just afraid, or are you one of them weirdos that secretly enjoys being abused? Does it turn you on?"

Without warning, he struck me in the face. The pain was so intense that I screamed. Tears sprang to my eyes. Then I felt something hot and wet on my lips, and I realised I was bleeding.

My hands came to my face, and the shopping bags fell to the ground. I heard the glass milk bottles shatter, and my stomach turned. When I lowered my hands, Tommy was watching me closely, his fist raised again. "Are you going to fight back now?" he demanded.

My hands balled into fists, and for one wild moment, I thought I would hit him. Then I remembered the other boys surrounding me, and my shoulders slumped. It was pointless.

"You're pathetic," Tommy spat. "You're not even worth the effort."

Then he was back on his bike, and I was alone.

I looked down at the ruined shopping. The milk bottles had broken, and the blood from my nose mixed with it, creating a thick, pinkish syrup that oozed over the veg.

The row my injuries caused that night was one of the worst. My dad had been increasingly agitated by the bruises and cuts I returned home with. On more than one occasion, he'd told me it was high time I "manned up" and started defending myself.

That night, however, he came home pissed. I was in my bedroom when he banged open the front door, and the moment I heard him, I tensed.

My mother's voice wasn't audible, only a soft rumble, but I knew she was telling him what had happened to me. My father's reaction was immediate and explosive.

"They broke his nose!" he roared, his speech slurring slightly. "They broke my son's nose, and he did nothing!"

My mother's voice came a little louder, and this time, I could distinguish what she was saying: "It will heal, Lenny."

"Heal, fucking heal. He should have given them broken noses, not the other way round!" Something thudded hard, and I suspected Dad had knocked over a chair in anger. "My son, my son, Lenny fucking Turner's son, getting beaten up. It makes me look like a fucking mug!"

"Maybe you should also be worried about him getting hurt!" my mother shouted, losing her temper.

That mollified my father a little. "Of course, I care. But he's going to have to learn to man up and defend himself, or this is going to keep happening. And it's not helping that you protect him, that you tell him it's okay to not fight back."

"I don't—"

"Where is he?"

I froze. Several tense moments later, my mum said slowly, "In his room…"

"*Eddy!*" My father's thunderous shout seemed to rock the house. Still unable to move, I listened as his footsteps drew closer. Then my bedroom door flew open, and my father, all six feet three inches of him, red-faced and broad-shouldered, muscles bulging as his hands curled into fists, stood over me. "You're coming with me," he snarled.

I followed him from the room without comment. As he led me out of the house, a sense of foreboding gathered and settled in the pit of my stomach. What was he going to do? Was he going to hit me for bringing him shame? Either that or he would beat Tommy and his friends up—which I secretly hoped would be the case.

But we walked the opposite way from the park. My dad said nothing for a while, striding ahead purposefully, but whenever I fell behind, he would come back, seize me by the arm, and march me forward. I was now more curious than afraid, and when we finally stopped, I looked around with interest.

"Here," he said gruffly, pointing at the squat, low building in front of us. Even this late at night, light shone from the building's windows, and I could see people moving around inside. Above the door, a sign read Dagenham Amateur Boxing Club.

I looked back up at Dad, comprehension clicking into place. "You want me to learn to box?" I said, my voice weak with nerves.

Dad knelt in front of me. After a moment, he placed his hands on my shoulders. I flinched at the touch, and his face softened.

"Listen, son," he began, his voice was gentler than I had ever heard it. "I know you think I'm hard on you. But there are things about this world you don't understand. Things I 'ave to teach you, to keep you safe. Life is hard and unfair, and this place, Dagenham... it's not an easy place to be different. Boys who aren't strong—who are into girly things or stand out from the crowd—don't survive. I've seen it happen many times. They're hurt repeatedly until it breaks them. I can't let that happen to you. And not just because you're my son. But because..." He cleared his throat, and a strange sensation overcame me; I think it was embarrassment. It embarrassed me to see my dad's emotions. He was always so strong and implacable. "Well, because I love you, son," he continued gruffly. "And I won't always be around to protect you. So you've gotta learn to defend yourself. Okay?"

His eyes were bright, his grip tight on my shoulders. Even through my embarrassment, I could feel another emotion stirring: love.

Wordlessly, I nodded, and Dad's anxious grimace broke into a smile.

"Alright then." He squeezed my shoulders one last time and released me. "Let's go meet my old boxing coach, shall we?"

Chapter Five

I stood at the threshold of the boxing gym, feeling the weight of my next move in every muscle. My heart pounded like a trapped bird in my chest, both eager to break free and terrified of what lay ahead.

The gym was loud and full of tall, muscular men who looked like they could kill me with one clench of their fists. As I came in, they cast appraising glances over me, then went back to sparring, punching bags, and working out with weights and ropes. I hadn't known it was possible to use ropes to work out, and I watched with wide eyes. When several men saw me looking, they scowled, and I wanted to melt into the floor. It took all my resolve not to run away.

These men reminded me of my father and the lads he watched football with, none of whom had ever seemed to like me. There were also a few teenagers, a couple of years older than me. I recognised a few of them from school. They were also much stronger than me, with well-defined muscles that glistened with sweat.

As I lingered in the doorway, I watched, fascinated, as the boy close to me, shirtless, hit his gloved hand rhythmically against a small punching bag attached to the wall. His muscles were tense, his face sharp with concentration. He looked like something out of the Greek myths we read in school, like an Adonis, with smooth, marble-like skin and perfectly sculpted muscles. His hair was long and blonde, and as I watched, a thick, lustrous lock came loose from his headband and fell in front of his bright blue eyes. He was exactly what a man should look like, I felt certain. The kind of son my father wanted. He was mesmerising.

The boy finished hitting the bag and wiped his sweaty forehead with the back of his hand. Quickly, I looked away, my cheeks burning. The boy's beauty had ignited a spark of something inside me—a clenching of my gut and a fluttering in my chest. These weren't unpleasant feelings, and I let the rush of admiration and pleasure consume me for a moment.

Then Shaun's words came back to me, cold and jeering: *Been off fucking a bloke, have ya?* My stomach lurched. Did these strange feelings mean I was…? I couldn't even think of the word. It was too frightening, so I pushed it deep inside me. The last thing I needed was to give my bullies any sign that they were right about me. So, as the boy raised his head, I looked away, my cheeks burning.

The boy's beauty made me feel self-conscious in my worn gym shorts, which were digging into my stomach. I knew I wasn't the skinniest person, but I felt extra podgy around these men.

"Alright, Eddy?" called one of the trainers, a burly man with a crooked nose and a broad smile. He raised his hand as he approached, and I returned my expression to neutral. "Ready for your first session?"

"Y-yes, sir," I stammered.

"I'm Cartwright," the trainer said, holding out a hand. Tentatively, I shook it. In his large, strong hand, mine felt particularly weak and noodle-like. "You're Lenny's boy, is that right?"

"Yeah…" I blinked up at him. "How do you know my dad?"

"We watch football together. And he used to come to the gym to train. Mean left hook," he chortled. "Wouldn't want to be one of those Millwall boys, that's for sure. He told me you'd be coming 'round today, asked me to show you the joint."

Cartwright led me around the gym, pointing out the training apparatuses that looked more like torture devices than athletic equipment. He introduced me to a few of the other trainers as well. Their eyes examined me, taking in my flabby arms and slight build, but they said nothing. After the tour, Cartwright gave me a pair of black wraps and showed me how to tie them around my hands.

"Won't I be wearing gloves?" I asked as he pulled the wraps tight around my fists.

"Eventually. But we're going to start with this."

"But… won't it hurt my hand if I'm not wearing a glove?"

Cartwright's eyes twinkled. "I don't think you'll be landing any punches for a while, son."

I wasn't sure if I should feel insulted or relieved, but Cartwright didn't seem to expect me to respond. He brought me into the ring, and I silently prayed that no one was watching as he showed me how to stand and hold my legs.

Once I was ready, he stood across from me. Then, without warning, he took a jab.

The force of it was so strong that even though his hand didn't touch me, the air whistled like a bullet had narrowly missed me. I stumbled back, and Cartwright let me get my legs underneath me before he jabbed again.

"Focus on your stance, lad," he instructed. "Feet apart, knees bent. Keep your hands up—protect your face."

I obeyed, but my body felt awkward and hesitant. Try as I might, I couldn't mimic the movements he was showing me. Each punch felt foreign and forced. Gritting my teeth, I willed myself to continue. I wasn't about to make a fool of myself on my first day, not when this might be my only chance to win my father's approval. He was so excited about it all. He was even paying for the lessons, and I knew he had little spare dough. This was something he wanted—no, needed—me to do, and maybe he was right: maybe it would finally get me over my distaste for hurting others; maybe it would help keep Tommy and his mates away from me; maybe it would finally earn Dad's respect.

At this last thought, my arm acted as if of its own accord, and it shot out in front of me, quick and darting, and hit Cartwright on the shoulder.

The grizzled trainer's eyes went wide. "Good job, lad!" he bellowed, clapping me hard on the shoulder. "I didn't see that one coming! Your eyes went all calm and inward there. I couldn't anticipate where you were going to strike. Very good. Now, let's try to put some power behind those punches, eh?" He chuckled and led me out of the ring toward a punching bag. As he lined me up in front of it, adjusting my stance, he said, "Remember, you're not just hitting them; you're trying to hurt them."

The words sent a shiver down my spine. Hoping Cartwright hadn't felt or seen it, I focused on the bag in front of me and then threw a right hook with all the force I could muster. The bag lurched, the impact reverberating through my arm like a shockwave. Even as the pain seared through me, I felt something else: the sickening thrill of power that came from feeling my full strength. I had never felt powerful before. For several seconds, adrenaline coursed through me, flooding me with euphoria. Like I could do anything. I felt like a king.

But the adrenaline dissipated, my euphoria vanished, and fear took its place: having power meant having power over other people. It meant being able to hurt others. That wasn't a power I wanted... Or was it?

"Oi, look at little Eddy!" someone shouted from across the gym. "He's not such a wimp after all!"

I turned and saw one of the older boys from school leaning against the ring's ropes, staring across at me. A wolfish smile played across his lips. At his shout, other people in the gym had turned to look at me, and I felt myself flush under their gaze.

"Focus, Edward," Cartwright barked, snapping me back to the task at hand. "Block out the noise and just keep hitting."

Block out the noise. But that was easier said than done. Even when Cartwright yelled at the older boys to leave me alone, I could still hear them sniggering from across the gym.

Now that I was self-conscious, it was harder to focus on Cartwright's teachings, and after another hour with little improvement, he let me go. I went home that night aching all over and woke up the following day even more sore. By the afternoon, when I dragged myself back into the gym, every single part of my body hurt.

"That's how it is in the beginning," Cartwright said when I told him I could barely lift my arms. "It'll get easier. You're killing the weakness in your body. No one said that wouldn't be painful."

And he was right. It got easier. Over the next few weeks and months, as I continued to go to the gym every day, the pain lessened. My muscles grew stronger. My stamina increased. Best of all, my body shed the baby fat that still clung to it. I became leaner, my muscles more toned. It was with awe that I watched the change take place. I never thought I could be one of those lads who was fit or strong; that type of lad belonged to another class of person. Someone like my dad.

Who was, of course, overjoyed by the physical change in my body.

"Lookin' sharp, Eddy, my boy!" he'd say to me each morning, ruffling my hair as he passed through the kitchen on his way out the door. "Keep this up, and you'll be winning featherweight championships; mark my words!"

But while my body grew stronger, and some of my practical skills at boxing increased, the one hurdle I couldn't seem to overcome was my fear of hitting others. Other than that first day, when I'd lightly punched Cartwright on the shoulder, I had yet to actually hit someone at the gym.

"What's going on in your head?" Cartwright asked me after one particularly gruelling session, during which I'd shied away from all his advances until my legs tangled beneath me, landing me hard on my arse. We were sitting on the edge of the ring, drinking water from paper cups. Someone threw a wet, sweaty towel around my neck. I felt sore, angry, and mutinous, embarrassed by my obvious inability to get tougher.

I shrugged in response to Cartwright's question, not looking at him. The Adonis, whose name I'd learned was Charlie, was sparring several feet from us with a friend, and my eyes were locked on him.

"I asked you a question, Eddy," Cartwright said gently but firmly. "Show me respect and answer me honestly. Are you afraid of being hurt? Is that the trouble?"

"I'm not afraid," I said, digging my toe angrily into the mat beneath me. "I get hit all the time at school. I'm used to it."

Cartwright's expression softened. "Then what is it?"

I took my time before answering. Across from me, Charlie threw a sharp upper jab that broke through his friend's defences and hit him on the jaw. After ascertaining that his jaw was fine, the other boy laughed, then threw his arm over Charlie's shoulder. "You got me good, fair and square." He grinned.

Looking away, I caught Cartwright's eye. "I just don't know if I want to hit you," I said at last. Even to me, I sounded surly and childish.

"Are you worried you'll hurt me?" Cartwright asked.

"That's part of it."

"What's the other part?"

My old man's face when he returned from the match, the wounds above his eye, the blood spilling out of it, coagulating in his beard, my mother's fear and anger—all of it suddenly flashed in front of my eyes, and I shuddered. Cartwright raised an eyebrow.

"You don't like violence, do you?" he asked quietly.

"I don't like what it does to people," I snapped. "Not just the people it hurts, but the people who commit it. And the ones who have to stitch you up when you come home covered in bruises."

"Why did you want to learn to box if you don't like violence?"

"My dad wanted me to. And I…" *Wanted to make him proud.*

Cartwright nodded as if he understood what was unspoken. He looked thoughtful, and after a minute or two of silence, he murmured, "I've known your dad a long time, Eddy. He's a good man, although flawed like all of us are. But I think I also know you pretty well by now, and you're not like him. You may have other flaws, but you don't have his."

"But I do," I said, more forcefully than I'd intended. I still wasn't looking at him, afraid he might see the liquid accumulating in my eyes. "Sometimes I feel the same anger and violence raging in me, too."

Cartwright stood and placed a hand on my shoulder. If he saw my tears, he said nothing. "All men have violence in them. That doesn't make you like your father." When I continued to say nothing, he sighed. "Maybe you have some of your father's anger. But you'll never know if you keep holding yourself back. It's better to know yourself, Eddy, rather than live in fear of your worst impulses. And you might surprise yourself." He squeezed my shoulder, then headed to the changing rooms, leaving me to think through and wonder at his words.

I walked home slowly that night. It was August 1971, and the days were growing shorter, the sun just setting over the identical terraced houses with tidy lawns. The belching smoke that rose from the Ford factory in the distance offset the splash of orange and pink on the horizon. To someone else, the factory might have spoiled the beauty of the night, but to me, to anyone from Dagenham, it was as part of the landscape as anything. It was even beautiful in its own way.

As I walked, I thought about Cartwright's words. He and my mum seemed to think I was different from my father, but I wasn't so sure. Could the apple really fall so far from the tree? If he was violent and angry, then it stood to reason I must be, too. Just because I had always had an aversion to violence didn't mean that the dark part of me wasn't lurking somewhere inside, buried deep beneath my fear and disgust.

So far, I'd kept the boxing from bringing it out. But I sensed that the darkness would come spilling out if I were to really let loose—if I were to hit Cartwright the way he wanted me to. And then I didn't know what would happen. Would it consume me? Would it hurt someone I loved? Or would it simply make me the man my father wanted me to be?

Such moody thoughts kept me distracted long enough that I wasn't paying attention to where I was going, and before I knew it, I realised I was passing through Pondfield Park. As the familiar sound of Tommy Burke and his gang's voices drifted towards me from up ahead, I wondered if there was something in my subconscious that had led me there on purpose.

Chapter Six

Shaun was the first to see me. As his eyes lit on mine, he grinned toothily. Then he elbowed Tommy, who was busy laughing with some of the younger boys and hadn't noticed me approaching. At Shaun's nudge, Tommy turned. The cigarette was halfway to his lips when he registered me, and it stayed suspended there, his hand frozen. His eyes raked over me, taking in my lean frame and new muscles. The sneer in them disappeared, replaced by a cold challenge.

I hadn't seen Tommy all summer, and this was the first time he was seeing the changes that boxing had wrought on my body. However, he didn't seem concerned as he tossed his cigarette to the ground and sauntered towards me.

"Well, well, well, look who it is," he sneered, his grin twisting his ugly face. "Little Eddy Turner got himself in shape. Get them muscles to impress the fairies, did ya?"

His gang laughed as they fell into place behind him, forming a semi-circle. They advanced, and I slowed to a stop. Sizing them up, I figured there were two I didn't need to worry about, one whom I could dodge easily enough, and two more who would fold from a quick uppercut. If I could bring myself to hit them.

Tommy stopped a few feet from me. He held up his fists in a lazy approximation of a boxer's stance. His eyes glittered. "Heard you've been learning to throw a punch. Let's see what you got, eh?"

I said nothing, although a cheeky part of me was tempted to correct his posture.

"Aw, come on now," Tommy taunted. "Give us a little demonstration."

"Careful," I murmured, low enough that I wasn't sure Tommy would hear me. It wasn't a warning to my opponent but a reminder to myself of the storm that was threatening to break.

But Tommy heard me and incorrectly assumed I was talking to him.

"Or what?" He laughed, his sneer widening as he stepped forward, fists still raised. "You'll punch me? No way. You're still just a weakling, no matter how much time you spend at that boxing club."

And in that moment, something inside of me snapped. The dam burst, and all the anger, pain, and humiliation surged forth like a tidal wave.

Without warning, without giving him a chance to guess my next move, my fist shot out like a bolt of lightning, striking him square in the jaw.

The impact was like thunder reverberating through my bones. It hurt more than hitting the punching bag—a lot more—and I almost cried out in pain.

The force of the blow propelled Tommy backwards, and several of his mates had to run forward and catch him before he fell to the ground. After a moment of confusion, he shook off his friends and pulled himself back to his feet. His eyes blazed.

And then he was on me.

The fight that ensued was brutal but swift. My breathing remained calm and measured as I dodged, weaved, and struck back against Tommy's blows with practised patience. I could feel the power in my muscles like coiled springs finally allowed to snap, each punch a testament to the effort I'd put into transforming myself physically.

And with each punch, pride swelled inside of me. Pride, and an overwhelming sense that I wasn't a failure. I wasn't just a king, like how I'd felt at the punching bag. Hitting Tommy Burke, I was a god.

It quickly became apparent that I was stronger and more dexterous than Tommy. What surprised me even more was the swaggering confidence the realisation gave me.

"Is that all you got?" I sneered after several minutes of dodging and parrying his blows and landing light jabs on his shoulders and face.

"Shut up!" Tommy howled. His voice was slightly hysterical. It only made me feel more in control.

Ducking under one of his wild swings, I pivoted on my heel, bringing my leg up in a sweeping arc that connected with the side of Tommy's knee. A sickening crunch echoed through the park, and he crumpled to the ground, clutching his injured leg.

I could have left him like that. He was down. If we were in the ring, I wouldn't have touched him. But we weren't in the ring. This wasn't a fair fight with referees and scoring. This was street fighting, and the only way to win was to show dominance. And after years of getting pushed around and beaten up by Tommy and his cronies, I would not let him off that easily.

I was going to make him suffer. I was going to make my father proud.

Tommy looked up at me, the words of surrender on his lips, but I didn't let him get them out. With all the force and power I'd built up over the last few months, I brought my fist straight into the side of his face. A thwack sounded through the night. Then he fell back onto the pavement, unconscious.

A ringing silence filled the park. The other boys stared at Tommy's prone figure, their eyes wide.

My breath was coming heavily, and sweat was running down my back. The exhilaration of the fight was coursing through me, the godlike feeling even more potent. But as I gulped down deep breaths, trying to slow my heart rate, the rush dissipated. My muscles relaxed. Blood no longer pounded in my ears. The sweat on my skin dried, bringing with it the sting of the cold night air. I shivered, and the hairs on my arms stood up. And as my body cooled, so did my anger.

I looked down at the lying, twisted body of Tommy Burke. Suddenly, it wasn't my enemy and bully lying unconscious in front of me, but a thirteen-year-old boy.

I crouched down next to Tommy's body. "Help me," I snapped at the nearest boy. "We need to put him on his side."

The boy obeyed, and together, we turned Tommy over into the recovery position.

"Is he... dead?" the boy asked, his voice small.

"Knocked out," I said, although I still felt for Tommy's pulse when the boy wasn't looking. "When he wakes up, tell him to put ice on the bump. It'll help it heal faster."

No one responded, and I glared at them. "Got it?"

The boys all nodded, still too disbelieving to speak. I stood and turned back the way I'd come. I'd take the long way home.

"Remember this," I muttered as I walked away into the darkness. But even I wasn't sure what I was supposed to remember: the surge of power at seeing the fearful, obsequious looks on the boys' faces or the sick dread that had curdled in my stomach at the sight of Tommy, unconscious on the ground.

When I got home, my mum was still up, although her hair was already in rollers. She took one look at my hand—which I was cradling to my chest—sighed, got up, and headed into the kitchen. A minute later, she'd returned with a bowl of ice, into which I set my throbbing hand. The relief was instantaneous, and I sighed as I sat across from her at the kitchen table. She lit a cigarette as I let my hand rest on the ice.

"Don't they make you wear gloves?" she asked after several minutes of silence. My knuckles were still red, and little flecks of blood were now floating in the ice water.

"They do," I conceded. "But I was mucking around with the lads after I finished sparring. Hit one too hard, I guess."

Her eyes narrowed, and I looked away. Shame burned my cheeks, but I was determined to push it away. I'd finally stood up for myself. This was a reason to be proud, not ashamed.

Twenty minutes later, Dad arrived home. In the doorway, he stopped short, his eyes travelling from my hand in the bowl of now-melted ice to my face, which was bruise-free. For a moment, his eyes gleamed. Then he glanced at my mum, and his expression returned to neutral.

"Good evening," he said as he came to sit down at the table. After kissing my old dear on the cheek, he looked at me. "Boxing injury?" He grunted.

"Yup." I looked down, not wanting to meet my mother's eyes, sure she could read the lie in them. The last thing I wanted was for her to think I was becoming like my dad, beating people up on the streets.

My old man patted me on the shoulder, and from the tightness with which he squeezed it, I knew he knew. Nerves, hope, and disgust all flooded me.

"That's my boy," he murmured as Mum gazed on, silent and watchful. "That's my boy."

No words had ever filled me with more joy, comfort, and foreboding. It was the first time I'd ever had my father's full approval. It was what I wanted most in the world, but it had come at a high cost. And what did it mean for the future? Would I have to continue beating up boys to win his approval? Would I end up becoming him?

Dad grinned as he sat down, unaware of the conflict inside me.

By the next morning, word of what I'd done had already spread throughout Dagenham. I wasn't expecting the news to travel so quickly. After all, Tommy wasn't likely to have told anyone that the kid he'd been picking on for years had knocked him unconscious. It must have been one of the other boys—probably still in shock and wanting to tell someone what he'd witnessed—who spread the news.

When I entered the boxing gym the following evening, the looks on the older boys' faces told me everything I needed to know. The moment they saw me, their expressions became wary, even a little disbelieving, but I knew that deep down, they were impressed. Maybe even a little jealous.

Ignoring the boys' looks and whispers, I went straight to my locker, head down, where I had just started to wrap my hands in gauze when I heard Cartwright call my name.

"Eddy!"

Cartwright was striding towards me, a frown fixed on his face. I braced myself, ready for him to clap me on the back and tell me how proud he was of me. But when he reached me, he folded his arms and continued to frown.

"I heard you were in a fight last night."

I nodded, a flicker of pride searing through me.

"And you kicked him in the knees and then knocked him out cold?" He raised an eyebrow, and I felt myself bristle.

"So what?" I snapped. "Tommy Burke has been picking on me for years. He had it coming. Shouldn't be a bully if he doesn't want to get what's coming to him."

Cartwright's expression softened, although his arms remained crossed. "But you're a trained boxer, Eddy. This Tommy kid isn't."

I slammed my locker closed and turned to face Cartwright, defiant. "So? Isn't that the point of learning to box? So I can defend myself from bullies?"

"The point of boxing is to learn how to control your violence," Cartwright said. "You're not a brute beast; you're an athlete, a disciplined fighter. That means you need to know how to control your anger and your violence."

"I can't win. I get signed up to box so I can learn to defend myself. And when I finally do, I'm told I shouldn't," I spat, suddenly and irrationally disgusted by Cartwright's moral posturing. In truth, part of me agreed with him, but I didn't want to admit that I was ashamed of my behaviour. Not when I'd finally earned my father's respect and the respect of my fellow boxers. "What am I here for if not to learn how to fight? I finally stood up for myself—which is what everyone wanted me to do!"

"I'm not unsympathetic, Eddy," Cartwright insisted, his voice now edged with something like worry. "I don't want those boys beating you up. But part of being a boxer is controlling yourself. To hurt an untrained kid... that's abusing your strength and training."

Cartwright put a hand on my shoulder, and although I wanted to brush him off, I restrained myself. There was something comforting about the gesture, and his eyes were kind. "We save our strength for the ring. Outside the ring, we only fight if we have to. Do you understand, Eddy?"

Although part of me still wanted to argue, I forced myself to nod and take a deep breath. Now that the anger and defensiveness were ebbing, I knew he was right.

It reminded me of our conversation about my father the day before. Lenny, I knew, would use his full strength on anyone who pissed him off. He was the brute beast that Cartwright had told me I wasn't. And no matter how much I feared I might be like my dad—that the same brutishness lived inside of me—I didn't want to be like him.

Cartwright seemed to read my thoughts because he murmured, "All of us have darkness inside us. All of us have rage. But being a man means we decide how we channel that darkness and keep it from doing real, lasting harm. That's why we box. It gives us an outlet for the pain, aggression and anger that comes with being a man in this world. Boxing gives us rules, a shape, and limits within which to express that rage. Then, when we're out of the ring, we can let go of it. That's the choice every boxer has to make: do you want to control the rage, or do you want it to control you?"

A current of understanding flowed between us. All I had to do was nod, and I knew Cartwright understood I had taken his words to heart. When I did, he smiled, then jabbed me below the chin.

"That's my boy."

It was the first time someone other than my father had called me that, and it made my heart swell painfully—yet wonderfully—in my chest.

"Now, look..." He dropped his hand from my shoulder. "I don't want you to think I'm only here to lecture you. I'm damn proud of you, son, for getting over your fear of hitting people. Sure, I wish you'd hit the kid more gently, but I'm glad you're past that."

"I really think I am," I said, flexing my hand as I remembered the feel of Tommy's face under my fingers. "It hurts a lot though, doesn't it?"

Cartwright chuckled. "That's why we wear gloves in the ring." He sobered slightly, looking me up and down. "Now, how would you feel if we signed you up for your first bout?"

"What?" My stomach swooped with anticipation and excitement, and I gaped at him. "Do you mean it? Do you really think I'm ready?"

"As long as you keep hitting with the accuracy and force that you hit that kid in the park, then yes, I think you're ready."

Maybe Dad was right, I thought, my stomach clenching with hope and fear. Maybe I was going to become a featherweight champion.

Chapter Seven

On the other side of the ring stood a boy around my age, broad-shouldered and smirking. He was a little skinnier than me but taller and scrappy-looking. His eyes told me the streets had been his training ground.

"Remember what I taught you," my father said in a low voice as he tightened the laces on my gloves. "You've got this."

"Thanks, Dad." I wasn't sure if I got this, but I was glad he thought I did. A year ago, he would have had no faith that I could win a fight like this. But here I was, standing in the blue corner of the ring, my father and Cartwright hovering around me, their expressions excited and full of nervous optimism.

For my first bout, I'd asked that my dad serve as my cutman. He'd done it before for friends in unofficial fights, and because he had trained as a boxer, Cartwright had agreed to it. Although he seemed a little worried Lenny would lose his temper and do something inappropriate, I think he suspected that my father's presence would motivate me.

He wasn't wrong. My dad didn't make me feel confident; if anything, it was the opposite. But his presence filled me with a grim determination to win. I could all too easily imagine the look of disappointment and embarrassment on his face should I lose, and I wasn't about to let that happen.

My opponent's eyes bored into me from his side of the ring like a predator stalking its prey. Jimmy Darcy was his name, and this was his third fight. I was told he was a brawler but had a temper, and if things were not going his way, he could get frustrated. "Emotional," Cartwright had called him. "It's an excellent test for you after the incident in the park. If you can keep your emotions in check, you'll win this one."

Tommy Burke, it turned out, had prepared me well for the ring. Except for the recent blip, all those years of bullying had taught me self-control.

Still, I was nervous going into this bout. Jim Darcy had been fighting longer than I had, and he had two bouts behind him. The first had been a draw, but the second he'd won, although not unanimously. I was probably a bit of a trial horse for him.

But we all had to start somewhere.

"You're gonna be great, Eddy," Cartwright said, clapping me hard on the shoulder. I looked up at him, and his eyes twinkled. "You've trained hard, and more importantly, you've got the determination. You want this. All you have to do is show Darcy and the judges exactly how much."

Unable to speak from the fear that my nerves would spill out of me as vomit, I nodded. Cartwright gave me one last encouraging smile, then stepped back. Dad handed me my mouthguard and grinned at me like this was the proudest day of his life—which it probably was. I turned to the centre of the ring.

Darcy had already stepped forward. He looked ready. He looked determined. Seeing this, I no longer believed I had what it took to box, let alone to win this bout. I was just a chubby, weak kid who'd been beaten up for years. There was no way I could best a born fighter like Darcy.

Tommy Burke's mocking face flashed before my eyes. His taunting words filled my ears. You're still just a weakling, no matter how much time you spend at that boxing club. My stomach clenched. Nausea coursed through me. I wasn't ready. This was going to be a bloodbath.

The bell rang, and the bout began.

Cartwright had been right about Darcy: he was fast, powerful, and aggressive. The moment the bell rang, he darted forward, clearly eager to be first. Without hesitating or waiting for me to move towards him, he threw a punch. Immediately, I was caught on the defensive. There wasn't a lot of space to back up, and I was afraid of being caught on the ropes. Pivoting, I used the fastest footwork I could summon to dodge and weave away from Darcy's punches until I was in the middle of the ring.

Here, I had more room to manoeuvre away from him. But his punches were so fast—even though his combinations were lazy—that it was difficult to do anything other than block him. For the first round, I danced around the ring, blocking his throws, parrying as many as possible, and trying to get some of my jabs in. Although I was good at defence, and Darcy didn't land many blows, I was tiring. My breath came in ragged gasps, and sweat trickled down my brow.

Because amateur boxing is judged on technical points rather than sheer raw power and KOs, I was likely losing by the end of the first round. Which didn't leave me much time to improve my situation, not with only two rounds left. But I had little time to think about this.

There was only a minute between the rounds, and I had to use that time to recover some of my strength.

Dad pulled me roughly into the corner as the bell sounded, signalling the end of the round. Removing my mouthguard, he sprayed water into my mouth. I gulped it down, then spit the rest into the bucket he offered.

"The kid's strong," my father said, speaking gruffly. "But he's not landing many punches. Your defence is good, boy. You just need to find a way in."

"Try attacking when he's on the offence," Cartwright said as he patted dry my sweaty neck and arms with a towel. "He won't be expecting that. He'll be waiting for you to attack during a reprieve."

"If he ever gives me one," I muttered.

"He will," Cartwright assured me. "But don't take it."

I wasn't sure how good this advice was, but I had to trust that Cartwright knew what he was talking about.

"Seconds out!" the referee called, and Cartwright and my dad wished me luck and retreated. Darcy and I once more faced each other in the ring. As the bell rang, he rushed at me again.

This time, I was ready. Even as I fell back and defended myself—feigning weariness—I paid careful attention to the speed and accuracy of his attacks. He always seemed to attack at the same speed and with the same combination. This meant if I could just get the timing right...

I'd never successfully landed a check hook during a sparring match. Cartwright and my other sparring partners were too good for that. A check hook was a punch that took an unsuspecting offensive attacker off guard. It was like a traditional hook, except you threw it while stepping backwards, on defence, timing the punch with when your opponent stepped forward. Cartwright made it too difficult to predict his timing, but Darcy was my age; he didn't have the years of experience Cartwright had, and his attacks were far more predictable.

I disentangled myself from him, and the next time he charged, I saw my opening. Stepping back as if I meant to dodge or parry his throw, I instead brought my arm around in a fast, hard hook, aiming right for the place Darcy was about to step into.

The punch landed squarely on Darcy's nose; a sickening, crunching sound emanated from him, and he fell back, clutching his gloved hand to his face. Blood streamed down. Too much blood, surely, for a broken nose. And as it dripped onto the ring at Darcy's feet, the onlookers screamed and gasped.

My stomach curled inward, and for one desperate moment, I thought I would be sick. The vomit rose in my throat, and I had to swallow it down.

After a flurry of commotion in Darcy's corner, his trainer threw a towel into the ring and looked at Darcy in disgust.

My dad roared, got in the ring, and hugged me. It was one of the rare occasions in my life where I could tell he was proud of me. He held my hand up in the air, and the referee did the same. The sound of ringing bells mixed with cheers and groans.

And then suddenly, the noise stopped. I could see mouths moving, but no sounds were coming out. I glanced at Darcy, who looked frustrated as his cutman put a white earbud up his nose.

"Blimey, Eddy!" my father exclaimed, and just like that, I could hear again. "That was one hell of a punch! You really nailed that bastard!"

Finally, my old man moved out of the way, and my coach moved forward.

"Good job, kid," he said, shaking my hand vigorously. He seemed to think for a moment, then pulled me into a one-armed hug. "You were brilliant! Did exactly as I said and executed it to perfection. Bloody brilliant, Eddy. Bloody brilliant."

I tried to smile, to feel the same elation that coursed through Cartwright's and my father's veins, but it wouldn't come. Fortunately, I still had my mouthguard in, which spared me the need to speak or smile. I felt excited and proud, didn't I? I tried to feel around inside of myself for the requisite emotions, but all I could feel was a somewhat numb relief. It was over. And I hadn't made a fool of myself or disappointed my dad.

In some strange, dark corner of my mind, I almost would have preferred being the injured one. I would have disappointed my father, but at least I would have had an excuse to never box again.

Even as onlookers greeted me, Mum among them, shaking my hand and congratulating me, I felt as if only half of me was present. The other half was already miles away, as far as I could get from the putrid smell of Darcy's blood.

Another wave of nausea gripped me, and I turned sharply to Cartwright.

"I need the toilet," I said as quietly as possible.

He nodded and waved away the people crowded around me. "Give the boy some space," I heard him say, as if from a great distance. "Clear a path, everyone. The boy needs to cool off."

Somehow, I made it through the packed gymnasium without running or looking too panicked. But when I reached the outskirts of the crowd, I didn't go into the changing room. Instead, I pushed open the gymnasium doors and sprinted out into the night. Behind me, I heard someone call my name, but I didn't stop running.

It was dark, and I wasn't sure where I was going or why I was running. But I couldn't stop myself. I just knew I had to get away. So I kept running, down one identical street after another, until I did not know where I was. I spotted an alley between two houses and darted down it. After several hacking dry heaves, I threw up everywhere, then got out of there before anyone saw me.

On the way home, my stomach settled, and my heart rate slowed. As it did, I was able to think through what had just happened. I'd won the fight, but it hadn't brought joy or pride. All I felt was disgust with myself. My stomach lurched again at the memory of Darcy's nose crunching under my glove, and I had to swallow back the bile. I was ashamed: ashamed to be like my father, returning home from fights with other hooligans; ashamed that I'd made him proud by doing something that felt so wrong to me; ashamed that I was becoming the type of man who hurt, not healed.

By the time I turned back onto the street where the Dagenham Boxing Club was, I knew what I had to do. The lights were still on inside, but as I drew closer, I couldn't see movement from inside. I was worried my dad had gone home.

When I pushed the door open, I was surprised to see that Dad had waited for me. My father was sitting in the corner with Cartwright, paper cups of coffee clutched in their hands.

The moment they saw me, both men stood. Cartwright looked worried, but my father's expression was hovering between anger and shame. He probably wanted to yell at me for embarrassing him but didn't dare in front of Cartwright.

"Eddy, are you alright?" Cartwright asked. He reached me in several long strides, placing his hands on my shoulders as he stared into my eyes. "What happened to you?"

"Just needed some air," my father said gruffly.

My father's face was hopeful. I wasn't sure if he was hoping I would lie or if he had convinced himself that this could actually be true.

But I would not lie so he could save face. Not anymore.

I took a deep breath. "Dad, Coach. I can't box anymore."

Cartwright's hands dropped from my shoulders as his face crumpled.

My father, meanwhile, looked incredulous. "Eh? Whatcha on about, Eddy? You just smashed that kid! You're a natural talent. Don't waste it!"

"I'm quitting boxing," I said, my hands curling into fists. "Don't argue with me, Dad. I've made up my mind."

"Don't go telling me you've made up your mind," my old man snarled. He took a threatening step towards me. "You've got the talent that I dreamed of having. I wish my dad gave me the same opportunities I'm giving you!"

"This is my life, Dad. Not yours."

"But you won!" Dad howled. "You won!" His eyes scanned over me, taking in my pale, shaking features, and his expression softened. "See here, you're just in shock, Eddy. You don't know what you're saying. Probably took a few too many punches to the head in the first round. Give it a few more fights—you'll grow to love it."

"I don't want to love it," I said as softly but forcefully as possible. "That's not who I am. It's who you are, Dad, but not me."

"It's who every man is," my father snapped. "From day one, men have been fighting. It's natural."

"No," I disagreed, and my eyes came to rest on Cartwright's, who so far hadn't said a word. He was simply watching me with wide, probing eyes. "I'm not a fighter, Dad. I don't want to hurt people. I care about people and their feelings."

"Feelings!" My old man snarled. "You sound like a poof! I won't have any son of mine sounding like a f—" He lunged towards me, and I barely ducked out of his reach.

"That's enough, Leonard!" Cartwright snapped. He strode forward and grabbed my father by the shirt, pulling him away from me. "I won't have you insulting the boy in my gym. That's not how we do things here. If the boy doesn't want to fight anymore, I won't train him." His eyes came to mine. "A boxer has to choose this life. He has to want it. Otherwise, it'll kill him. And if Eddy doesn't choose this, then none of us can force him."

The tension in my shoulders lessened, and I smiled at Cartwright. He smiled back, although I could tell it was an effort.

"But, Eddy..." he continued more quietly, "I just want you to be sure. Your dad is right: it was only your first fight. It can be quite a shock the first time. But it will get easier; it will get better. And you're a natural. It would be a shame to lose a talent like yours..."

But I had never been so sure of anything in my life as I stepped forward and held out my hand. "Thank you for all your training, Coach. I'll never forget what you did for me in this gym. You taught me to stick up for myself, and for that, I'm eternally grateful. But I'm just not a boxer."

Cartwright clasped my hand. "I understand, and I respect that. Good luck, son. We'll miss you. And if you ever change your mind... you know where to find us."

As I turned and headed towards the changing room, I heard my father arguing with Cartwright. He was shouting at the coach that he shouldn't have sided with me.

He might never accept my decision, I reminded myself as I unwound the gauze from my hands. You might have lost his approval forever.

It hurt more than I cared to admit. But I couldn't force myself to be someone I wasn't just so he might be proud of me.

Chapter Eight

It was a bright, hot day—unseasonably warm for September—and the sun was searing through the bustling stadium, almost blinding me to the sea of claret and blue around me, the distinctive colours of West Ham United. The stadium was crowded and loud, the fans restless from the heat, and I twitched every time they let out a deafening roar. The anticipation in the air was palpable, the air laced with the sickening smells of sweat, beer, testosterone, and cheap pies. It was an environment that led to violence. A tinderbox waiting to be set on fire.

I glanced over at Dad, who was in the middle of an animated conversation with several members of the Mile End Mob. I knew these lads. They'd been coming around the house since I was small, each time with even more crooked noses and deeper, nastier scars on their faces. They'd never warmed to me—except they thought I might be a boxing champion—and had mostly left me alone since I'd quit.

Things with Dad were another story. He was always storming around the house, muttering about what a disappointment I was. Even though it had been a month since I'd quit boxing—the summer was over, and I was back in school for the third year—he still hadn't given it up.

Mum had suggested that he take me to a West Ham game. She thought it would bring us closer.

"He's never been interested in football," Dad had complained when she suggested it. "And I don't want to spend ninety minutes explaining how the game works."

"Please, Lenny," I'd heard her say, her voice low. "He misses you. I know he does."

But Mum had insisted, which was how I ended up at the late September home game of West Ham United versus Everton.

"Oi, Eddy!" one of Lenny's mates shouted, thrusting a plastic cup of lager into my hand. "Drink up, son! The beer will make it easier to knock out some Scouse cunts after the game."

Resisting the urge to tell this idiot that alcohol would make me a worse fighter, not a better one, I nodded and took a tentative sip of the flat warm liquid. It tasted foul, but I didn't dare make a face. The lads were watching me closely, and I wasn't about to give Dad another reason to be disappointed in me. So, instead, I forced a smile and focused on the players warming up on the pitch.

Admittedly, they were fascinating to watch. The footballers moved with grace and power, their muscles rippling beneath their jerseys—a stark contrast to the hefty bodies and slow movements of the men I'd known at the boxing gym. Both were beautiful in their own way, though, radiating health and discipline, masculine beauty...

My heart fluttered, and I clapped a hand to my chest. My stomach clenched, and a ripple of... something... spread through me. It was like stepping into a warm bath on a cold day: warmth starting in one spot, then spreading through me, bringing an easy contentment. It was the same feeling I'd gotten whenever I'd watched Charlie boxing.

Once again, the pleasant feeling gave way to a wave of nausea. Stop staring at the players, I seethed at myself. Don't let them be right about you.

But a sinking feeling had taken hold of me, and dread filled me even after I'd forced myself to stop admiring the footballers.

"Keep an eye out, Eddy," another of Dad's mates said, putting a heavy hand on my shoulder and pulling me out of my strange, confusing thoughts. "Things could get rough if we lose."

"Or if we win," another hooligan chimed in, grinning maliciously. "Either way, some Northern Monkeys will go home in a London hearse."

I had to turn away to hide my eye roll. It was pitiful how these men would find any excuse to fight. It was one thing to be a sore loser, but to be a sore winner as well... Even when their team won, my father and his friends still wanted to bash skulls in, preferably the skulls of the losing teams' fans. They had no grace in victory.

"Leave the kid alone," Dad said. "He wouldn't fight the Everton fans even if they came right at him." I flushed with embarrassment and turned to look at him, but he was still staring out over the pitch. He hadn't spoken to or made eye contact with me since we'd arrived at the match. It had been like this since I quit boxing: he mostly ignored me. And while this was better than constantly hearing how disappointed he was in me, it was very isolating.

Dad's mates gave each other quizzical looks but said nothing, and I moved farther down the terraces, away from them.

As the match kicked off, I tried to enjoy the spectacle before me, the skilful footwork, and the electrifying pace of the game. The "beautiful game" wasn't wholly uninteresting to me, and despite what my father thought, I knew the rules. And even if I didn't care much about the sport, I could still appreciate the skill involved, the sheer athleticism of the players, the graceful fluidity with which they raced up and down the pitch, their hair sparkling in the sunlight...

But it was hard to enjoy the game when I couldn't shake the unease that gnawed at my gut, the sense of impending doom that clung to the game like a shadow. Dad and his friends were like a ticking time bomb waiting to go off. As they got drunker and drunker—their shouts louder, their slurs more offensive—I could feel the tension building, the explosion approaching. While I'd never witnessed their violence firsthand, I had seen the aftermath of it many times, and it scared me.

But while the game continued, my fears went unrealised. I had just begun to relax by the time the final whistle blew, signalling a narrow victory for West Ham.

Dad and the other members of the Mile End Mob were instantly on their feet, screaming and bumping chests in a decidedly caveman-like ritual that had me once more rolling my eyes. My problem wasn't football; it was football fans: the strange masculine displays of dominance and violence that somehow bonded them to one another. It was as alien to me as if they came from a different planet.

I was still sitting when Dad spotted me. Grinning from ear to ear, he pushed through his friends until he was at my side.

"Come on, get up!" he shouted, seizing me by the arm. I was so surprised he was speaking to me again that I let him pull me to my feet. My beer sloshed onto my shoes as I stood, soaking my feet. "At least show some enthusiasm."

"Woo hoo, we won." I was glad we'd won. Maybe it would put him in a good enough mood that he wouldn't start a fight.

Of course, I was being naïve.

The Everton fans were furious at their narrow loss, and the sweltering heat, combined with their drunkenness, made them rowdy. They were yelling derisively at our side of the stadium, and the West Ham fans were shouting back as good as they got. The ICF blokes were boisterous. For a minute, the crowd teetered on the edge of violence as both sides worked themselves up. Then, like a tidal wave crashing on the beach, it broke.

Violence erupted as Everton fans charged our side, unleashing pandemonium. Suddenly, cups flew through the air, people screamed bloody murder, and Everton fans surrounded me. Amid it all, the Mile End Mob lads swung their fists wildly, their expressions feverish.

"Get stuck in, Eddy!" Dad bellowed. "Show 'em what you're made of!"

"No, Dad," I shouted back, although I wasn't sure if he could hear me over the screaming of the crowd. It suddenly hit me that he might have agreed to bring me along because he hoped a fight would break out. My stomach lurched. Maybe he had hoped that fighting Everton fans would reignite my desire to box.

However, Dad was gone before I could think to ask this, hurling himself into the fray. More and more Everton fans had reached our side of the stands, and both sides were clawing and swinging at each other with abandon, their eyes bloodshot and their jaws slack.

I glanced around, searching for an escape route—but it was too late. An Everton fan, bloodied and bruised, lunged at me, and I only just dodged his blow. When I stood up, I found two more advancing on me, grinning like maniacal idiots. Slowing my breath, I looked between them. They were both large and beefy but clearly drunk and seemed slow. It would be easy for me to take them. But that would require fighting; I couldn't parry my way out of this one.

Just then, Dad came back into view. He saw the two men moving toward me, and his eyes lit up.

"I got you, son!" he shouted over the crowd. Right in front of me, he punched a small Everton fan in his way, knocking him over. Then he was by my side, grinning toothily. My stomach curled as I saw the blood from the man he'd clobbered on his knuckles. "We can take them," he yelled, gesturing at the two Everton fans before us.

They lunged, and Dad caught the first one with a clean uppercut. The other made straight for me, and I had a split second to decide: do I fight or let him knock me down?

My instincts and my need for my father's approval roared at me to fight back and defend myself. I knew I could easily. But another, stronger part of me was screaming at me not to listen, for once, to my own values instead of my father's desires.

The Everton fan hit me, and the world spun out of focus. Stars danced before my eyes as I crumpled to the ground. Somewhere above me, I heard Dad shout, then clock my attacker, who grunted and retreated.

Dad's face appeared above me, twisted with disgust and shame.

"Pathetic," he spat. "All that boxing training, and you still let yourself get done."

The pain was radiating from my jaw, making it difficult to speak. Each breath came in ragged, like the air had turned to broken glass, and my head throbbed.

"Get up, Eddy," Dad shouted. "Get up, for fuck's sake!"

I pulled myself up and steadied myself on trembling legs. My heart was pounding like an angry fist against my ribcage. I clenched and unclenched my fists, willing away the all-too-familiar pain of being punched.

"Y'know, Dad," I said, unexpectedly and inappropriately amused by the whole situation, "I think I've found my true calling: professional punching bag."

Dad shot me a glare, unaffected by my attempt at humour. "You're a fucking embarrassment."

That's when it hit me: even though I'd quit boxing, Dad still hadn't given up hope I was going to follow in his footsteps, that I would become a football hooligan, or at least a "lad's lad" who drank pints with the boys until all hours of the night and wasn't above throwing a punch or two.

Dad had never understood who I was. He'd never tried to understand. So once the fighting was over, I let him know, definitively, who I was.

"Look, Dad," I began, pulling myself up to my full height. I may have been shorter than Lenny, but the summer had changed more than my height; I didn't feel diminished by him anymore. Our eyes met: his blazing, mine controlled. "I know I'm not like you and your mates. But I've got other strengths that don't involve fighting."

"Strengths?" Dad snorted derisively. "What strengths, Eddy? Being a coward?"

"I'm not a coward," I fired back, anger flaring. "I could have done that bloke, but I chose not to because I'm sick of hurting people. That's not cowardice. That's compassion."

"Compassion?" Dad sneered. "You think compassion will help you survive in this world?"

"Maybe not," I admitted. "But it's who I am. And I won't change that for anyone." *Is that true, though? A sly voice inside my head whispered. Remember how you felt looking at the footballers? You won't admit that part of yourself, surely?*

I shook my head, trying to rid myself of these intrusive thoughts. Dad shook his head as well. He turned and walked away, leaving me standing alone, battered and bruised.

Chapter Nine

Although things with my dad remained tense that year, at least my position at school had improved. The other boys had left me alone since I'd knocked Tommy Burke out. I wasn't sure if this was because I'd shown Tommy he couldn't push me around, or if he was grateful that I'd put him on his side and had told his mates to leave me alone. I suspected it was the former, but I hoped it was the latter. It also could have had something to do with the bout I'd won. While people at school didn't follow amateur Junior boxing, I knew that word had gotten around about the fight.

Regardless, my reputation at school had undergone a positive shift. And while I wouldn't call myself popular or even well-liked, the students exhibited a newfound wariness around me. If I wasn't a weakling to be made fun of and bullied, they didn't know what to do with me. I was still too odd and into "feminine" things to be considered a lad, but I was too strong and threw too good a punch to be taunted anymore.

By October 1971, my classmates had decided it was better to ignore me. This suited me perfectly fine. I still had a few friends—all girls—and the third year was so much more rigorous than the second year that I spent most of my time studying.

That all changed at the beginning of November.

It was between classes, and the corridors were full of students. Tommy Burke and his gang were cutting a path through the crowd, and out of some old instinct, I pushed myself out of the way when I saw them coming. Usually, Tommy and I never acknowledged each other, and this time was no different. He didn't even look at me as he walked by, but Shaun, always the loyal sidekick, glared at me.

I raised my eyebrows at him as if to suggest that if he wanted to say anything to me, we could take it outside. This was a bluff, of course. I wasn't interested in fighting anymore. But Shaun didn't know that.

Shaun's face paled. For a moment, I thought he was afraid of me. But then colour continued to drain from his face. The speed at which he turned was so fast that I almost reached out towards him, afraid he might faint.

And then, in a moment that seemed to stretch for an eternity, Shaun staggered and crumpled to the ground like a marionette whose strings had been abruptly severed.

"Shaun!" My scream reverberated down the corridor. All around me, the once-ebullient throng of students dissolved into chaos, their voices becoming confused and panicked.

"Move!" I yelled, shouldering my way through the crowd. People fell back at my shout, making way for me to reach Shaun.

I dropped to my knees when I reached Shaun's side and quickly assessed the situation. His chest was rising and falling in shallow, erratic breaths, and his face had become an unsettling shade of grey. His skin was clammy, and his eyes were unfocused.

"Someone get a teacher!" I shouted, suddenly aware that the surrounding students had fallen silent. There was the sound of someone sprinting away, and I hoped they had gone to tell a teacher to call an ambulance.

"Eddy..." Shaun gasped. His eyes were wide with fear and pain. "I... I can't..."

"Where does it hurt?" I asked. "Can you show me?"

"It's my chest..." He was struggling to speak, and I felt a pang of worry that I was costing him much-needed energy. But I had to know what the problem was. "My arm, too. Tingles."

"Your arm?"

He flopped his left arm, and an icy fear seized me. It couldn't be... Shaun was fourteen years old. There was no way he could have a heart attack. Unless it was something genetic, which was rare but possible.

"Stay with me, Shaun," I murmured, my voice steady even as my hands trembled. "You're going to be alright."

Then his eyes fluttered closed, and Shaun stopped breathing.

Fear gripped me. But despite the paralysis of panic, my instincts kicked in.

With a steadiness I hadn't known I was capable of, I placed the back of my hand against Shaun's nose to check his breathing. There was nothing, no warm air against my hand. Moving my fingers to his neck, I pressed down hard, looking for a pulse. Nothing.

Shaun's heart had stopped. He wasn't breathing. He was going to die. He was already dead.

My fingers were slippery with sweat, and my back was drenched. I knew what to do, but I had never done it before, not like this. I'd learned how to administer CPR when playing "doctor" with my friends, and we'd been taught at the boxing gym, just in case. But reading theory and practising on dummies was very different from doing it in real life, on a real person, with half your school watching.

But I didn't have any choice. Every second I hesitated was a second Shaun's life slipped away. Tearing off my jacket, I rolled up my sleeves and brought my hands to his chest.

"Alright, mate, I'm going to start CPR. Just hang in there," I whispered, even though I wasn't sure he could hear me. I then began pressing down in firm, rhythmic compressions, counting aloud to keep pace. "One, two, three..."

As I counted, doubts and fears whirled through my mind. What if I'm doing this wrong? What if I can't save him? What if he dies right here, on the floor of our school?

And, selfishly, Will people think I let him die because he used to bully me?

After thirty compressions, I switched to rescue breaths. Pinching Shaun's nose shut, I placed my mouth to his and blew air into his mouth. Once, then twice. Each breath felt like a prayer, a plea to the universe to spare him.

"Come on, Shaun," I muttered under my breath as I lifted my mouth away. "Don't give up on me now."

But Shaun didn't stir, and when I held my hand under his nose, I still couldn't feel any breath. It hadn't worked.

I began another cycle of chest compressions and rescue breaths. Soon, my hands were aching, and sweat dripped down my brow. But I refused to give up. My hands moved with deft, instinctual precision, pushing down on Shaun's chest in a steady rhythm. Time stretched around me like a shroud, obscuring everything else. I didn't know how many cycles of chest compressions and rescue breaths I'd done. It could have been five or fifty. The surrounding noises had faded until there was only Shaun and me.

Then someone touched my shoulder, and I almost lost track of my compressions in the middle of a cycle.

"Edward, are you alright? I've called an ambulance." It was Mr Green, the maths teacher. He crouched by my side, his hand on my shoulder and worry creasing his face. I barely had time to register him before I returned to Shaun.

I returned to the count inside my head. Twenty-three, twenty-four, twenty-five.

Shepherded by Mr Green, the crowd shifted back, granting Shaun and me a small pocket of air amidst the crush of people. Mr Green's presence had pulled me from my focus, and I was now acutely aware of time ticking by, of how little time we had before Shaun would be beyond help. The average person could go only four to six minutes without oxygen before it caused lasting damage to their brain. I didn't know how long Shaun had been without oxygen, but I knew it was getting close to the point of no return.

"Come on, Shaun," I snarled, though it was as much a plea to myself as to my old tormentor. "Don't you dare give up on me now!"

And then it happened. With the force and suddenness of a geyser shooting up from the ground, Shaun gasped, sucking in air, and his eyes flew open.

I nearly yelled from the shock and caught myself just in time. Removing my hands from his chest, I immediately cradled his head with one hand and placed the other on his neck. Sure enough, his pulse had returned. It was faint, but it was there.

Jubilation flooded me. Jubilation, relief, joy, and even a tiny flicker of pride. Shaun was alive. He hadn't died. I had saved his life!

Shaun blinked up at me and tried to speak, but I shook my head. "Don't talk," I said. "Save your energy."

His face crumpled, his eyes filled with tears, and to my shock, he began to cry. I kept my hand cradling his head, holding him as he cried.

It was the strangest feeling of my life, to hold the boy who used to bully me as he cried in my arms.

Mr Green let out a shout of relief and moved forward.

"Shaun!" he cried, his voice thick with emotion. "You're alive!"

"You had a heart attack," I said calmly to keep Shaun from getting more upset. "But you're alright now. The ambulance will be here momentarily."

"Eddy saved you! He gave you CPR and everything." Mr Green smiled radiantly at me. Sweat was pouring down his face, which was very red. He looked worse than I felt, and I was the one who'd been giving CPR.

Shaun, meanwhile, was blinking up at me. He was still crying but seemed to have calmed a little. I couldn't read the look on his face, and I averted my gaze. I didn't want to see anger, disgust, or even gratefulness there. To be honest, I didn't know what I wanted to see.

There was a commotion down the corridor, and I looked up to see several paramedics racing toward us. They were carrying medical bags and a stretcher. At the sight of them, relief once again coursed through me.

When they reached us, they carefully lifted Shaun and set him on the stretcher. They then began attaching devices to him, which I assumed would monitor his heart, blood pressure, and breathing. I stood and took a step back to give them space.

"He was gone," Mr Green said to one. "But Eddy here gave him CPR, brought him back."

The paramedic glanced at me as he fitted an oxygen mask over Shaun's mouth and nose, his expression surprised and impressed.

"Quick thinking, kid," he said. "You probably saved your friend's life." With the oxygen mask now fitted over Shaun's face, the paramedic placed his hand on my shoulder. "You should think about a career as a paramedic."

Then, he and his colleague were lifting the stretcher. They moved away down the corridor, Mr Green following in their wake.

I stayed behind, watching them go. Now that it was over, I felt so tired that I thought I might collapse. But even amidst my exhaustion, I was exhilarated. I had saved Shaun's life. I had saved Shaun's life! And then there was the comment from the paramedic: You should think about a career as a paramedic.

It had only ever been a game with my friends, but as I stood in the corridor, my classmates skirting me warily, unsure whether to congratulate me, I realised what I'd always known: I was meant to be in the medical profession.

Chapter Ten

Shaun didn't come back to school for several weeks. When he finally did, the school organised an assembly to welcome him back. He'd been diagnosed with a congenital heart disease, which the doctors assured him he could manage with medication. It wasn't fatal if caught early. This meant he wouldn't have to have surgery unless his symptoms got worse and he needed a heart transplant.

I heard all this from Mr Green, who kept me up-to-date on any new information the school got on Shaun's condition. Strictly speaking, he probably wasn't supposed to divulge medical information about another student to me, but I think Mr Green wanted me to know what had become of the person I'd saved. And I appreciated it. For days afterwards, I woke abruptly every night, wrenched from sleep by nightmares in which I couldn't perform CPR on Shaun; my arms and torso were waterlogged and unable to move. In those dreams, Shaun always died.

Which is why I was relieved and excited when he returned to school. I wasn't expecting anything from him, of course. Certainly not a thank you. But having him back meant that things could return to normal; I could return to going unnoticed.

Upon Shaun's return, the corridors were loud and crowded as students tried to get a glimpse of him. He entered with Tommy Burke, and while some of his usual swagger was gone, he looked happy. As students called out to greet him, he smiled shyly. At last, several students came over and patted him on the back, and he grinned more widely. It wasn't until he reached the end of the corridor, near where I stood by the chemistry classroom, watching silently, that someone shouted, "Oi, Shaun, you like kissing boys?"

A wolf whistle and a spate of giggling followed this. Shaun stopped walking at once, and his face flushed. Tommy, meanwhile, swung around as if looking for the source of the comment.

"What did you say?" he snapped at no one in particular. No one answered, of course, but several more people giggled. My stomach felt as if it had dropped out of me. Part of me wanted to shout that even if I were gay, I'd never want to kiss the boy who bullied me, but I knew to keep quiet.

"We didn't kiss," Shaun said too loudly. "It was CPR."

More sniggers. Heat was also beginning to burn in my cheeks and down my neck. Shaun wasn't looking at me, but I knew he had seen me because he was looking everywhere but where I stood.

Tommy cracked his knuckles. "Whoever said that, say it to my face."

There were several moments of silence, and then a boy stepped forward. He was in the second year but already large, with beefy arms and broad shoulders. I think his name was Brandon. He didn't look intimidated as he sized up Tommy Burke.

"You telling me you didn't think that was gay?" he leered at Tommy. "Your best mate kissing that Eddy bloke?"

I could feel eyes on me, but I didn't look around. I continued to stare at Brandon, Shaun, and Tommy, my mind racing. How had they discovered the secret flutterings, the bubbles of pleasure that rose when I looked at footballers or watched Charlie boxing? It wasn't possible. I didn't know what they meant, so how could anyone else?

Tommy opened his mouth as if to repeat Shaun's line that CPR wasn't the same as kissing but then changed tactics. He closed his mouth, set his jaw, and snapped, "Yeah, Eddy kissed Shaun. What was Shaun supposed to do? He was unconscious. He had a bloody heart attack."

"Whatever," Brandon sneered. "I know what I saw. Two blokes on the ground, snogging."

"Then you're a fucking idiot," Tommy hissed.

Brandon smiled. His big, flabby lips curled back to reveal large, uneven, yellowed teeth. "At least I'm not a queer. Or friends with one."

There was more laughter. Tommy looked as if he was about to punch Brandon right in the middle of the corridor, but then Shaun put a hand on his arm.

"Leave it," he mumbled.

Tommy turned to stare at him. "He called you a queer!"

Shaun shrugged. "Yeah, and I've just had a heart attack. I'm in no fit state to be fighting people. Let him think what he wants."

Tommy's eyes narrowed as if trying to assess how he should respond. Finally, he jerked away from Shaun. "Ah, you liked it!" he snarled. He didn't sound convinced, but I suspected he wanted to save face in front of the other students. But he wasn't done. "Don't touch me, you dirty fucking shirt lifter!"

Several people gasped, but a few also laughed. Shaun's eyes, meanwhile, went wide, and the hurt in them was so acute I felt a painful jolt in my chest. Tommy gave Shaun one last furious look, then stormed away down the corridor, barging into me as he passed.

Across the corridor, Shaun stared at me. His hands were clenched into fists at his side, his lips were curled, and his eyes were wide. If you think about cartoons where characters' faces go red, and steam comes off of them, that was what he looked like. "Look what you've done. You should have let me die!" he shouted across.

And do you know what I felt? Guilt. Guilt for saving him. Because of me, he was now going to be bullied.

I didn't wait for Shaun to storm past me. Instead, I turned away and trudged down the corridor. I wasn't angry; I just wanted to cry. All I ever did was hurt people, no matter how hard I tried to do the opposite.

The headmaster held an assembly that afternoon. He'd invited parents, too, and as we students filed into the school hall, I saw my mum and dad sitting together in the front row. They were sitting in a place of honour since the headmaster planned to give me an award for saving Shaun. Mum looked around as the students came in, and she smiled and waved when she saw me. Dad's expression remained more muted, and he didn't wave. I looked away; Dad's reaction to me saving Shaun had been predictable:

"You saved the boy who you used to beat you up?" he'd asked, incredulous. "Sounds to me like he got what was coming for him."

"Leonard!" Mum had gasped. "That's a child you're talking about!"

Dad had paused, then flushed, as the realisation of his words hit him. "You're right," he'd said apologetically, then continued to grumble, "Still, asking us to take a day off work to celebrate the fact…"

As if Lenny's lack of pride in me wasn't enough, I was also having trouble with all the attention currently directed my way. Years of bullying had made me averse to being noticed. I preferred to feel invisible.

I felt ill at ease in my body as I sat down in the third row, on the opposite side of the aisle from my parents.

Our headmaster walked up onto the stage, and silence spread throughout the hall. He coughed and tapped the microphone. Feedback reverberated through the room, making parents groan and kids clap their hands over their ears.

"Apologies," he mumbled into the mic. "Welcome, parents, to Robert Clack. We asked you here today to welcome back our student, Shaun Windham, who suffered a heart attack three weeks ago. It was a frightening experience for all our students, but for Shaun and his family, it must have been a terrible ordeal. We'd like to extend our best wishes to Mr and Mrs Windham and tell them how happy we are that Shaun has made a full recovery and returned to school. Please join me in welcoming Shaun back with a round of applause."

The audience applauded dutifully. I turned in my seat so that I could see Shaun. He was blushing, and I felt a little bad for him again. It couldn't be easy to be singled out for having a heart attack and collapsing in front of the entire school. That wasn't exactly what someone wanted to be remembered for.

Then I remembered the hatred with which he'd looked at me, and I pushed any feelings of sympathy away.

"We also wanted to take this opportunity to say a heartfelt thank you to another student," the headmaster continued. His eyes searched the audience until they found mine, and he smiled. "I'm speaking, of course, about Edward Turner. Eddy, would you mind coming up here, please?"

Getting out of the row was difficult, and I kept tripping over students' feet. But as I reached the end, I stumbled down the aisle and up the stairs to where the headmaster was waiting for me, hand outstretched. I shook it, and he beamed at me.

"Eddy acted with remarkable speed and skill when Shaun fell ill. Thanks to his quick thinking and expert CPR knowledge, Shaun is still with us today. The school would like to thank him for his bravery, competence, and grace under pressure. We are presenting this award to him"—the headmaster motioned to another teacher, who stepped forward from the wings of the hall holding a small trophy—"in order to show our gratitude, admiration, and pride."

The other teacher handed the headmaster the trophy, and he held it up high. "This Award of Courage and Services Rendered to the School is awarded to Edward Turner. We are excited to see all the remarkable things you do with your life, Eddy."

He turned to me, still beaming, and handed me the small, shiny trophy. It looked gold but was light, reminding me of gilded chocolate coins from Christmas stockings. The metal was cold to the touch. I stared down at it in my hands, too bashful to look at the audience, who were applauding loudly. It was bad enough to be put on display like this, but to do so for something that had humiliated Shaun and made him hate me more was even worse.

"I'm sure that Mr and Mrs Windham would also like to thank you," the headmaster continued, and my stomach lurched. The last thing I wanted was to interact with Shaun's parents. But sure enough, moments later, the Windhams—Shaun in tow—were mounting the stairs. Then they were shaking my hand. Mrs Windham was crying, and Mr Windham patted me on the shoulder and called me son. Shaun looked horrified, but he tried to arrange his face into one of polite gratitude as he shook my hand. He didn't quite meet my eyes.

Then it was over. Everyone applauded again. The Windhams left the stage, and I slouched back to my seat, my face burning.

After the assembly, the school served refreshments at the back of the hall. The headmaster gathered around my parents, and I watched from a distance as they basked in the glow of his attention. Mum smiled more than I'd ever seen her, and even Dad seemed to have perked up. I could only relax once the Windhams had left, but even then, I felt nervous and on edge. I was sitting on the floor, back against the wall, not talking to anyone, when Mum found me.

"Hey, you," she said as she approached. She was smiling, and her cheeks were pink. A loose strand of hair had come undone from her coiffure. She was holding a cup of tea, which she held out to me. I accepted it, and she slid down the wall to sit on the ground next to me.

"This is nice," she murmured.

When I only grunted, she nudged me playfully. "I know you don't like attention, but it's important to be acknowledged for the good deeds we do."

"I didn't do it to be acknowledged," I said, unsticking my throat. "I just wanted to save Shaun's life. Anyone else would have done the same."

"No one else did the same," Mum pointed out.

Uncomfortable with the praise, I fidgeted. "I'm not a hero," I insisted, more waspishly than I'd intended. "I just... reacted, you know?"

My mother gazed at me for a long moment, then nodded. "I understand. But as a parent, it's nice to see my kid get an award for helping someone and not for, well..."

"For fighting?" I supplied.

She laughed. "Yes. When you won your bout, I was happy because you won. But this is different. You saved someone's life, and that's something you should be immensely proud of."

"Yeah," I muttered. "This feels more me."

She tweaked my cheek. "It does."

We lapsed into silence, both of us watching the headmaster chatting with Dad.

"The Windhams seemed appreciative," she began tentatively.

I looked at my feet. "Shaun isn't."

"Didn't he used to bully you?" When I nodded, she frowned. "He probably doesn't enjoy having to thank the person he used to push around."

"No, he doesn't."

Mum reached out and brushed a lock of my hair back from my forehead. "I'm proud of you, Eddy. Not everyone would be selfless enough to save the kid that used to bully them."

Again, I shrugged. "I didn't think about that in the moment. All I could think was that this was a person, and he needed help. It didn't matter if he was someone I liked or not. Still…" Mum looked at me quizzically. "It would be nice if he didn't hate me for it," I finished.

Mum sighed. "God put you on this earth to help people, Eddy. Unfortunately, not everyone will be grateful for that."

Dad chose that moment to laugh loudly, and we both looked at him. "I know what you mean," I said.

"You help people because that's who you are, Eddy," she continued. "Don't let anyone take that from you."

"I won't, Mum. I want to go into medicine like you did. But I know Dad will never let me be a nurse."

Mum sighed and paused for a moment. "Maybe not a nurse… but I'm sure he will come round to the idea of you becoming a doctor."

"He might come round to the idea of it. But training to be a doctor takes a long time, and there's no way Dad will put his hand into his pocket to support me through it."

Mum's response was to fold her arms and set her jaw. "Leave that to me."

Chapter Eleven

In the autumn of 1976, just before my eighteenth birthday, I received the acceptance letter from St. George's. I was sitting at breakfast with Mum and Dad when the post arrived, and as I ripped open the envelope from my dream medical school, my parents watched on. My mother's expression was tense, and she had her fingers crossed. Dad looked like he was hoping for bad news.

"I'll expect you to pay rent," he snapped as Mum and I danced around the kitchen thirty seconds later. She was hugging me, half-crying, as I spun her around.

Dad's words, as they always did, brought me hurtling back to earth. "If you're going to be staying here while at uni."

My mother dropped her arms from my waist. Wiping her tears from her cheeks, she returned to the kitchen table. When I turned to face my dad, he was scowling.

"Actually, Dad, I was thinking of moving closer to the university." I remained standing as I turned to speak to him and held my head high. This was something I'd given a lot of thought. While I'd save money if I stayed with my parents (even paying them rent would be less than renting near St George's), it was time for me to get out from under my father's oppressive shadow.

Dad snorted. "And how will you do that if you don't have a job? Or does that acceptance come with some sort of scholarship?"

"It doesn't," I admitted. "But I'm planning on getting a job. Maybe I can work at a pub, or..."

"You should work at the factory with me!" Dad slammed his hand down on the table, making the cutlery rattle. "Not going off to some fancy uni south of the river just to learn how to bandage people up!"

"Leonard," my old dear said sharply. "We've discussed this! Eddy has worked hard to get into St. George's. It's the best medical school in the country. He can't work at the Ford factory when he has the brain he does. He's got to use it, to make something of his life."

For a moment, Dad looked as if he was about to hit her. His face went pale, and he raised a hand. It was shaking with rage. "What you trying to say? That I've wasted my life?"

"Don't speak to her like that," I snarled, stepping forward. In the past year, I'd grown taller than my dad, and as he looked up at me, there was half a second when fear clouded his face. It might have been years since I'd boxed, but looking at my height and strength, he must have realised it was still possible for me to hurt him.

Then he laughed.

"Or what? We both know you'll never throw a punch ever again."

"I will if you continue to yell at my mother," I said as calmly as I could manage. However, I don't think my father was fooled because he smirked.

"Lenny, it's not a competition," Mum said quickly. She reached out and tried to take his hand, but he pulled it away. "You've always provided for me, for us. I'm so proud of you. But Eddy is our son. We should want him to have a better life than we had."

Dad stood abruptly, knocking over his chair. It clattered to the ground, and Mum flinched. "So now you're saying I didn't give you a good enough life, is that it?" Mum opened her mouth to respond, but he turned away. Without meeting my gaze, he stormed past me and disappeared down the hallway.

Silence filled the space he'd left. For a minute, neither Mum nor I looked at each other.

"He'll come round," she murmured finally. "It feels like a rejection of him. He thought... he thought you'd follow the life plan he had for you."

"I've been working towards this for years," I said, throwing the acceptance letter on the table. "He's known for years that I want to be a doctor."

"Yes, but I think he hoped you weren't serious." She looked up at me, her expression desperate. "Or he hoped that once it came to it, you'd change your mind."

I folded my arms. No matter how she looked at me, I wouldn't take pity on my father. Not anymore. "Well, I didn't change my mind. And I'm serious about what I said: I will get a job and find a flat near the university. I can't live with him anymore. Not if he hasn't let go of this idiotic notion that I'm going to be a boxer, or a hooligan, or a factory worker."

"I understand," she murmured. "But, Eddy... just know you're always welcome here if things get too hard on your own."

From Dad's bedroom, a crash sounded, rattling the entire house.

Mum and I looked at each other, and I shook my head. "I don't know if that's true."

Despite the gnawing feeling I'd once again disappointed my father, I put him and those feelings aside as soon as I moved out of my childhood home a few weeks later. Finding a job was easy enough. On my first day walking through Brixton, I found a pub that was hiring, and after a brief interview, they brought me on to help behind the bar.

Finding a flat wasn't more complicated. London in those days wasn't like it is now, where flats are impossible to find and prohibitively expensive. There were flyers all around the university advertising for flatmates. After looking at several options, I moved into a house with a group of second-year med students. I figured they'd be working as hard as I was and that I could learn from them, maybe even ask for their help on particularly hard assignments.

The property was just off of Tooting Commons, on Franciscan Road, a terraced house with large bay windows on both the ground and first floors. My room was on the first floor, at the front, overlooking a small park. I had very few possessions, all of which fit in the tiny space. The bedroom had once been the master suite, but the landlord had converted it into two rooms. The boy in the other room, Raj, was from India and one of the brightest people I'd ever met. He and the two other girls who lived in the house, Betsy and Deborah, were best friends. And contrary to my expectations, they liked to throw big parties and do drugs more than they liked to study. On my first evening there, they invited me to sit in the back garden with them while they drank cans and smoked weed.

"Have you ever had this before?" Betsy asked me as she handed me the joint. Blue smoke curled up from the red cherry at its tip, filling my nose with an earthy smell that was not unpleasant. We were all sprawled on sun chairs, watching as the last rays of sunlight disappeared over the tops of the terraced houses. Reggae was blaring from the neighbours' house, where students were having a party.

I shook my head. "My dad would kill me if I ever tried it."

"How quaint," Betsy said, shaking her head. "A boy from Dagenham who doesn't do drugs." As far as I could tell, she and Deborah were from posh families. Their accents sounded like they were from West London, and their clothes were nicer than anything I'd seen any girls in Dagenham wear.

"Don't be a snob," Deborah said, throwing her a dirty look.

"Where I'm from, hash is legal," Raj said. "They sell it on the streets, cooked into desserts. It's called bang."

"Go on, try it," Betsy said, her voice patronising as she wagged the joint at me. "You'll like it."

"But we're medical students," I protested, even as I took it. In truth, I was curious about marijuana. I was eighteen and free of my family for the first time; of course, I wanted to experiment. But the dutiful son and serious medical student in me were both screaming at me to resist. "Isn't it bad for you?"

"Nah, man, it takes you away from reality," Deborah said. She smiled and winked. "It'll make you a better doctor."

"What do you mean?"

Deborah sat up straight. She was sitting opposite me, and as she leaned forward, her knees knocked against mine.

"Doctors deal with ill, seriously ill, and dying people daily. It's not like any other profession. And how do you detach yourself from that when you get home? You get fucked up and forget what you have to deal with when you are at work. Trust me, every doctor you've ever seen before gets fucked up when they are not working."

"Are you already high?" Raj asked with a snort.

Deborah rolled her eyes. "You don't believe it's true, just like everyone believes their mum and dad have never had sex," she snapped at him. "But they do."

"I think she has a point," I mumbled.

"Don't be an arse licker," Raj said, but he sounded amused, not judgemental. "Just because Debbie's good-looking doesn't mean she's not talking bollox."

Debbie stretched out a leg and lazily shoved Raj with her foot. Her toenails were painted black, I noticed. Her legs were also unshaven. I'd never seen a girl without shaved legs, and my eyes lingered too long on her thigh. When I looked up at her, her dark eyes were boring into mine.

"Don't tell me you're disgusted by a woman's body hair," she said, her eyes narrowing.

"Of course not!" The idea was so funny that I actually laughed. "I think it's cool."

Debbie leaned back in her sun chair, smirking. "Women's lib is going to change everything. Just you wait. Have you read Gloria Steinem? Bell Hooks? Audre Lorde?"

I shook my head, and she raised her eyebrows. "Well, just you wait. It'll change your life."

"Debbie is a feminist," Betsy said, smirking at me. "Feminism is in vogue, you know."

"I'm a feminist," I said, without thinking.

Raj, Betsy, and Debbie all stared at me.

"What are you talking about?" Debbie demanded. "A man can't be a feminist."

"Why not?" I met her gaze and didn't look away. A lock of her auburn hair had fallen in front of her eyes, but she didn't seem to have noticed. "My mum was one of the sewing machinists who led the strikes at the Dagenham Ford factory in sixty-eight. She was the one who taught me all about women's rights and the struggle to get them."

"Well, you'll fit right in here, then," Raj said, taking the joint from Betsy and hitting it hard. He coughed as he exhaled. "Inside the house, instead of getting high and listening to music, we like to talk about feminism and our confrontational relationships with death."

Debbie snatched the joint from Raj. "You've got to understand doctors are not robots and—" She stopped speaking, a hazy, distant look coming to her eyes. The three of us stared at her, transfixed, until she burst out laughing. "Fuck, it just hit me!" she screeched as she dissolved into a fit of giggles. "I can't even remember what I was saying!"

Betsy and Raj laughed, and I watched with quiet amusement as they writhed around on their sun chairs, laughing hysterically.

"I bet you thought I was going to say that smoking wacky baccy helps us find ourselves or something like that?" Betsy asked me, gulping at the air between fits of giggles.

"No"—I grinned—"but it looks like you are having a lot of fun."

Debbie swiped the lighter from the table in front of Raj and re-lit the end of the joint. Then she offered it to me, her eyes twinkling. "Want to try?"

This time, I didn't hesitate.

Later that night, after Betsy and Raj had gone to bed, Debbie said we should make food and sit on the roof and stargaze. She was too high to operate the stove, so I made pasta with butter for us. Then we climbed out through the bay windows in my room to the roof.

We were probably too drunk and high for what we were attempting, but with the confidence of youth, we didn't even hesitate as we clambered out onto the shingles and half-climbed, half-walked up to the apex of the roof.

There, we ate directly from the bowl—too lazy to use plates—and stared up at the stars.

"So h-how did you end up here?" Debbie asked abruptly after several minutes of silent stargazing.

"What?" I was so entranced by the stars that it took several seconds to realise what she'd said. "Oh... I climbed out the window with you."

"No, silly... I mean, university?"

"It's a long story, but I worked really hard. No one from my school has ever made it to university before."

Debbie looked surprised. "You're real w-working class, aren't you?" She didn't sound judgemental, merely curious.

She bit her lip and looked at me shyly. "I forget that... well, that w-working-class blokes can be intellectual..."

"Well, I don't know if I'm an intellectual," I said with a shrug. "But when I was in the third year, a boy in my class died, technically, and I saved him, so—"

"Wait, what?" Debbie grabbed my arm. "You've saved a life already?"

"Uh... yeah?" I blushed, unused to how she looked at me, almost as if she admired me. "It was a freak thing. He had some sort of genetic condition that caused a heart attack in the middle of school. I knew CPR, so I... saved him."

"Fuuuuck," Debbie said, looking into space. "I've got to admit, I'm quite jealous."

I didn't answer for a long moment. Shaun's pale, lifeless face swam in front of my eyes. Even after all these years, I could still remember the feel of his fragile body under my hands as I compressed his chest. I could still remember the fear like it was yesterday, but also the calm sense of sureness that I could save him.

"I wouldn't be jealous," I said at last. "I think he sort of wished I'd let him die."

"Huh?"

"Oh, just... he used to bully me. He and his best friend, Tommy Burke. But after I saved him, everyone started making fun of him for being gay." When Debbie looked confused, I explained, "Because of the rescue breaths."

She snorted. "Well, he sounds like a fucking idiot. Everyone at your school sounds like a f-fucking idiot." I had never heard a girl swear so much, and I liked it. I smiled at her, and she grinned back and threw her arm around me. "It's a good thing you got out of Dagenham. You're with your people now. We appreciate you, and we don't think you're gay for s-saving someone's life."

"I guess I'm just not used to hearing that." The warmth of her arm on my shoulders was unfamiliar and strangely comforting. I couldn't remember the last time someone my age had touched me like this.

Debbie released her arm and looked away. "You hear it, d-don't you? My stammer?"

She still wasn't looking at me, so I said quietly, "Yeah, I hear it. But I didn't earlier."

"I've always had it, and when I was younger, people used to make fun of me. Bully me, too." She turned back to me and placed a hand on my leg. "So when I went to college, I decided I was going to become the most confident bitch I could be. I reinvented myself and made myself tough. I took speech therapy. And it worked. Even when I did stammer, I'd become so c-confident that no one dared to make fun of me. And the stammer got better. It only comes out now when I'm n-nervous."

"Why are you nervous?" I whispered. My heart was pounding in my chest, and I had a feeling that hers was, too.

Debbie's eyes stayed fixed on mine. They seemed to burn with the same brightness as the stars above us. Then she brought her free hand to my cheek, and my stomach squirmed. It didn't feel exactly like the heart flutterings I'd experienced for boys, but it seemed close enough that relief flooded me. At last, I had a crush on a girl.

"You're cute," she murmured. "And you're real. Do you know that?"

I forced myself to speak. "Erm. I don't know what to say to that?"

Her hand slipped to my neck while the other moved up my thigh. She leaned towards me until her lips were brushing against mine. "Then let me show you."

Chapter Twelve

Debbie's presence in my life was an unexpected, happy addition to those early days at uni. Classes started the next week, and I was immediately so overwhelmed that I was grateful for her constancy in my life. My classes were harder than any I had taken in secondary school, harder even than learning to box. And while I had been at the top of my class in Dagenham, where there wasn't much competition, I was far from the brightest student at St. George's. Many of my classmates had come from posh backgrounds and had attended preparatory schools. They knew more than me, were faster to answer questions in class, and were less shy to make their opinions known. Compared to them, I felt like a failure. In fact, several times during those first few months, I thought about throwing in the towel and giving up entirely. Only Debbie—and the thought of facing my father—kept me from returning to Dagenham with my tail between my legs. She believed in me. And since I could count on two fingers the number of people who had believed in me—Mum and Cartwright—this meant everything.

"Ignore all those knobs," Debbie told me after one particularly difficult lecture, during which a professor had grilled me on the lymphatic system. As I stuttered out an answer, some boys sitting behind me, who had attended Harrow, sniggered. "The world has pampered them their whole lives, and now they have far too high an opinion of themselves."

"Maybe... but that doesn't change that they're better than me," I said, trying hard to keep the bitterness from my voice.

"Hey!" She turned and grabbed me by the shoulders, forcing me to stop and look at her. "You got into St. George's, same as they did, and without any of the privileges they had."

I suspected she was defensive of me because my stammering reminded her of being bullied as a girl, but I appreciated her loyalty. And her support quickly became something I couldn't live without.

By the end of September 1976, Debbie had practically moved into my bedroom. Raj probably would have preferred if we had slept in Debbie's room, as the makeshift walls between our rooms were thin, and there were many nights when he would thump on the walls to get us to quiet down.

Not that I was ever loud. Even at eighteen, I was still shy and painfully conscious of others' opinions—a relic from my days of being picked on—and the last thing I wanted to do was disturb Raj and Betsy. But Debbie was loud. She considered it her feminist duty to "reclaim her sexuality" and learn not to "perform for the male gaze." She hated pornographic films where actresses squealed like little girls. Instead, when we made love, she would grunt and moan and make animalistic noises that simultaneously aroused and frightened me.

In truth, most things about sex frightened me. I was happy to do it with Debbie, as it seemed to make her happy, but each time, I had to push down the anxiety that inevitably arose. There was always a logical answer to a medical problem: a diagnosis and a cure—or, more rarely, death. But with making love and emotions, there was no one right way to do it, and there were no simple answers to the complicated feelings they elicited—as I was learning.

Debbie hated it when I said that we made love.

"Don't say that just because I'm a woman," she told me one night when she was on top of me, my back pressed into the thin mattress of the bed as she rode me. Debbie liked to take charge and be in control. That was fine by me. I didn't know what I was doing. Debbie was my first in every way, and it was a relief when she told me what to do, how to please her, and what she would do to me.

"Women can fuck just like men do," she continued as her nails bit into my shoulders.

"Does that mean that we're not boyfriend and girlfriend?" I asked, struggling to concentrate as her breasts bounced above me.

Debbie frowned down at me. "Of course we're not. We're just shagging."

Afterwards, we lay together on the mattress, still naked, and smoked a joint. Debbie didn't shave her armpits, and as she passed me the joint, I caught a musky whiff of her—simultaneously sweaty and spicy. The smell was soothingly refreshing and alive after days spent dissecting cadavers.

Debbie propped herself on one arm to watch as the thick blue smoke curled out from my lips.

"About earlier—that's alright, isn't it?" she asked. "That we're just shagging, not dating?"

"It's alright," I said. "You're in charge." Debbie laid a hand on my chest, right above my heart.

"You're not the kind of boy I usually fall in love with," she said. As the wacky baccy fogged my brain, it was hard to understand the meaning of these words. At last, they clicked into place, and I turned to look at her. She was watching me closely, barely blinking.

"Usually, I fall for arseholes," she continued once she had my attention. "Last year, I dated a fifth-year surgeon who told me I didn't have what it takes to become a doctor. And in college, I mostly slept with the boys who never went to college."

I pushed her hair back from her throat and leaned forward, pressing my lips against where her shoulder met her neck. I'd noticed in the past that she liked it when I kissed her on the back, and she rewarded my perceptiveness with a moan.

"Mmmmm, keep doing that," she murmured.

I kissed along her shoulder until I reached her armpit, and then I flicked my tongue out, tasting her sweat and hair. She giggled and pushed me away. I grinned at her.

"What made you want to be a doctor?" I asked.

She didn't answer right away. For a minute or two, she played with my hair, smiling down at me. Then she sighed. "My mum always wanted to be a doctor, but that wasn't possible back in her day. So, I went to med school for her. My dad wasn't very supportive. He wanted me to study finance, like my brothers. But I don't want to become another corporate suit. My dream would be to help young mothers who are hooked on drugs. Maybe I could even go abroad and be a doctor for kids with malaria, somewhere like India." She had a faraway, dreamy look in her eyes. "But people always doubt me. The fifth year, he told me I was idealistic but spoiled and didn't have a good work ethic. He said I smoked too much dope."

"That was shitty of him," I murmured.

She shrugged. "Yeah, well, he was a wanker. Turned out he had a girlfriend back home in Kent. He broke up with me by telling me they got married and he ought to stop cheating on her." She shook her head. "But you're not like him or any of those guys. You're sweet. And you're here for the right reasons."

"So are you." When she gave me a sardonic look, I sat up. "No, seriously, you are. There's nothing wrong with being idealistic. And if you want to go to India, or anywhere, and save lives, then I bet you will. You're smart, and you're passionate."

"Thanks, Eddy. You're a sweet kid." She tweaked my nose as if trying to reestablish that she was the one in control—that we were just shagging—but the deep blush in her cheeks and the warmth in her eyes gave her away. I said nothing. It was okay if Debbie wanted to act like this was a casual hookup. If that's what aligned with her feminist values, that was alright by me. But I knew she felt something more for me. I knew in how she looked at me or how she'd sometimes open her mouth to say something, blush, and then change her mind. And I knew in how she would roll over and spoon me from behind when I turned away in my sleep.

No one had ever liked me before—not counting my youthful encounter with Lucy and Sharon—and Debbie's feelings for me were flattering. It felt good to be accepted for who I was, and after years of bullying, Debbie felt safe. And while the fluttering feeling in my chest didn't happen with Debbie, I was fond of her, even protective of her. I sometimes privately agreed that she smoked too much wacky baccy, but I knew she'd be a brilliant doctor—much better than me. She was smart, courteous, and never afraid to voice her opinions. I knew she'd listen to her patients and advocate fiercely for them. If I was going to have a girlfriend, I wanted it to be someone like Debbie: someone solid and safe, talkative and outgoing, who would allow me to be my shy, quiet self.

But sometimes, I also felt more anxious than excited to see her. In every interaction, I had the feeling I was letting her down. She never said this, but I could sometimes tell in the way she frowned into the distance or grabbed my hand to hold. It reminded me of when Sharon had asked if I liked her, like there was some subtlety to the question I was missing, some nuance I couldn't quite grasp.

By November, we were spending almost all our time together. When we weren't studying together in the library, she visited me at the pub, or we cooked at home. On one of my rare phone calls home, I even mentioned I had a girlfriend, which excited Mum.

"Don't tell Dad," I said after she'd finished gushing.

"Why not? He'll be so excited."

"That's why," I said, twisting the phone cord in the students' lounge. "I don't want something to go wrong and disappoint him again."

"Fair enough. But maybe you can tell him over Christmas. Or better yet, invite her home with you!"

"I don't know, Mum... I think she has plans." I didn't want to tell my mother, but Debbie was supposed to go skiing in Switzerland with her family over the Christmas break. Her family lived in Surrey and was very wealthy. She'd shown me pictures of their house. It looked more like a castle than a house to me. She had also let slip that her parents were paying her rent. "Maybe she could just come to dinner sometime?" I suggested instead.

"Of course, love. Whatever you think is best."

But at the beginning of December, Debbie became withdrawn. It started with her telling me she needed to study alone because her grades were slipping. This surprised me since, as far as I knew, Debbie was still doing excellently in all her classes. Certainly better than I was, as I was still struggling to keep up with my classmates. She then stopped coming to the pub during my shifts. In class, she wouldn't sit next to me. I tried to catch her eye, but she wouldn't look at me. At night, she would still sleep in my room, but she had become surly and withdrawn. When I tried to initiate sex, she'd slap my hand away or tell me she felt ugly and fat. If I withdrew, she accused me of losing interest in her. Eventually, she told me she needed to get better sleep and would be returning to her room.

"What's going on with you?" I asked her that evening. She'd made a rare stop at the pub just as my shift was ending. As I wiped down the bar countertop, I studied her face. She was sitting stiffly on a bar stool, not looking at me. "Have you met someone else?" I asked. My stomach felt like lead, but I had to ask. "Because if you have, I'd rather you just tell me. I know it's awkward because we live together, but I can handle it."

"It's not that," Debbie said. She still wasn't looking at me, but the end of her nose had turned red. I stopped wiping down the bar and peered more closely at her. There were tears in her eyes, and her lip was trembling.

"Debbie..." I threw the cloth into the sink, deciding I'd finished enough of what I was doing. I asked the other barman if I could have a few minutes and then came around to her. She was trembling as I took her in my arms.

"What is it?" I murmured in her ear. "Whatever it is, we can figure it out together."

"Let's go outside," she whispered. Even quiet, her voice sounded hoarse. "I don't want people to hear this."

Outside, it was cold, and slushy rain fell lightly around us. Christmas lights wreathed the pub, giving the street a red and green glow. Holiday shoppers crowded the pavement, so I took Debbie's arm and led her to the alley behind the pub.

"Tell me what's going on," I said once we were ensconced in the alley's darkness. As I spoke, my breath came in a foggy cloud before me.

Debbie took a deep breath. Then she began to sob.

It took several minutes for her to calm down enough to make any coherent sense. Only then was I able to make out what she was saying.

"I'm pregnant," she wailed, the tears still running down her cheeks. "I'm pregnant, Eddy, and I'm f-fucking s-scared."

Initially, I felt shock. My whole body went stiff, and goosebumps erupted up my spine. Then my stomach churned, and for a moment, I thought I might be sick.

It had never occurred to me that Debbie might become pregnant. Sure, we didn't always use condoms, but she was so passionate about women's sexual freedom that I had assumed she was on some kind of birth control. And a baby was just so completely foreign a concept to an eighteen-year-old having his first sexual experience. It was too adult to happen to someone like me.

But as Debbie's words sank in and their reality hit me, I felt something else: excitement. A baby was a way out. It would mean I would need to leave uni and get a job. Instead of giving up, I would be leaving to take care of my family. It would spare me the humiliation of admitting to my parents what a colossal mistake I'd made by thinking I could become a doctor. They might not love the idea, but they'd be getting a grandchild, and my dad could no longer accuse me of acting like I was better than him.

"Debbie..." I murmured, rubbing her shoulders as if to warm her. "That's... amazing. I mean, yes, it's scary. But it's also kind of exciting, isn't it?"

"Is it?" She looked up at me through waterlogged eyelashes. "But w-we're so y-young, Eddy. We have our whole l-lives ahead of us. We can't have a baby right now..."

"It'll be hard," I agreed, my mind already jumping ahead to scenarios I could barely conceptualise, let alone understand, the consequences of having a child. "But we can do it. Your parents will help us, surely. We can get our own flat, I'll get a job... You can even stay in uni!"

"Eddy, slow d-down," she said, placing a hand on my chest. Her voice sounded alarmed, and the return of her stammer meant she was nervous. "Let's not get ahead of ourselves. I don't even know if I want to k-keep it."

My stomach dropped out of me. Of course, Debbie wasn't sure if she would keep the baby. I'd been so immediately excited that I hadn't even stopped to consider that there was an alternate option. "Of course," I hurried to say. "It's your choice entirely. And I'll support you if you decide to get an abortion. But... If you decide to keep it, I want you to know I'll also support you. And I'll be there, every step of the way, to be the father I... wish I had."

I could just make out Debbie's expression in the half-light from the street. Even though she still looked afraid, there was also a half smile on her lips that hadn't been there before. "Do you really m-mean it?" she whispered.

"Of course I do," I said, pulling her into me and wrapping my arms around her. "You don't have to be afraid of anything. I'll take care of you." I truly meant it, too.

We stood in the alleyway for several minutes, just holding each other. Then I released her and tilted her chin up.

"I think it's time I introduced you to my parents. They're going to be grandparents to this baby, after all."

"Why?" She looked doubtful. "It's not like we need their blessing."

"No," I agreed. "But you're family now. And I'm sure they'll want to help us."

She deflated. "A little help would be nice. And I don't think I can ask my parents. They'll kill me if they find out I'm pregnant... They have such high hopes for my future."

"Well, I've already disappointed my father so much I doubt it can get any worse," I joked. What I didn't say out loud was that Dad would probably be excited I could get a girl pregnant at all. He'd be thrilled I was man enough.

Chapter Thirteen

Dad's reaction, however, was not what I had imagined.

"She's what?" he bellowed two nights later as we sat in my parents' small dining room. Mum had just served the first course, and both of them had frozen, staring at me from across the table as I delivered the news.

Debbie and I sat next to each other, holding hands. Her eyes were downcast, but I glared defiantly at my father.

"Debbie is pregnant," I repeated.

Slowly, my mother sank into her seat. "Are you sure, dear?" she whispered, looking at Debbie. "Have you been to a doctor?"

"We are doctors," I reminded her.

"Not yet," my father barked. He seemed to have aged considerably in the three months since I'd last been home. Either that or I hadn't noticed the greys appearing in his hair and beard and the wrinkles forming on his forehead when I was busy studying to get into medical school. But now, in the harsh light of the overhead lamp, he looked much older than his forty-four years. I had to remind myself that my father had worked in a factory his entire life. The manual labour had aged him, as had, undoubtedly, his many violent encounters with fellow hooligans. "You're still in your first year. You still have many years of being a penniless student ahead of you before you become a doctor. How do you expect to support a child without a salary?"

"I was thinking of quitting," I said, squeezing Debbie's hand reassuringly. "I'll get a job and work full time."

Debbie looked up at me sharply, but I kept my eyes on my father. I hadn't told Debbie I'd been thinking about quitting uni, but she must have realised it was an option. Meanwhile, my father sat back in his chair and crossed his arms.

"After that whole song and dance about how you wanted to get a fancy university degree and become a doctor, you're going to drop out, just like that?"

I flushed with anger. "It wasn't a whole song and dance. Being a doctor has been my dream since I was a kid."

"Which is why I doubt very much you're prepared to quit to become a plain old blue-collar worker, like your old man. You said you were above that."

"I never said that," I spat, my colour rising. The last thing I wanted was to have this argument again, especially in front of Debbie. But Dad had a particular talent for getting under my skin.

"What your father means to say," Mum cut in quickly, "is that you worked hard to get where you are. It would be a shame to give all that up."

"Things change," I pointed out. "Life happens. And I think it would be a bigger shame to not care for my child."

When both still looked unconvinced, I threw up my hands.

"I think you both are losing sight of what matters here! Debbie is going to have a baby. You're going to be grandparents. This is good news! A cause for celebration!"

"Celebration?" Dad stared at me, incredulous. "My eighteen-year-old son bringing home his pregnant girlfriend and threatening to drop out of the uni I'm helping fund is hardly a cause for celebration."

My hands curled into fists as if remembering my long-dormant boxer instincts. "You were against me going to medical school!" I yelled. "Don't act like you give a shit if I quit now!"

"I won't pretend I approved of you attending medical school," my old man snapped. "But first you quit boxing, then you spit on the life I wanted for you, and now you're throwing away the education you were so convinced you wanted? You can't finish anything, Edward. And I very much doubt you could stick with being a father, either. You'll probably abandon your child to pursue something else in a couple of years."

I stood up quickly, releasing Debbie's hand. For several tense seconds, I was sure I was about to hit my father. Dad seemed to think so as well. He put his hands on the table as if about to get up.

"Don't you dare say that again," I breathed. "Don't you fucking dare." It took all my effort to keep from leaping across the table, seizing my dad by the front of the shirt, and giving him the beating he'd had coming to him for years. Only my stubborn desire to not become my father kept me where I stood. "Not only would I never abandon my child, but I would never bully him the way you spent my childhood bullying me. I'm going to be ten times the father you were. Just you wait and see."

Dad merely sneered.

Debbie, meanwhile, was tugging on my arm. "Sit down, Eddy," she whispered. "Your father is just in shock."

"You don't know him," I snapped at her. "He'll take any excuse to make you feel small."

"Please, Eddy, calm down," Mum said. Her eyes were pleading, and seeing the pain in them, I finally lowered myself into my chair. However, I continued to glare at my dad.

"We just want you to think this through," my old dear continued. Her voice was small, barely more than a squeak. "Both of you. You're both young, smart kids with bright futures ahead of you. We'd hate to see you have to give up your dreams because of an unplanned pregnancy."

Next to me, Debbie looked down at her lap, and I thought I heard her sniffle. I put my arm around her shoulder, but she shrugged me off.

"Oh, love, don't cry," Mum said, reaching across the table and taking her hand. "Everything will be alright. You'll see. It's happened to many girls before you, and it'll happen to many after. Do... do your parents know?"

Without glancing up, Debbie shook her head. "They'll k-kill me," she hiccupped. Her voice sounded choked, and I felt a jolt of dread at the misery I heard there.

"There, there," my mother crooned. For a split second, I got an image of what my mother would have been like with a daughter. Another jolt, this time of jealousy, shot through me. Would she have preferred that? I wondered. A girl she could have dressed like a doll, and who never came home with bloodied knuckles and bruises on his face?

My mum, meanwhile, continued to comfort Debbie. "We'll help you out, alright? Your parents don't have to know if you decide not to keep it. It can be our secret."

Debbie finally looked up. Tears streaked her cheeks. But for the first time since she'd told me about the pregnancy, she didn't look half-crazed with fear. A look passed between her and my mother, a look that I instinctively knew wasn't for me: a look that only two women who knew what it was to carry life inside of them could ever understand.

"You'll help me?" Debbie murmured, and my mother's hand tightened on hers.

"I'll help you," Mum whispered.

Debbie was silent all the way back home. We took the Tube, and she sat stonily beside me, not saying anything. That night, she slept in her own room. By the time I woke up the next morning, she was gone. I didn't see her until that evening when she knocked on my bedroom door while I was studying.

"I'm going to get an abortion," she said without preamble as she perched on the end of my bed. She wasn't quite looking at me, and as she spoke, she trembled.

I closed the medical textbook I was reading and scooted forward on the bed. "Are you sure?" My voice sounded unsteady.

She looked at me then. There were no tears in her eyes. In fact, it was a steely glint I saw there. "I know you're not happy about this—" she began, but I shook my head.

"No, I'm okay with it," I said quickly, despite disappointment curling in my stomach. "My mum was right. You have so much planned for your life. You want to go to India. Travel the world, saving lives. Help women recover from addiction. And I want to..."

What did I want out of life? Medical school hadn't exactly been the resounding success I'd been expecting. I had been all too eager to give it up at the first chance.

"You want to make your father proud," Debbie finished for me. My eyes flickered to hers, and their cold disappointment made my cheeks flush. "You want his approval. And you won't get that if you have a baby out of wedlock at eighteen. Or if you drop out of medical school."

"Debbie, that's not—"

"There's no use denying it, Eddy. No matter what you do with your life, you will be haunted by the need for his approval."

I wanted to argue with her, to tell her she was wrong, but I knew, deep down, that she was right.

She sighed and gestured at her stomach. "It makes you think about the future, doesn't it? It's like, if you're going to terminate, then you have a d-duty to the baby to live a great life. To achieve your d-dreams. To make it w-worth it."

I swallowed. "I don't know if that's a good way to think about it. Then feelings of guilt will plague you if you're not 'living fully' or achieving enough."

But the steeliness in Debbie's eyes only seemed to grow. "I think I need to make it worth it. That means no more drugs. No more partying. And I think you should try to make it worth it, too." She looked at me. "Which means not dropping out of medical school just because it's hard."

I wanted to argue, to tell her this wasn't the reason I wanted to keep the baby, but somehow, I knew it would be useless. Debbie knew me better than anyone. She knew I was lost and looking for an out.

"Anyway," she said, shaking herself. "I got the name of a d-doctor today from a friend. She had an abortion last year. I called him, and he scheduled me for an appointment in three d-days."

"Wow, that's soon..."

"Yeah. But I just want it out of me so I can m-move on, you know?"

I looked up at her. "Do you want me to come with you?"

She shook her head. "That's not necessary. My friend said she'd pick me up."

"I'd like to—" I began, but she continued to shake her head.

"No, Eddy. This is something I have to do on my own."

Three days later, it was a Monday. In class, I couldn't concentrate. I didn't know when Debbie's appointment was—she had been cagey all weekend—but I assumed it was during business hours. That night, I waited up for her in the living room. She didn't come home. I fell asleep on the settee, a cup of tea in my lap, and woke the following day when Raj came downstairs. Debbie still hadn't come home.

Later that day, two slightly older boys who shared Debbie's dark eyes and auburn hair showed up and introduced themselves as her brothers. There was no spark of recognition in their eyes when I told them my name, which made me think Debbie had failed to mention me to her family. They told me that Debbie was ill and wanted to be home for a little while, that they'd come to collect her stuff. I watched in shocked silence as they packed up her room. When I told them I had some of her things in my room, I thought one of them would crack a joke about me sleeping with their sister. But they said nothing. Didn't even look at me suspiciously. It hit me then that Debbie had never told her family about me. The realisation hurt more than I thought it would. Of course, she hadn't wanted to keep my baby; she had never taken me seriously as a boyfriend. She was probably ashamed of her working-class boyfriend from Dagenham, I thought bitterly.

Before they left, both brothers shook my hand.

"Do you know when she'll be back?" I asked, finally unsticking my throat. The eldest brother looked at me like I was crazy. I don't know why, but that was when I realised Debbie wasn't coming back. It wasn't just the pregnancy and the partying lifestyle she had gotten rid of; it was me. Any reminder of the baby, the abortion, and the brief brush with the life she could have had.

That night, as I lay in bed, I thought about Debbie's words to me about making the abortion "worth it". She had many plans for herself, and I knew she'd accomplish them all without me and a baby slowing her down. What were my dreams? For so long, that had been medical school. Debbie was right that dropping out just because it was hard would be a waste. Dad was right, too. I'd worked so hard for it. I couldn't give up now.

I frowned up at the ceiling. The old man was impossible to please: angry when I wanted to go to medical school and angry when I didn't. It was infuriating.

Debbie's other words came back to me: No matter what you do with your life, you will be haunted by the need for his approval. Well, she wasn't right. There was still time for me to become the man he wanted me to be. And if I didn't have Debbie and our baby to make proud, was it so wrong to want to make my dad proud?

But how could I do that while still staying in school and becoming a doctor? It was too late for me to become a boxer, and I wasn't about to become a football hooligan.

I turned over on my side, punching the pillow as I thought hard. There had to be some other way to be the macho man he wanted me to be without sacrificing all I'd dreamed of and worked for to become a doctor.

Then it came to me. It was so simple and perfect that I couldn't believe I hadn't thought of it sooner.

The next day, I visited my local British Naval Recruitment Office to enquire about signing up after finishing my studies.

Chapter Fourteen

In the spring of 1981, I graduated from St. George's, University of London, with a Bachelor of Medicine, Bachelor of Surgery, and immediately entered the Britannia Royal Naval College's induction course at Dartmouth. I wanted to get through the officer and medical training as quickly as possible to begin practising medicine, like all my peers who were finally out in the workforce after five long, gruelling years of medical school.

The officer training was surprisingly fun; it's what I imagine being a Boy Scout would have been like. I learned field-craft skills, map reading, and survival techniques; how to discharge weapons; ceremonial traditions; and, best of all, basic seamanship, navigation, and boat handling. Having grown up in land-locked Dagenham, I'd done nothing like it before. I enjoyed the work and found that it came naturally. The physical training, although demanding, reminded me of my boxing days. I'd tried to stay fit during medical school, but it had been difficult to keep up a rigorous exercise routine while studying eighty hours a week. Still, I was in relatively decent shape when I started at Dartmouth, if undisciplined. After three weeks at the BRNC, I regained the strength and stamina I'd had when I won my first and only boxing bout. The training and discipline came easily after boxing, and I quickly fell into my old exercise routines.

The other new officers were different from my medical school classmates. They were less insular in their tastes and interests and certainly more of the tough guys my father had always wanted me to be. I'd gotten along with my classmates but had made no close friends on my course during my five years at St. George's. After everything with Debbie, I realised that getting close to people would only impede my goals. And love, I'd learned, was messy and painful without nearly enough upsides.

Loneliness was an old companion; its weight was a familiar burden on my shoulders. I'd spent most of my childhood and adolescence alone. What were a couple more years? Once I was a medical officer in the Navy, I would allow myself friendships, maybe even relationships, again. But not until then.

The experience with Debbie had scarred me. After she moved out, she became reclusive, focusing on nothing other than her studies. Raj and Betsy rarely saw her either, and when they did, they reported that she had no interest in continuing her friendships with them. After the semester, she transferred to another medical school.

"I think the abortion was really painful for her," Betsy told me one quiet night in February when we were sitting around the fire, drinking beers and studying. "She wanted to be as far away from the memory of it as possible."

I understood that. If I could have transferred away from St. George's, I might have. But it had taken everything in me to get into the university. I couldn't throw that opportunity away, not after what I'd already sacrificed to pursue my dreams.

But by the time I arrived at Dartmouth, my memories of Debbie and the abortion were fading. The feelings of loss, abandonment, and guilt were still present. But now that I was finally out of London—and far away from anyone who knew about the abortion and the life I could have had—I began to let go of the sadness I still carried with me.

The constant exercise and clean sea air cleared my mind, and the clarity gave me a new perspective and focus. And I was part of a team now. Medical school had felt like a never-ending competition between every student. We couldn't be happy about one another's successes; we were too competitive, too ambitious, and too determined to be the best. However, in the Navy, teamwork was essential. I wasn't trying to be the best; I was trying to work in tandem with others to make us all the best—and, more importantly, keep us all alive. This ethos of teamwork suited me well, as I'd always felt unworthy of individual glory, especially since being honoured for saving Shaun's life. My success mattered to me little, apart from how it could help others. And if those others were my fellow officers, then I was happy.

So even though some of the training and physical demands reminded me of boxing, the part of boxing I'd liked the least—hurting others and trying to dominate them—was absent. I could enjoy the camaraderie of working with my fellow officers rather than trying to beat them.

At the end of the six-month course, in early April, I assumed the role of General Duties Medical Officer. As part of the Royal Marines, my superiors assigned me to the M squad of 42 Commando, based in Bickleigh Barracks just outside of Plymouth. The Royal Marines were the elite amphibious force of the Navy, held at the ready for rapid-response assignments. I was surprised this was where I'd been assigned, but my commanding officer explained the decision on my first day.

"Usually, these lads have to go through commando training," he told me on my first day on duty. "But you were such an exceptional medical officer that we wanted you here."

"I'm honoured," I said as he ushered me into the operating theatre where I would work.

My CO harrumphed. "You're still green, if you don't mind me saying so. Fresh out of school. But you're one of the most competent medical officers we've seen, and... we will need the best of the best."

I swallowed. Even though I felt I was ready—and was eager to prove myself in the line of duty—I knew the CO wasn't wrong. I'd never practised medicine under the conditions of combat. Still, I'd always done well under pressure. My professors had been effusive in their praise of this quality.

"Is there something I should know, sir?" I asked at last.

He sighed and ran a hand through his hair. "I don't know. None of us ever know. But you should follow the news. World events affect you now that you're a Royal Marine."

"Are you talking about Argentina, sir?" Days earlier, the Argentinians had invaded the Falklands. I'd been closely following the controversy in the Falklands ever since the scrap metal workers landed on the islands.

" 'Course I am," he harrumphed. "Looks like it's gonna be war. It's like I always say: diplomacy can only get you so far. Enough carrots; it's time for the stick."

"Diplomacy broke down over a decade ago," I said carefully. "If the islanders had agreed to a leaseback scheme in eighty, then maybe that would have satisfied the junta, but it's unlikely, as the British government was proposing a ninety-nine-year leaseback and Argentina was insisting on just ten years."

The CO gazed at me, his eyes unfocused. It was clear he didn't know what I was talking about.

"Argentina has wanted the islands back for decades, and while our government mostly sees them as a nuisance and barrier to trade in South America, the islanders themselves, who are of British descent, refuse to cede sovereignty to Argentina," I amended, hoping this would make a little more sense.

"Ahhh, so you have followed current events!" The CO thumped me on the back. "I knew I made the right choice bringing you in."

That night in the barracks, my fellow commandos were equally fixated on the Argentinian invasion.

"I didn't even know where South Georgia was until the metal workers took over," the man on the bunk across from me joked as the room buzzed with theories and speculation about the Falklands. "Had to look it up."

"Talk about hell and gone," another agreed. "Beats me that there's anything down there we even want."

"It's a matter of national pride," a tall dark-haired man said. At once, the chatter in the room stopped, and everyone turned to look at the new speaker. It was as if no one wanted to miss out on what he might say.

I watched the tall dark-haired man from where I stood by my bunk. He stood by his bunk as well, shirtless. Even in the dim light, I saw that his body was flawless. He had a toned six-pack and perfectly sculpted arms. It was his face, however, that arrested me the most. He was delicately beautiful, with wide, dark eyes framed by thick black eyelashes, an aquiline nose, high cheekbones, and full lips like a woman's. But while his beauty might be feminine, his body was decidedly masculine. The contrast was alluring.

"Thatcher is weak," the man continued. "Unemployment is high, and she's just giving up our territories. No wonder the Argies think they can just take them."

"The milk snatcher should never have proposed giving Hong Kong back to the Chinese," I said defiantly.

Heads turned to look at me, but I had eyes for no one but the dark-haired man. His eyes came to mine. As they slid onto me, something in my body seemed to shake loose. It was as if I was shedding something or unlocking a heavy door and letting a breeze blow through it, lightening me. My stomach immediately clenched, and the familiar fluttering returned to my chest. Warmth flooded me, and I had to struggle to keep from smiling.

"That's right," the man said, and his eyes lit up. "Which is why it's important we respond to the metalworkers'—and Argentina's—aggression promptly and decisively. We aren't about to let Britannia become the laughingstock of the world, beaten by a military dictatorship on the other side of the world, are we? We're going to fight back against these wankers, aren't we?"

The men roared with him, and I joined in. Suddenly, people were fist-pumping each other—me included—and excited talk had broken out throughout the room.

I turned back to my bunk. I had just pulled my shirt over my head when I felt someone behind me. Turning, I found myself face to face with the man. He was smiling at me.

"Quite the patriot, aren't we?" he asked. His smile, I couldn't help but notice, extended all the way to his eyes, which were sparkling.

I shrugged, trying to play it cool even as my heart hammered. "Had it drummed into me from my dad when I was a kid. Sorry, I'm not normally like that. I think the emotion got the better of me. I'm a medic, so I'm usually calm."

"Ahhhh, so you're the new medic?" He looked me up and down. "I heard they were bringing another one in. So you're here to look after me?"

"Hopefully, it doesn't come to that."

He held out his hand. "Sergeant Theodore Bennett at your service."

"Edward Turner," I said before grasping his hand. His skin was warm and rough to the touch. As I shook it, a strange jolt went through my stomach, like when you're in a car that goes over a speed bump too quickly. Unnerved, I quickly dropped his hand. Bennett, however, didn't seem to notice anything odd.

"Well, Turner, it's nice to meet you," he said. "Something tells me we're going to be friends."

Five days later, on 9 April 1982, 42 Commando set sail from Portsmouth aboard the recently requisitioned SS *Canberra*. Our destination: the Falkland Islands. As we cruised out of Portsmouth Harbour and into the English Channel, the sea spray biting through the air and Sergeant Bennett's arm flung loosely around me, I had a feeling that life would never be lonely again.

Chapter Fifteen

Teddy and Eddy. In the week that it took us to sail to South Georgia, that's what we became known as. Teddy and I were inseparable. In the evenings, when we had time for recreation, we played volleyball on the deck of the SS *Canberra*, kicked around a football, and even sparred. Teddy had never boxed before, and he loved it when I told him about my brief boxing career. He even insisted I teach him what I still remembered.

Although I'd never enjoyed hitting people, I loved boxing with Teddy. For one thing, he didn't really want me to hit him. To him, sparring was a way of keeping in shape. And we didn't have gloves, so we couldn't go for any real punches without hurting our hands. This could have put Teddy in danger out in the field. For me, it could mean the end of my career. As a medical officer, I had to have steady, injury-free hands.

Technically, I ranked above Teddy, but he was the leader from the moment we met. I followed him for the same reason everyone else did: it was easy. Teddy was charismatic, charming, and a natural leader;

easygoing during leisure time, serious and professional while on duty. And after that first night in the bunks, he was always by my side.

Teddy thought I was the smartest person he'd ever met. He was constantly quizzing me on history and current affairs, trying to find gaps in my knowledge. I'd always laugh at him when he did and assure him, for the hundredth time, that I was not that smart. I'd just had a lot of lonely years, both in secondary school and university. Reading and memorising facts has always been the refuge of lonely kids. I was no exception to this.

Teddy had been popular his whole life. He'd grown up in Blackpool, where he'd had a series of rotating girlfriends, scores of friends, and a happy, supportive family. The son of a commercial fisherman, he'd spent his early years out on boats and had grown up swimming in the frigid waters of the Irish Sea. Both experiences had made him an excellent sailor and the perfect candidate for the Royal Marines. Considering a formal education to be only for the posh, Teddy had foregone university in favour of signing up. Since then, he'd risen quickly through the ranks to sergeant, buoyed by a much-publicised act of heroism during a stint in Northern Ireland when he'd gone back into heavy gunfire to rescue an injured Marine. I suspected he would be at least a colour sergeant by the end of his tour in the Falklands. He was still young, though, just twenty-five, and had ambitions to rise to lieutenant colonel of the Royal Marines. I knew he would get there.

The SS *Canberra* was also the first place I ever got to practise medicine as a professional. While we hadn't seen combat yet, soldiers had minor injuries while on the ship, including a few sprained ankles from evening athletics, cuts and scrapes, and burns on the kitchen staff. I also had to teach first aid to the commandos. This made me nervous, as I didn't like public speaking. But Teddy's repeated shouts of encouragement during the training helped to ease my fear and make me feel less like an inarticulate freak.

I'm sure that part of what made Teddy befriend me was that he sensed I was someone who had always needed a protector. Maybe that's also why I had chosen a life in the Royal Marines: I liked the idea of following orders and having a strong, commanding authority figure to obey. Perhaps it was my issues with my father. I'd needed him to be someone I could follow and rely on, but he'd been a violent and unreliable hooligan without a sense of right or wrong. In the Marines, there was a code of honour. I knew that when I followed orders, I would be doing what was right and honourable. There was something freeing in knowing that and letting go of my decision-making to follow someone else's. And while the Marines gave me that on a macro scale, Teddy gave it to me on the micro level. Not that he tried to push me around or tell me what to do. He was no bully, no Tommy Burke or Shaun Windham. But he was the decision-maker in all our interactions, and that worked perfectly for me. I understood that my ceding leadership to him meant I was under his protection. I knew Teddy would have my back if anyone tried to bully me again. And there were a few close calls when some boneheads wanted to give me shit for what they perceived as my "feminine" mannerisms. It wasn't anything terrible, just a few snide comments in the canteen, but each time, a few words from Teddy were enough to shut them up.

Under Teddy's protection, I was safe, perhaps for the first time in my life. No one would hurt me when I had him on my side.

Once we landed in South Georgia, however, I was assigned to the hospital ship SS *Uganda*. I didn't see Teddy for some time. While still technically part of 42 Commando, I no longer saw my battalion daily. The ship was anchored off the coast, and it was here that I treated my first combat patients. It was one of the most exhausting, challenging, and stimulating experiences of my life.

Compared to other British conflicts, the Falklands War saw very few casualties. That being said, we were still busy every day, treating patients on both sides of the war. The days were long, and the work was constant. By the end of April, I couldn't fathom how medical professionals had survived during higher casualty conflicts like WWI. I couldn't even imagine the exhaustion of the medical staff during that war, when thousands and thousands of wounded and dying were brought into hospitals and where they had so little of the tools and medical knowledge we now possessed. I didn't like to think of how many people must have died of perfectly curable ailments.

In mid-May 1982, I was feeling claustrophobic inside the SS *Uganda*. I'd never spent so much time inside a ship, and the other medical officers, all of whom had seen conflict zones before, laughed when I asked if it was always this bad.

"Being a Marine is as psychological as physical," one old-timer told me. "Man isn't made to be at sea for long periods. We need ground beneath our feet: good, growable soil."

Despite this, the older medical officers never seemed to grow restless like I did. But I think they took pity on me because when the Army took a meat-processing facility on Ajax Bay and converted it into a field hospital, some medics put in a good word for me to get transferred over.

"It'll be good for you," my Regimental Medical Officer told me. "You'll see more acute injuries that need immediate action, which will be great training." Some triage doctors went as far forward with the line as possible, which we supported from the floating hospital. I supposed that since I'd acquitted myself well in the hospital ship, I had proved I had what it took to work in one of the Advanced Surgical Centres.

The slaughterhouse where I arrived on 23 May was one of the strangest places I'd ever seen. It reminded me of the Ford Dagenham factory, except it was full of injured people. In the smaller rooms, where butches had once bled animals from hooks, there were now operating theatres. Humans—both Argentine and British—were being cut up by surgeons mere feet from butcher blocks and grinders that had once been used to slaughter animals. It was eerie, to say the least. And I loved it.

I thought often of my dad when I worked at the slaughterhouse. He had also worked on an assembly line in a factory like this. And even though I was doing something utterly foreign to him, I knew that a part of him would be proud to see me working in such a place. It would make him think we had something in common at long last.

Those long, hard days in the slaughterhouse were exhausting, but the endless, methodical work also cleared my mind. It was as if the tiredness burned away any distracting or unimportant thoughts. All I had left were the most vivid memories, the most honest assessments, and the hardest truths.

It was during these long hours that I thought most about my dad. We hadn't spoken since I'd told him and my mum that I was shipping out to the Falklands. That wasn't because we weren't on good terms. It was just harder to call from the ship, and I didn't make the effort.

Things had been good between us those past few years. Unsurprisingly, he'd applauded my decision to join the Royal Marines. It had seemed to wipe away all memory of Debbie's abortion and his fury at me for getting her pregnant. He said that joining up had finally made him proud, that I was a "real man" now.

Mum, of course, had been less than thrilled. She'd worried, of course, about my safety. She didn't want me to see combat. It was only after reassuring her that medical officers rarely saw combat and that enemy fire rarely came near hospitals that she relaxed a little. I think it disappointed her I had again chosen a violent path, a career defined by its relationship to combat and war. I think it reminded her of Dad's hooliganism. But at least I was going there to heal, and I think she would have liked that we treated both Argentine and British soldiers exactly the same.

Even if it hadn't been a mandate of the Geneva Convention, we still would have treated our own soldiers and prisoners of war equally. Our oath was to the British Crown, but as physicians, we had also taken the Hippocratic Oath, and this overrode any others. It didn't matter if it was an enemy combatant on our table or our own bunkmate; we treated them the same, and we always treated them in order according to the severity of the injury. This meant we sometimes worked on an Argentine with worse wounds before a Brit. I was sure this caused some grumbling amongst our soldiers, but I just had to learn to tune it out. Block out the noise. This was what it meant to be a doctor. It was probably my favourite part about serving in the Falklands: not just knowing in theory but actually practising the values I held dear: to save everyone, regardless of nationality, race, religion, or creed. In the hospital and operating theatre, we were all equal, all God's creatures on this earth. And we were all worth saving.

It was something that Dad never would have understood. But it made sense to me, instinctually.

I thought Teddy would understand this, too, but we had our worst argument—and the one that nearly broke me—about this code of ethics near the end of the war.

He was on a few days of leave and came to see me at the slaughterhouse. Morale was low. The day before, the Argentines had dropped bombs on Bluff Cove just as several troop transport ships were unloading, killing dozens of British soldiers. Although the final count was still unknown, it was by far the largest number since the start of the war. Those who survived were severely burned. Since then, burn victims had inundated the slaughterhouse.

Although we were busy, my CO gave me an hour's break to visit with Teddy. He probably knew I'd be better able to perform my duties after seeing my friend. Teddy and I walked towards the water along a stone road that cut through a field of long, uncut grass. He lit two cigarettes and handed one to me. Together, we smoked in silence, looking out over Ajax Bay.

"It looks like Northern England here," Teddy said after a long time. "Or Ireland. And I thought South America would be hot and tropical."

"We're as far south from the equator here as Portsmouth is north of it," I said, forcing a laugh.

Teddy glanced at me, his expression confused. "How do you know that?"

I shrugged. "I looked up the longitudes."

Teddy laughed hollowly. "You really are the smartest person I know, Eddy."

His compliment sang through me, and despite the cold and brusque wind, I felt warmth throughout my entire body. Teddy shifted, pulled another drag on his cigarette, and threw it into the grass.

Then he turned to me. When he spoke, there was an aggression in his voice I'd never heard before. "But if you're so smart, why are you treating Argentinians like you'd treat our own boys?"

"What?" The question caught me off guard, as did the vehemence in Teddy's eyes. He'd never looked at me with anything other than admiration, respect, and fondness. But now, he'd narrowed his eyes, clenched his fists, and scowled. Fury emanated from him.

"Why do you treat the enemy the way you'd treat our own boys?" he repeated.

I knew better than to shrug. Instead, I stood up straighter, squaring my shoulders. "Because I have to," I explained quietly. "And... it's the right thing to do."

I didn't have to add this last part. A few years earlier, I might not have. I wouldn't have wanted to alienate someone who seemed to like me. But I was a doctor now; I'd taken my oaths. And I would not sacrifice my beliefs for anyone. If I couldn't change for my father, I didn't think I could change for Teddy.

It was not, however, what Teddy wanted to hear.

He scowled even more deeply, and I could see his anger rising. "Don't tell me it's the right thing to do when hundreds of us are lying dead in Bluff Cove!" he shouted. "You've seen the burns! You know what they did!"

"I'm a doctor, Teddy," I said. "These are the laws of humanitarian treatment during wartime, as set out in the Geneva Convention. Doctors have to treat everyone, regardless of their affiliations."

"Who cares about Geneva?" Teddy snarled. "War is kill or be killed. No one cares about Geneva when you are on the battlefield."

"This works both ways," I pointed out. "If you were injured on the Argentinian side, their doctors would also treat you."

"I'd rather die!" I raised an eyebrow at his theatrics. His face flushed, and he turned away from me. "I don't care if it's the law. It's wrong, and if you were a true patriot, you'd stand up to it."

"And be dishonourably discharged?"

Teddy whirled around. "You wouldn't be! Not for that."

"Yes, I would. It violates international law."

He snarled at me. "Well, what you're doing now violates every law of human decency! And any friend of mine would know that."

My heart stuttered in my chest. "Teddy..." I began. I reached for him, but he pulled away.

"I might die," he spat at me. "It takes every ounce of courage I have to face that every day. Meanwhile, you're in here, saving the people trying to kill me. If I am killed by someone you've treated, then I hope you can live with that."

He shoved past me, striking me in the shoulder. The sting of his shoulder against mine felt exactly like Tommy Burke's had, all those years ago, just after he'd rejected Shaun when Brandon called him queer.

Because I'd saved him.

It was my fault. It was always my fault.

There was something wrong with me, I knew then, as I watched my only true friend walk away from me. There was something wrong with me that I wanted to save people, not hurt them. Dad had known it, Tommy Burke and Shaun had known it, and now Teddy knew it, too. It didn't matter that saving lives over the past few weeks had been the best experience of my whole life; it didn't matter that I'd found my calling and worked hard to achieve it; it didn't matter that I was obeying international law and doing my duty for Crown and Country. I would never be a real man because I didn't have a killer's instincts or a thirst for revenge or domination. And because of it, I would never earn Dad's approval.

Chapter Sixteen

Teddy left that evening. He was needed back with 42 Commando. We didn't speak before he left. I saw him enter the slaughterhouse, shake hands with the Regimental Medical Officer, and leave. He didn't even glance in my direction. Of course, I was busy treating a burn victim, so I couldn't have spoken to him even if he had. But it still hurt.

I didn't know this then, but 42 Commando was part of the assault on Mount Harriet on East Falkland that would directly lead to the end of the war.

It was the middle of winter in the Southern Hemisphere, and the weather on the Falklands was punishing. In the ensuing conflict, Teddy and his fellow commandos would battle through icy sheets of rain, strong winds, and mud so deep it took two men to pull anyone out of it who fell. But they would take the mountain, thus pushing closer to the capital, Stanley. The Argentinians would surrender three days later.

Of course, I knew nothing of this that night as I lay in my bunk, my mind going over the day's events. Teddy's rejection had cut me.

My father's rejection had always hurt. Tommy's and Shaun's bullying had destroyed my self-confidence. But the way Teddy had looked at me went beyond this pain. It wasn't just a feeling of self-loathing but a feeling of loss. The closest I could equate it to was the feeling of someone you loved dying or losing an unborn child—one sting I knew all too well.

I saw some awful things that played havoc on my mind. But that evening, the memory of Teddy's rejection took all my attention. I just couldn't stop thinking about it or him.

But what did it mean? Was a man supposed to feel this way about another man? Or did that make him…

I had asked myself this question once before, then immediately buried it deep inside me where no one could find it. This time, I let myself finish the question: Did it make me gay?

The question sent an icy shiver down my spine. For years, I'd been avoiding this question. But now I had to consider the possibility. After all, I couldn't discount the heart flutterings that had often accompanied my feelings for boys, which I had tried to ignore or explain away. Memories of Charlie the Boxer and the West Ham footballers filled my head. All elicited a feeling like bubbles were erupting in my stomach, and if I had to give these a name, I would call them desire.

Desire for other men. The thought was dirty and shameful. Almost too terrifying to face. Immediately, Brandon's voice reverberated through my head. *At least I'm not a queer. Or friends with one.*

Queer. Queer queer queer. It echoed through me, one of the dirtiest, most shameful words I'd ever heard.

Then Tommy's words, dripping with vitriol: *Don't touch me, you dirty fucking shirt lifter.* And other words I'd heard over the years, mostly from my father:

Does Eddy always play with girls?

Been off fucking a bloke, have ya?
Do they always play those girly games?
You sound like a poof!

I closed my eyes as if this could block the sounds from my head. They persisted, resounding through me like my mind was an empty canyon.

But I couldn't be gay, surely. I'd loved Debbie. We'd almost had a baby together. If that didn't make me straight, what did?

I turned over on my side, my eyes still closed as I tried to remember exactly how I had felt about Debbie. Yes, I had loved her. But had it been romantic? Debbie was the coolest person I'd ever met. And she'd understood me. We'd both been bullied as teenagers and were both doctors. And she'd made me feel things no one had before—wanted, treasured, and alive. Making love to her had felt good, if mildly terrifying. But looking back at it now, I realised I'd been passive throughout the relationship. I'd let her pursue me, seduce me, and move into my room. Never had I taken any initiative. It wasn't because I didn't like her, but because I felt none of that pulsating sexual desire that I'd read about in novels or seen in films. None of that carnal, half-violent, half-sensual desire to pursue, to hunt down one's prey and make them yours.

But when I thought about Teddy, the deep, aching need to make him mine filled my veins with electric blood.

Heat came to my whole body, and I sparked. My eyes snapped open. Even in the dark, I could see Teddy, a vision of him, as if surrounded by light: shirtless, like I'd first seen him, a slight smile on his lips. In this vision, he was walking towards me, his khaki trousers low on his hips, revealing the deep V leading down to his pelvis. As he advanced, he unbuttoned the trousers until he'd revealed just a hint of blonde pubic hair. Then his hand disappeared down his trousers as he gripped himself. His eyes rolled back into his head, then closed. He threw his head back and groaned. Moaned. Eddy.

It was as if all the lights of the universe came on at once. As if I'd stood in a darkened house and thought I understood what it looked like. But now, as the lights illuminated every nook and cranny, every beautiful detail and undusted corner, I could see that I'd known nothing. I hadn't even known what I didn't know. I'd thought love and sex were letting something happen to you. Now I knew that love and sex were burning needs that nothing could satiate except the feel of your lover in your arms.

The realisation that I loved Teddy, that I wanted Teddy, was simultaneous relief, exaltation, grief, and fear. I knew I could never tell him and that the love I felt would forever remain secret. I probably wouldn't ever be able to tell anyone. This would be a secret I'd carry until my grave. If my father found out, he'd probably kill me.

But at least I knew. At least I finally understood the part of me that felt different. The part of me I'd always been running from, hiding beneath my solitude. I wasn't entirely sure how I hadn't figured it out sooner. Perhaps my father's early warnings that I was a "poof", that I was feminine and played girly games, had led my brain to shut down any confirmation of his assessment. My brain had probably been trying to protect me from the shame and self-loathing that would have followed had I realised I was gay while still under my father's roof.

Or maybe I just hadn't met the right person. There'd been no one until Teddy.

But was this true? I wracked my brain, trying to remember. A sudden image of the older boy at the boxing gym came to me. Watching him spar with his friend. My stomach lurched at the memory, and the same warm feeling spread through my body. I almost laughed. So that's what it was.

But then there was the fear.

What would happen to me now? How would I hide this part of me for the rest of my life? Did this mean I would never have a spouse and family? That my parents would never have grandchildren? Would I always live in fear of being found out? And what if I couldn't do it? What if I gave in to my temptations and pursued a romantic or sexual relationship with a man? What if he outed me to my family? And what if he rejected me?

It's almost laughable now, but as I was first discovering my sexuality, my greatest fear was that I would meet the man of my dreams and that he would reject me. In that way, I was no different from anyone else, straight or gay, experiencing their first crush and realising, for the first time, that pursuing those you really wanted meant risking getting hurt.

This is common for gay people, I've discovered. We hide ourselves for so long—often even to ourselves—that when we finally discover our hidden passions, they can bring on a second adolescence.

I lay awake for hours that night, alternating between fantasies of Teddy and me—in an alternate universe where he returned my affections, and we could be together—and less appealing imaginings of what it would be like to tell Mum and Dad about my realisation. So much was new, so much I barely understood. But a certain euphoria roared through me that night as Teddy prepared himself for battle somewhere far away. Even if I didn't love the answer as to why I'd always been different and disappointed my father, at least I finally knew what it was.

When we got word of what was happening on Mount Harriet, my fear was immeasurable. I had to keep reminding myself that this was 1982, not 1915. The number of casualties in this war would never come close to those of either World Wars. These weren't boys in trenches crossing the fields of Europe, bayonets strapped to their backs. This was modern warfare. Still, fear seized me like a fist to the stomach, leaving me breathless and stunned.

The Forty-two Commando was amongst those who were taking the mountain. And if Teddy were to die, and the last thing we'd said to each other had been in anger... For the first time in years, I prayed to some nameless, faceless deity above me. Bargaining. I would give up my love for Teddy and never even think about it again if it meant he would live. I'd never think of another man as long as I lived, if only he survived.

When the junta surrendered and we gathered in Ajax Bay to celebrate, I looked for him everywhere. And when 42 Commando rode into town, and I glimpsed him above the heads of everyone, his smile giddy, his hair thinner and flecked with grey—probably from stress—but still glittering in the sunlight, I forgot all my promises. I didn't believe in God, anyway. My love for Teddy was immutable. And I marvelled again that it had taken me so long to recognise the desire in my heart. Because looking at him now, it seemed impossible that I had ever thought I was straight.

Amidst the celebrations, Teddy found me. I thought he was looking for me because when he saw me, the strain in his eyes relaxed, and a broad smile broke out on his face. Before I could say anything, he seized me and pulled me into a tight hug.

"Eddy..." he breathed into my neck. "We won! We beat the bastards!"

"We did," I laughed into him. His body was hard and warm. I could have let it envelop me for hours. Days. Years.

Teddy released me and held me at arm's length. "Look, Eddy, I want to apologise," he began. "What I said to you before—it was wrong."

"Don't apologise," I rushed to say. "I understand why you were upset. I know it's hard to understand for anyone who's not a doctor."

But Teddy shook his head. "No, but it was wrong. I'm not a monster or a war criminal." He laughed as if the idea was ludicrous. "I was angry and scared after Bluff Cove."

"I understand. It's really okay."

Teddy grinned. "Okay, good. Because you're my best friend out here, Eddy. And when I was up there on the mountain, shitting water and my toes freezing off, I thought about the argument and how badly I came across. I don't hate you, Eddy. I don't. I..." He hesitated, a burning look filling his eyes, and my stomach clenched with expectation. For a moment, it seemed as if he were about to utter words I could only conceptualise in dreams.

Then he clapped me on the arm. "You're my brother. And nothing will ever change that." He pulled me close again so our foreheads touched and clasped me behind the neck. "Brothers?" he murmured.

"Brothers," I agreed. My breath was coming in short, ragged gasps, but I hoped he assumed that was because of the adrenaline of the moment, not my desire to kiss him and rip the clothes from his body.

This time, I didn't wait for him to hug me. It was me who pulled him close. Wrapping both my arms around his back, I held him. Tightly as first, and then more loosely; gently. We swayed on the spot, our bodies wound around each other. Time seemed to slow. Noise faded. Until it was just us. Us and the knowledge of what could have been in another world.

Nothing happened that day or on the way home to England. I'm still unsure if Teddy knew what his body had communicated or if he felt anything for me other than brotherhood. I'll never know if he was straight and oblivious, gay, bisexual, or something else entirely: that rare person who falls in love with someone of their own sex just once but never acts on it or understands it. But whatever Teddy was, it didn't matter. Whether we were brothers or lovers, I was thankful to him for having awakened me.

As we sailed back into Portsmouth Harbour, where cheering crowds of upwards of thousands greeted us, waving small Union Jacks and singing rounds of "Rule Britannia", it hit me I had awakened to more than my sexuality. I had awakened my self-confidence. Before, there was fear and shame, but now I felt powerful and sure. I was a war hero. The pride and joy of my nation. For years, I'd been hiding. I'd hidden so well that even I hadn't known my true nature. But I wouldn't hide anymore. I was strong enough to be honest about my truth. And if others didn't like it, then to hell with them. Even my father.

"What do you think you'll do next?" Teddy asked as he stood beside me on the ship's deck, waving at the crowd lining the dock below us. The wind was up, ruffling his hair, and his cheeks were pink from the brisk cold. "Will you remain in Portsmouth?"

I glanced sideways. Teddy looked hopeful, and it broke my heart as I shook my head no. "All this violence... It's too much for me. I like to heal people, but it's difficult for me to be around all this warfare. I think I'll put in for a transfer to an NHS hospital."

Teddy nodded, although I could see the disappointment lurking in his expression. "But you'll stay in London, right?"

This time, I hesitated. I wanted to stay in London, near Teddy. But I also knew that if I was going to live my truth honestly and openly, then I couldn't hang around my Marine buddies.

"Probably not," I admitted. "I might go up north, try a change of scenery."

"I understand," Teddy said. Another slight hesitation, and then he slipped his arm around mine. "Stay in touch, though. Don't be a stranger."

"I won't," I promised. But I already knew I was lying. Already, I knew I would never see Teddy again. He was a sacrifice I had to make to live the life I wanted. But there were others I couldn't sacrifice, others I wouldn't give up, and now I had to tell them the truth.

Mum and Dad had decorated the living room with an enormous banner that read Welcome Home Eddy, Hero of the Falklands. I laughed when I saw it, then kissed my mother on the cheek.

"I'm not sure I'm the hero of the Falklands," I said, and she laughed and pinched my cheek.

"You are to us."

Dad, who had been helping to bring my bags in, shuffled into the room. When I turned, he didn't break eye contact with me, and his expression was solemn. He held out his hand.

"I'm proud of you, son," he murmured as I shook his hand. His voice sounded a little hoarse, and his eyes were bright. If I didn't know better, I would have thought he was about to cry. "I've never been so proud of anything or anyone."

My mother handed me a beer, and I turned again to look at the banner. "You know," I began softly, "being in a war zone makes you think. You're risking your life every day, and it forces you to ask yourself: if I died, would I have led a good life?"

"You have led a wonderful life!" Mum exclaimed, sounding surprised. I turned back around to face her. Her brow furrowed. "You're a doctor. And a Royal Marine!"

"Yes," I conceded. "But I also haven't been honest with myself, with both of you—with anyone—about who I really am. And when I'm not being honest with myself, it also means I'm not living the life I really want."

My father was frowning at me. "What are you talking about, Eddy?"

"Mum, Dad..." I steadied myself. "I'm gay."

The room became still and silent. Neither of my parents moved. Time felt elastic, and I didn't know how long I stood there, waiting for them to respond. Nothing felt real, and I kept expecting to realise that I hadn't spoken the words aloud, that Mum and Dad were still waiting for my confession.

Then, my mother half-laughed and glanced at my father. His expression had become very dark.

"What did you just say?" he whispered. My stomach knotted, and dread spooled out to every corner of my body. Sick, nauseating dread.

"I'm gay," I said more quietly, less confidently. "But I'm still the same person. Nothing about me has changed except whom I love."

For all my boxing skills, I didn't see the punch coming. It landed hard on my jaw and flung me backwards. Then Dad was on me. His other fist connected with my throat, and I gasped, unable to draw breath. Behind him, I heard Mum scream.

"No son of mine is a poof!" my father roared as he punched me again in the face. Everything hurt. My face was on fire. There were tears on my cheeks—or maybe it was blood. "Hit me back!" he shouted. "Hit me back and prove you're not a queer!"

"I won't fight you, Dad!" I screamed, and he hit me again.

Then Mum joined the fray. She pulled my dad off of me, still screaming wildly, and I rolled away. Despite my pain, I sprang to my feet.

"You still won't fight me," he growled. "All those years in the Marines, and you're still weak. At least now I know why."

"I'm not weak," I said, standing up straight. "I'm a marine. A boxer. A war hero. Being gay doesn't make you weak."

"Just get out," he snapped, turning away.

I looked at my mother. "Mum..." I began, holding out a hand toward her.

"You should go," she whispered. Her face was pale, and tears clouded her eyes, but she looked resolute.

I stared at her for a long moment, then dropped my hand. When I reached the door, she said quietly, "Don't tell anyone, Eddy. You could lose your job." I turned back to look at her, and she elaborated. "No one wants a gay doctor touching them."

Abandoning my bags, I wrenched open the door and stepped out into the warm summer night. Behind me, my father shouted, "Never come back here! You're dead to me!"

My mother's sobs followed me out of the house.

I didn't look back once.

Chapter Seventeen

After the fallout with my family, I could no longer bear to be in London, so close to them. So I put in for an assignment at an NHS teaching hospital, and they sent me north to Sheffield, to the Royal Hallamshire Hospital. As much as I had enjoyed my time in the Royal Marines, being away from 42 Commando and Portsmouth was a relief. Everything there reminded me of my father and the circumstances that had led to him beating me like I was a football Millwall hooligan. I'd always known about my father's capabilities for violence, but I'd always thought—or naively hoped—that his violence would never turn on me. Growing up, I'd known of other hooligans who beat their wives or smacked around their children. But Dad had never been like that. Whatever violent urges lay within him, he had saved them for the football stands. Which was fortunate for him because if he'd ever laid a hand on my mum, I would have had no difficulty in forgetting my promise that I'd never fight again. I wouldn't have hesitated to beat him if he hurt my mother.

But that had never been the case. He'd never hurt his family. Until now. I supposed my being gay was the last straw: the realisation of all his fears. Despite his effort to make me a lad's lad, I'd still turned out to be the nancy boy he'd lived in fear of.

The transfer up to Sheffield came at the perfect time. I knew I couldn't ever reach out to Dad again. Mum, too, was off-limits. She'd tried to protect me from my father, but I hadn't exactly heard words of support, either. And if I got in touch with her, Dad might turn his violence on her. I had to protect her from that. Which meant keeping my distance, at least until things calmed down.

But despite the relief I felt after moving to Sheffield, the latter half of 1982 was still a dark time in my life.

Sheffield reminded me of Dagenham. It was an industrial city, and the factories that lined the skyline brought back both happy and difficult memories of home. But it was a world away from everything and everyone I knew, and profound loneliness characterised those first few months. Not only loneliness but depression. I'd never really known depression until then. Even in my lonely days before, I'd at least known I had my mother in my corner. Now, I was all alone. Rejected. Cast out. The bruises on my body healed, but the psychological pain did not. If anything, it only intensified. After long shifts at the hospital, I would come home, eat a tin of beans without heating them first, and then drink vodka straight from the bottle until I passed out in my bed, facedown, still in my scrubs.

I woke every morning with a cottony feeling in my mouth and a blistering headache. I'd force down some paracetamol, drink a glass of water, and go back to the hospital.

During this time, I became skinny, losing all the muscle mass I'd put on in the Royal Marines. I became skin and bones, and my cheeks and eye sockets hollowed out. I looked like a skeleton, even as I advised my patients how best to care for their bodies and stay healthy. If they ever wondered how a man who looked so close to death could give out such advice, they said nothing.

One night, after I'd drunk half a bottle of vodka, I decided, spontaneously, to go out. I was off for the next three days, so I thought maybe I could risk drinking even more. I stumbled from my shabby, unfurnished apartment and made my way through the deserted streets of Sheffield. It was late, and a chill in the air pierced through my coat. My flat was in a sedate area, and as I passed rows of terraced houses, I glimpsed the blue flicker of television screens through thin curtains. Turning resolutely away from my residential area, I made my way across town, to where I could hear the muffled sounds of discos down alleyways and the happy chattering of young people enjoying their youth and vitality.

I knew what I was looking for but didn't know how to find it. I hoped the universe would send me some guide, and I'd instinctively know to follow him.

The universe, for once, provided.

In a seedy area, I passed several brasses, all in tight skirts and low tops. A man at the end of the street watched me. He didn't look like a pimp. For one thing, he was wearing a leather harness, and the way his eyes swept over me told me he wanted me, or at least wanted me to think he did. More likely, he just wanted my money.

But I had more than enough money. Why not give some to a man like this? I had what he wanted, and he had what I wanted.

"Looking for a friend tonight?" the man asked as I continued to let my eyes linger on him.

I nodded. "Where can we go?"

His eyes swept over me again. "Yours?"

"Sure. But I want to party first."

"We can go to the Checkers Society. They're hosting a disco just around the corner."

"What's the Checkers Society?"

He looked at me as if I was an idiot. "They run social events for fags."

"Underground discos?"

The man snorted. "There's nothing underground about fags in Sheffield. They say three days in Sheffield does more for a gay man than three years on Valium."

"Right..." This seemed too good to be true, but I didn't want to annoy him by asking more questions. He motioned me to follow him, and we walked back down the street together. When he turned left down an alley, I followed.

Halfway down the alley, he stopped. I paused as well. My heart rate picked up. What if this man meant to rob me? In my pockets, my fingers tightened on my wallet, even as my pulse raced.

But instead of robbing me, he motioned for me to unzip my trousers. "I'll blow you now if you pay for me to get into the disco," he said.

I swallowed. A dark, dirty alleyway wasn't exactly the place I'd dreamed of having my first sexual experience with a man. Nor had I hoped it would happen with a stranger. A rent boy, no less. But this guy was hot, his muscles straining against the black leather harness, and I was twenty-four and still untouched by a man. I was afraid that it would never happen if I said no now.

At last, I nodded. The man smiled, then dropped to his knees in front of me.

It was over quickly. Too quickly. I barely even had time to appreciate how good it felt before I finished, and embarrassment and shame were flushing my cheeks.

Afterwards, as he led me down the alley, he looked at me sideways. "You're straight, aren't you?"

"No." I frowned at him. "Why would you think that?"

"Because you've never heard of the Checkers Society. And because you just came like a fifteen-year-old losing his virginity." He clapped a hand on my shoulder. "Hey, it's okay. Lots of straight guys like to experiment."

"I'm not straight," I snapped. "I'm just..." But I didn't know how to finish that sentence. It was too shameful to tell him I had only recently discovered I was gay. I was too old, surely, to just realise I was gay. And it was more humiliating than I could imagine, admitting that this was my first sexual experience with a man.

"Here we are," he said. We'd arrived outside a door that looked like it led to an abandoned building.

"Are you sure?" I asked, looking around.

"Of course." He knocked on the door, and it opened to reveal a large, burly bouncer in a leather harness and little else. He looked at my companion, then at me.

"He cool?" he asked, nodding at me.

"He's cool."

I paid the entry for both of us, then followed my escort into a dark, crowded bar filled with men. Disco music was blasting, and strobe lights filled up the place. It was a sensory overload, and as I got my bearings, my new friend disappeared into the crowd. I knew there was no point in going after him. He'd find someone else more attractive and more confident to buy him drinks.

As the man disappeared into the crowd, I realised I hadn't even asked him his name. My first male lover and I didn't even know his name. Another reminder that these feelings were something to be ashamed of, best relegated to anonymous, emotionless encounters.

I had never particularly liked bars like this, but as I looked around, I tried to act natural, like I belonged. After making my way to the bar, I ordered a vodka tonic.

"What are you, a girl?" someone called from next to me. I glanced over to see a tall, bearded man, broad-shouldered and muscular. "That's a girl's drink."

"N-no," I sputtered, suddenly nervous. Being called a girl brought back painful memories of my father.

I must have looked terrified because the man touched my shoulder. "Relax," he said more kindly. "I was only takin' the piss. It's okay to be a girl here. Here, let me make it up to you, buy you that drink."

Ten minutes later, we were in a bathroom cubicle, and this time, it was me on my knees.

My experience with oral sex was virtually nil. Even with Debbie, she'd preferred to take control and do things to me. And as I performed this act for the stranger, I couldn't stop wondering if I was doing it all wrong. My teeth kept getting in the way, and I wasn't sure if my rhythm was good. But the bearded stranger didn't seem to have any objections. He came quickly and, afterwards, kissed me on the mouth.

It was my first kiss with a man, and it took place in a dirty bathroom cubicle. Even more than the blowjobs, it cemented something inside of me. The man's beard was scratchy, but his lips were soft. And I knew as we kissed against the toilet that I had found what I was looking for. Not this man, necessarily, but men. This was what had been lacking with Debbie: the feeling of rightness that reverberated through me. All my shame and embarrassment melted away at the feel of his mouth on mine. And while I kissed him, all thoughts of my father's rejection disappeared. It was only me and this strange man. Even the dirty toilet cubicle faded away.

That night, I brought home a third man. The whole time, I never once thought about my father kicking me out of the house. It was the first time I didn't think about it in months.

The following day, after the stranger was gone, I stood in front of the mirror and looked over my body critically. My thinness was alarming. I looked sick. It was time to get back into shape. If I wanted to keep bringing men home—and keep drowning out the memory of what my dad had done to me—then I needed to not look like I was on death's door. And I needed to fill all my waking hours with men.

Soon, my nights became filled with anonymous men, their bodies beautiful but forgotten by first daylight, their faces blurring together until I could no longer be sure, when approaching men at discos, if they had been my lovers. Not that it mattered. I wasn't trying to rack up a high body count. Newness was not what was important to me. It was a need to fill the long, frosty nights with a warm body, to bring companionship to what otherwise would be loneliness, to fill up the space in my head that would otherwise have echoed with my father's disapproval until I was a twisted, demented thing.

And it worked. The constant stream of hot, sweaty bodies at night kept me from lingering on what I wanted to forget. During the day, I had the hospital to distract me. There, the constant stream of sick, injured bodies also drowned out the noise of my own memories.

Block out the noise. That was the important thing to remember. I had to block out the noise by any means necessary.

Thus, I existed for over a year, drifting in and out of my life, asleep to everything that mattered.

And I might have stayed like that, my nights full of anonymous sex, my days full of anonymous patients, had it not been for Brian.

Chapter Eighteen

To understand how Brian entered my life, we need to look back to March 1984. After I had been living in Sheffield for almost two years, the miners' strike started. Formerly a keen observer of world events, I stopped keeping up with news after having experienced war in the Falklands. I kept away from knowing too much to prevent triggering painful memories from resurfacing.

Despite my best efforts, ignoring the strikes in my new city was impossible. Everyone talked about it. The strikes began in March, and with them came a feeling of unease that blanketed Sheffield. I could see the effect everywhere I went: from the looks on people's faces, to the large numbers of middle-aged men I saw in pubs in the daytime, to the chit-chat from nurses whose families were miners.

I had been trying to ignore the chaos, but something changed in June. I was working in A & E when the door burst open, and a group of four or five men rushed in carrying an injured man between them. He was a few years older than me and in terrible condition—his body was bruised and beaten, his clothing torn, and there was a deep cut on his forehead, bleeding profusely. Both his right arm and left leg were bent into awkward angles.

" 'Elp!" one of the men carrying him cried out, desperation clawing at his voice. " 'E needs 'elp!"

"Bring him over here," I commanded, clearing space on a nearby gurney. The men hurried over, and together, they deposited him on the stretcher.

They stepped aside, leaving me ample space to do my job. Despite the obvious exhaustion on their weary faces, they stayed in a tight circle around the stretcher, refusing to take a break and sit down. I couldn't help but notice that these men were hardened. They reminded me of my father in that way; they'd both been prematurely aged by years of manual labour.

"Stay strong, mate," one of the men whispered to the man on the table, gripping his hand tightly. "Tha'll pull through."

"Tell me what happened," I said as I assessed the damage.

"Got caught in a scuffle with the plod," another chap growled, his fiery temper plain to hear. "We 'ad five thousand demonstrators whilst they mustered an equal number of officers, and they weren't showing any leniency."

Suddenly, something made sense. "Are you part of the miners' strike?"

Several men bristled at my question whilst one straightened himself up as if expecting me to condemn them. "It makes no difference whether we are or not—tha still has a duty to aid him."

"Don't worry," I said, holding up a hand in what I hoped was a friendly gesture. "My mother was part of the Ford factory strikes, so I understand the struggle you are going through—not that it would matter. Even if I were against your cause, I'm a doctor, and we can't turn people away."

The miners looked satisfied with this answer because they nodded and relaxed.

"Where did this take place?" I asked.

"Rotherham. We would've carried him to t'local hospital, but it's overwhelmed."

"What's his name?" I asked the closest one.

"Brian," he grunted. "He took t'brunt of it, 'cause he knows he's t'strongest of us lot. He's a good one, Brian is."

"Can you hear me, Brian?" I asked gently, leaning over my patient. "Brian, my name is Dr Turner. Can you hear me?" The injured miner's eyes fluttered open, glassy with pain but defiant all the same.

"Aye," he gasped, struggling for breath.

"Good," I murmured, a hint of relief in my voice. "I need you to stay with me, alright? We're going to get you patched up, but I need you to trust me."

"Oreyt," Brian whispered.

As I set to work, the same stillness and concentration came over me that always did when I was working. I'd heard this described as "flow state", and it was what I experienced then, triaging Brian, patching up the wound on his face, dressing all the bruises, and prepping him for the surgery that I guessed was inevitable.

"Doc?" Brian murmured, his eyes fluttering open and searching for reassurance.

"Right here," I said, offering him a small smile. "I won't let you down, I promise."

"Ta." His eyes slid shut once more.

The other miners had sat down by now, and I drew the curtains around his bed to ensure Brian's privacy. Then I began to cut open his shirt.

"Whatcha doin'?" he grunted.

"Easy now," I murmured. "This is going to hurt." I held Brian's gaze as I eased a dislocated shoulder back into place. He let out a gasp of pain as the arm popped in, then gritted his teeth. His grey eyes brimmed with tears, but he kept himself still and didn't gasp or cry out again.

"Ta," he said as he gave the shoulder a tentative shrug. "It's like yaz done this before," he quipped.

I'd heard the joke a million times before, but this time, I let out a half-hearted chuckle—it was almost comforting, a slice of normal in the chaos. Brian grinned, and our eyes met. It was hard not to notice the well-defined muscles of his arms, chest, and toned abdomen. Brian was handsome, big and burly, with broad shoulders, a thick neck, and a well-defined jawline. His eyes were grey, yet still warm and friendly, and he had sandy blonde hair that he wore long. It kept falling in his eyes.

I forced myself to keep my voice neutral and professional. "You took the pain well. I've seen soldiers twice your size who were begging me for painkillers."

Brian gave me a small grin. "I've been in worse tangles than this, believe me. I just wish I belted one of 'em."

I moved around to the end of the bed to get a better look at his leg. It was clearly broken, but I needed to assess how bad the damage was.

"So this isn't a case of you should see the other guy?" I teased lightly.

Brian laughed hollowly. "Gi over. But under other circ'mstances—" He broke off, looking me over. "Sorry, went and forgot whose company I were in."

"Don't worry, my dad was a football hooligan, so I'm used to violence being glamorised."

Brian didn't try to hide his surprise. His eyebrows shot up, and he tried to sit up.

"Don't," I said, gently pushing him back onto the pillows. "You'll hurt yourself."

"The spawn of a football hooligan and a trade unionist. Not what ah'd expect from a doctor. Makes me think different of you, if ah'm honest."

Brian's eyes roamed over me with interest, taking in every detail of my face. Despite myself, I found myself blushing. I wasn't used to being looked at so closely. Men at the discos usually gave me a quick once-over before deciding whether or not to take me home. But Brian looked at me now as if he was actually curious about what he might discover. I was suddenly glad I'd decided to start caring for myself again and get back into shape. I wasn't so bad to look at these days.

Not that Brian cared about that, of course. I knew he wasn't gay. But still…

"Your mum and her lot proved strikes can bring abaht change. Tha should be right proud!" Brian remarked.

"I am." I tried to smile, to show some of the pride I felt, but it was difficult to talk about my mother without bringing back up the pain of my last encounter with her.

"Well, she sounds like a reet good woman," Brian said. He was watching me carefully, and I had the distinct impression he'd seen some of the conflict cross my face.

"She is," I agreed. Then I came around the bed and gave Brian a very serious look. "Brian, I'm afraid I have some bad news. It looks like you are going to need surgery done on this leg. As quickly as possible, to ensure the best possible outcome for your mobility."

Brian's face went pale as he whispered: "Could I lose t'ability to walk?"

"That's a possibility." I tried to keep my voice as neutral as possible. "We won't know more until after the surgery."

An hour later, as I watched Brian being wheeled away to the operating theatre, I felt an odd sensation like it was a family member being wheeled away. Usually, I was numb to my patients' injuries, even to their occasional deaths. One had to be, to be a doctor. Empathy was why you got into the game, but it would burn you out quickly if you let it.

But with Brian, there was something different. Maybe it was because he reminded me of my parents' working-class background: a trade unionist unafraid of a fight, just like my dad and involved in the strikes, like Mum. Looking back, I think I felt that a hole that had been empty since my parents vacated my life had finally been filled.

Brian was in the hospital for a week after his surgery. During that time, he tried to maintain an upbeat attitude. This, even though he'd been told by the surgeon that he would always have a limp.

I visited him as often as I could, whenever my duties allowed me a few spare minutes. Not that I was the only one. He was very popular; besides family members, rafts of miners visited him. He was like a hospital celebrity. In fact, he got so many packets of Fox's Glacier Mints that we could have opened our own sweet shop. I noticed, though, that no girlfriend turned up. No wife, either, or any children.

Not that it matters, I told myself for the hundredth time. He's definitely not gay.

Not that it mattered. Even if we could never be more than friends, I still appreciated the easy companionship. It had been a long time since I'd had a friend.

Despite my attraction to Brian, I kept going to Checkers Society's discos, determined to keep to my usual schedule and my repeated mantra that I never wanted a relationship. But the discos were starting to feel flat and predictable. I found myself bored during them, my mind wandering as I picked up men and even during sex. Wandering to Brian and how he was doing.

The day the hospital discharged him, I visited him one last time to wish him luck. I'd caught him in a rare moment alone as he was sitting on the end of his bed, putting on his jacket. He still couldn't walk without help—his leg still in a cast—and a wheelchair was waiting for him by the bed.

"Aye up, Dr Turner," he said, looking up and smiling as I came into the room. "Here to admire your work?"

"Actually, I brought you a present."

"Wow, that really is service. I hate to give that woman any credit, but maybe Thatcher was reet when she said, 'The NHS is safe with us', eh?"

"I have to be free of political bias in my role as a doctor, but between me and you—I don't like Thatcher either. The gift is only something small. A pair of boxing gloves I've had since when I used to box. Don't worry. They are adult-size, and I only wore them a few times. They're sentimental to me, that's all. Hopefully, they will remind you to hit back next time."

Brian laughed but then refused to take the gloves. "I appreciate the sentiment, but I just can't take summat that means that much to you. Now, if you have some o' them Fox's Glacier Mints, well, that's a different story. Can't rightly recall the last time I had one o' those," he said with a wink.

"Nonsense! I want you to have them. I'm never going to get any use out of them again."

Then it hit Brian—excuse the pun.

"Tha were a boxer?"

"Hard to believe, I know."

"Maybe tha can take my place on t'picket line. We could do with someone who can throw a punch."

I blushed, and Brian continued, "Ah'm not good enough ta go on any more demonstrations. In fact, tha' surgeon reckons ah'll ne'er be able t' work down t' mines again. Not with a limp."

Although he was trying to maintain a cheerful facade, I could tell that Brian was devastated. His shoulders had drooped, and there was a melancholy in his eyes that I had only ever seen hints of before.

"I'm very sorry," I murmured. "I don't know what I'd do if I couldn't be a doctor."

Brian grunted. "Ya see, lad? Sometimes a man's got a callin'. I know mining might not seem like much, but it's in me bones. Me old man was a coal miner, just like his old man before 'im. It's me community, me family, me home. If I can't do it... I don't know what I'll be. Probably an outcast, ya know?"

"You won't be an outcast," I said fervently, going to stand next to him. After a brief hesitation, I placed a hand on his shoulder. "No one will blame you for this injury. You were fighting for your friends' and family's jobs. It's not your fault you can't work in the mines anymore."

"You're right," he said. His eyes were very soft as they met mine. "But I'm lost, Doc. I don't know where to go next."

My hand tightened on his shoulder. "I've been lost my whole life. You'll find your way. Strong people always do."

Brian was quiet for a minute or two. His silence went on for so long that I worried he wanted me to leave. Then he looked back up.

"Ah'm chuffed our paths crossed, Doctor Turner. Maybe not in thes' circumstance, but ah'm glad they did, nonetheless."

"Me too. And for the record, my name's Eddy."

"Maybe we'll cross paths again when t' times are better, Eddy," Brian said, sighing.

"I hope so," I replied.

We shook hands, and then a nurse arrived to help him into the wheelchair, and it was time for me to leave. As his family greeted him in the lobby, then wheeled him outside, I watched from afar. The hole in my heart opened again, and I didn't know how I would fill it.

Chapter Nineteen

Once Brian departed from the hospital, I took a good, hard look at my life. Frequenting discos and engaging with random men for sex was only providing temporary pleasure, I realised. It distracted me but did nothing to fill the void that had haunted me ever since my dad banished me; for that, I had to search for a place that felt more like home.

It had become evident to me that miners were my people up north: hard-working, working-class lads who were happy to stick up for what they believed in, even if it meant they got a beating. I resonated with that, so I sought out pubs that miners frequented.

When I stumbled upon these pubs, they evoked memories of the ones my dad used to take me to as a child. They were simple and unpretentious, filled with people simply living their lives. My father would have been proud that these were the kinds of pubs I was drinking in whilst in Sheffield.

Understandably, at first, the regulars suspected me of spying on them—a stranger from London appearing in their pubs coincidentally at the same time as the riots. But once someone noticed me at work and told others I was a doctor—not a police officer or journalist—they were more friendly.

At last, two months after I'd quit going to the discos, I was sitting alone at a pub, nursing a pint on a rowdy night, when I felt someone put their hand on my shoulder.

"Aye up, Doctor—Eddy, wasn't it? Sorry, I've never been great at remembering names."

Brian was standing behind me, smiling from ear to ear. He looked better than when I'd last seen him: healthier, more filled out, happier. His skin was glowing, and there was a ruddiness to his cheeks that could have had to do with having recovered from his injuries or the half-drunk pint of lager in his hand.

For a moment, I was speechless. Although this was what I had been hoping for months, I still couldn't believe it had finally happened. "Brian!" I finally exclaimed. "How are you?"

"Ah'm reight, Eddy! Wot yer doin' drinkin' wi' us common folk?"

I opened my mouth to protest, then saw the gleam in his eyes. He was taking the piss. I closed my mouth and smiled. "I guess I miss my working-class roots," I said.

He laughed. "Reet, that means I won't be 'fraid to introduce you to me mates. Come on, let's go meet 'em."

Brian ushered me away from the bar to a table, where he introduced me to a group of lads who looked like they would have bullied me in secondary school. They were all large, beefy, and intimidating. But either they were different from the Tommy Burkes of the world, or Brian vouching for me meant I was okay because they were nothing but friendly as they invited me to sit with them.

"Eh, this is t'doctor who first got me stitched up," Brian explained. "He's t'reason I still 'ave use o' this leg at all." He gestured at the one he'd injured and grimaced.

"Should 'ave chopped his leg reet off," one of Brian's friends joked. Quickly followed by another who said, "Ey, t'drinks are on us tonight."

I tried to protest, as I had been drinking significantly less these past two months, and I was a bit of a lightweight, but the lads wouldn't hear of it. Soon, I'd drunk more pints than I knew what to do with, laughing uproariously at everything Brian's friends said and hyper-aware of Brian next to me. The pub was so crowded that he was right up against me, his bicep pressed firmly into my shoulder. I was acutely aware of the physical touch, and even when I cramped, I didn't dare move for fear of losing it. Never once did Brian look at me in a way that implied he thought anything of—or even noticed—this physical contact. But I could think of little else. I'd touched many men since moving to Sheffield, but none had elicited such a sudden and intense desire in me. But with Brian, even this small, accidental touch inflamed me.

At around two in the morning, the pub closed, and Brian and the lads pulled me out with them into the crisp night air. It was August, but the nights were cool this far north, even in late summer. The lads wanted to keep the party going, but Brian said he had to turn in. "Ah'm sure th' doctor does too," he said, waving vaguely at me. " 'Ee won't be in any fit state t' heal anyone tomorra if 'e drinks anymor."

I hadn't told Brian that I didn't have to work until the afternoon, but I said nothing as I allowed him to steer me away from the others, back towards what I assumed was his home.

Once we were alone, he sent me a coy look. A smile was cocked on his lips like a loaded gun, and his eyes were sparkling. "Fancy a nip of summat?"

I raised an eyebrow. "I thought if I did, it would affect my ability to heal people tomorrow."

"Quiet now." Brian grinned sloppily. "Just one quick'un won't do no harm."

"What do you have?"

"Port and cognac."

I laughed. "And here I thought you weren't posh."

Brian grabbed my arm, and together, we made our way to his flat. He was chatty the whole way there, but once we arrived, he grew quieter. As he prepared two glasses of cognac, I wandered around his flat, looking at everything.

The flat was remarkably clean. Even the bathroom, which I assumed would be dirty and disgusting, was immaculate. The many men's houses I had been to during my two years of anonymous sex were typically complete dives. I found that young men didn't know how to take care of themselves, let alone a flat. But Brian was tidy and clean, and I admired that about him.

For a lad's lad, he also had a remarkable amount of art on the walls. In the living room, I stopped in front of a print of a young man, his 1950s-style haircut messy and his arms covered in spindly tattoos. He was beautiful, but that wasn't the reason the picture took my breath away; it was because I knew, instinctively, that a gay man had taken the photo. Only a gay man could have perfectly captured this man's delicate yet masculine beauty.

"This is very good," I said as Brian entered the room. "Who did it?"

He handed me a cognac. "Robert Mapplethorpe. Tha's Dennis 'Smutty' Smith, t' bass player in Levi an' t' Rockats."

I nodded. I knew the band, but I was unfamiliar with Mapplethorpe. In answer to my unasked question, Brian explained, "E's a photographer from New York, int 'e? Gay as they come." Brian gave me another sly smile. "But tha already knew that, din' tha?"

My breath caught in my throat. I kept staring at the photo, unable to look at Brian. Fear flooded me. Was that why Brian had brought me here? Had he guessed I was gay and now planned to beat me up?

It seemed unlikely, considering Brian's kindness, but I was so used to men attacking me that I couldn't discount it entirely. I wanted to believe this was a tender moment between us, but all my experiences screamed at me to run, to protect myself, that I didn't deserve a man's affection.

When I glanced up, however, it was to find Brian smiling at me. His hands were in his pockets, his shoulders a little hunched. Despite the shyness of the stance, his grey eyes were alight with desire. He took a step towards me, and then another, until we were so close that the tips of shoes were touching.

"If yer were wonderin'," he murmured. And then he kissed me.

In the past two years, I had kissed many men, but none were like that kiss: soft and hard all at once, warm and wet, sweet yet demanding. I wasn't sure if Brian was just a better kisser or if the fact that I knew and liked him made it even better. Either way, it sent chills up my spine, and a deep ache awakened in my belly.

Brian tasted like cognac and smelled of everything I loved: sweat, spice, and a woody aftershave. My senses drank in his scent, his taste, and his feel. He pressed against me, not forcefully but not too gently, and I could feel the strength and hardness of his taut limbs. His arms circled around me, his fingers running through my hair. Then, one hand came to my cheek, and he stroked it. He kissed me once more, lightly, and pulled back.

His eyes were twinkling. "I've been wantin' t'do that since t'moment I opened me eyes and saw t'good-lookin' doctor comin' to me rescue."

I wanted to have a perfect response to that, something romantic and sexy, but my brain felt as if it wasn't working. Brian had just kissed me like his life depended on it. Brian had kissed me. Just seconds before, I'd thought he was straight. And now he'd kissed me.

"You have?" I finally breathed.

"Aye, I 'ave. But I were feard I'd ne'er run into tha again." His thumb continued to stroke my cheek. It was the most blissful feeling I had ever experienced. "I even thought abaht goin' back t' th' hospital but didn't wanna freak ya aht."

"So... you're gay?"

It was a stupid thing to say; of course he was. But I was still so astonished that I had to be sure.

Brian laughed. "Folks are always taken aback. Ah doon't look like what they reckon gays ta' look loike. I s'pose it prevents me from gettin' t'worst sorts of bother, but it can be reet difficult when ah'm tryin' to 'it on someone."

"You were hitting on me?" I seemed temporarily incapable of asking anything other than stupid questions.

Again, Brian laughed. "Aye, of course I was! Couldnae ye tell? I had me arm around ya all neet..."

"I just thought that was how Yorkshire lads are. Matey, you know?"

His hand went from my cheek to my neck, pulling me towards him. Our lips collided harder this time, and then he kissed me so deeply and passionately that my entire body quivered with unsatiated need. Brian's lips were surprisingly soft, enveloping mine, drawing long, wet kisses from me. His tongue flicked lightly into my mouth, and I responded with my own.

"I'd like ta be more than yer mate," he murmured between kisses. I laughed as he kissed my throat, nipping at my Adam's apple.

"Yes, I think that's obvious," I half-laughed, half-moaned back. With each of his kisses, my confidence grew, and suddenly I couldn't hold back anymore. My hands came to his chest, and I was touching him all over, greedy for him, needing every inch of him.

Somehow, we stumbled our way to the bedroom. Then Brian was undressing me. "I wanna do this slow-like, romantically," he said as he fumbled with my shirt buttons. "But ah don't feel like ah can wait."

"Don't go slowly," I gasped. "Take me."

He grinned up at me. "Oh, I'm gonna tek ya. Then tha'll stay 'ere, and in t'morning, I'll be t'one takin' care o' ya in bed."

"Oh, so you'll be the attractive doctor?" I teased. I couldn't believe this was happening. Everything felt giddy; it was too good to be true.

"Aye," he said. "An' I'll be examinin' ya very closely now."

Later on, or rather in the early hours of the morning, after we had been up for countless hours entangled in each other's embrace, we lay side by side. I was fighting the urge to doze off when Brian touched my skin with his fingers. I was hesitant to succumb to sleep because I feared that when I awoke, this moment would be nothing but a dream. Come daylight, I couldn't tell if our love would still be possible. Only during these twilight moments did it seem like anything was achievable. I didn't know what would happen when we sobered up.

"Did you always know I was gay?" I asked Brian, as much to keep myself awake as to satiate my curiosity.

"Nah straight off," he said. "I knowed I wanted you reet away, but it weren't til ya came to visit me after surgery that I knew."

"How did you know?" This I was very curious about. Was it so obvious? Or just something other gay men could sense?

"It were in t' way ya looked at me," Brian said, grinning craftily. "And t' attentiveness. I don't know fer sure, exactly. I dunno if others would know, but I did."

Brian continued to trace his fingers along my back while I thought about this. "I'm always afraid of people knowing," I admitted. "Especially my colleagues and patients. That's why I work out so much, try to bulk up. I want them to think I'm straight. Maybe it's cowardly; I was beaten up a lot as a kid for being seen as gay. I didn't even know then—I had a girlfriend in uni because I didn't know I was gay—but others did. And if they knew at work… Well, I could get fired."

"Aye, I get ya." Brian's voice was soft. "It can be right scary t'be out, like."

"Are you out?"

He nodded slowly. "But I'm proper lucky. Sheffield's reet left-wing. As long as tha's working class and a trade unionist, folk couldn't give two shits about thy sexuality. Just keep it quiet like, don't go shoutin' it from t'hills."

"My father…" I swallowed, unbidden tears coming to my eyes. This was hard to say, but I wanted Brian to hear it: to know me and all the pain I carried. "He threw me out when I told him. I'd just returned from the Falklands. I thought my being a war hero would soften the blow with him. But it didn't. He beat me up and then threw me out."

Brian's eyes had sharpened on me, and he touched my chest, right over my heart. Several long moments passed, during which my heart seemed to beat for Brian alone. "I'm sorry that 'appened to you," he murmured. "I promise ya, as long as you're mine, ya will always be loved fer who yer are."

That's when I let the tears fall: the tears I had held in for two years. All the pain and hurt and anger came bursting out of me. Brian pulled me close, and he held me as I cried. He whispered soothing words, never once making me feel like less of a man. In his arms, it was okay to be emotional and vulnerable. In fact, it was what made me strong.

Chapter Twenty

A few weeks later, I found myself cosied up in a pub in Sheffield with Brian. Over conversation, he explained that while he supported worker's rights wholeheartedly, he rarely went out to protest for gay rights. He simply didn't have the time, he said, when he was working full time in the mines. He spoke about how he imagined the two causes merging into one, a dream come true for him. As an example, Brian recounted how the Gay Rights at Work Campaign had held conferences in Sheffield in '81 and had sponsors from all the major trade unions. This had led many to believe the unions and gay rights organisations would become allies, but so far, it hadn't materialised. That was what Brian wanted most for his life: to fight for both causes together.

"So why don't you make it happen?" I suggested. But he told me it wasn't that simple.

"Unions 'ave got their members' well-being at t'forefront, while many gay rights organisations prioritise identity above all else. But they's both tryin' for t'same darn thing; it's just their methods what sets 'em apart. Gay rights groups tend to be more rebellious, which can clash wi' t'more structured approach of unions. And them unions might see the 'gay lifestyle', like goin' out clubbin', as a bit too flashy."

Brian punched the table, and a few people looked over before returning to their beers. With clenched fists and a hushed but angry tone, Brian continued. "I oft find meself in t'middle, defendin' t'gay movement to t'unions and t'unions to t'gay community. It's reet silly really. We shouldn't be agen each other. We're on the same side against Thatcher."

"Being gay doesn't make you left-wing, though," I reasoned. "I'm sure there are plenty of rich gays in London who love the Tories and hate the unions."

"There are," he agreed, then he smiled slyly. "I thought tha' were one o' them. But as tha's not, I reckon 'tis time ta introduce thee to mi fam'ly."

My eyes widened, and I raised my eyebrows. I didn't realise we were at that stage, but it meant a lot that we were.

The following year was the happiest I'd ever experienced. Although life brought us some tough times, Brian and I were a team and could overcome any obstacle together. One of those challenges was Brian's lack of employment. The union had given him a nice pension, but it wasn't enough for long-term financial security. Far more difficult than worrying about money, however, was the psychological strain of being unable to work. None of the miners had jobs because of the strike, and to keep busy, he wrote letters to union members and spoke at rallies. But darkness was still looming; when his colleagues eventually returned to their jobs, Brian couldn't join them.

Although Brian faced this new reality with as much cheerfulness as he could muster, it wasn't easy for him. He'd grown up thinking he'd spend his whole life as a miner, and overnight, he'd lost his career—and, more importantly, his identity. Being a miner in Sheffield meant something. It was a career to be proud of. As far as the miners were concerned, they had the most important job in England: keeping houses lit and warm through the winter. That's why the strike was so dear to their hearts. They didn't want everyday people to suffer, but they knew that if the pits were closed, they would lose everything: their livelihoods, history, and identity.

Except Brian had lost that anyway, overnight.

And although he tried to remain positive, there were days when he couldn't bring himself to get out of bed. On these days, I would take sick leave from the hospital so I could take care of him and try to cheer him up.

In December, we moved in together. He gave up his flat and moved into the larger one I could afford on my salary. I also insisted he not pay rent. Not until he could work again at whatever it was he pursued next. After some consideration and more time on his hands, he also volunteered for CHE, which was the political arm of the Checkers Society.

It was around this time that we first started thinking seriously about AIDS.

The whispers and rumours of a mysterious illness in America that only affected gay men had begun in 1981. Back then, I hadn't thought about it in the context of being gay, as I hadn't even realised my sexuality. My interest in GRID, as it was known then, came from a professional curiosity. But with the advent of the war, my concern over this illness vanished, as my attention was taken up by trying to keep my fellow soldiers alive. I still hadn't given HIV much thought during my promiscuous days in Sheffield. In 1982, Terry Higgins became the first person in the UK to die of an AIDS-related illness, at least to the medical establishment's knowledge. We still had no idea how it spread, how prevalent it was, or even what the prognosis might be.

Many of the gay men I knew thought it was a hoax designed to scare people out of being homosexual. But by 1984, there were one hundred and eight recorded cases of AIDS and forty-six deaths, and we could no longer ignore the disease. In fact, as a physician and gay man, I suspected that these numbers were astronomically low. Brian and I were starting to hear numerous stories of young gay men in Sheffield, Manchester, and London who were dying of the mysterious illness. We heard these stories through the new friends we made at the CHE, who had been paying close attention to the new virus.

After joining the CHE, Brian finally allowed me to drag him to several discos. We never partied hard, as Brian had a distaste for what he called "bourgeoisie excess", but for the first time in his life, he had other gay friends. They were more worried about the disease than we were. Brian had never had many sexual partners, and my party days were long behind me. But sometimes, late at night, after drinking a little too much, I would check my body for any sores, which were supposed to be the telltale signs of the "gay plague".

On these nights, after Brian fell asleep, I would slip into the bathroom, remove all my clothes, and examine my body in the mirror. Running my hands over the places I couldn't see, I'd feel for anything rough or unusual, any place that was sensitive. At the feel of any moles or a shadow on my chest, my heart would hammer, and sweat would drip down my back. But there were never any sores.

I never told Brian that I looked for them. I wasn't sure he knew just how promiscuous I'd been before we met. He wouldn't have judged me, but I still felt secretly ashamed. It was probably just leftover shame from my father, but for whatever reason, it felt wrong to have had lots of anonymous sex in the past.

In contrast, being with Brian felt better, more acceptable. If it weren't for the fact we were both men, we could have been any twenty-something, monogamous couple in England.

Another much harsher blow came in March: the defeat of the miners' strike. I'd never seen Brian so low. For weeks afterwards, he could barely leave the bed. He didn't eat and barely drank. During those weeks, he shrank into himself. I think he blamed himself. He felt he could have done more if he hadn't been injured. Which was silly. The strike was so much bigger than just him. But I understood how he felt. If we'd lost the Falklands War, I knew I would have blamed myself, regardless of how irrational it was.

To cheer Brian up, in the late spring of 1985, I surprised him with tickets to the Live Aid concert in July. The upcoming concert had taken over much of the news, and everyone I knew wanted to go. I hoped it would be a pleasant distraction, not to mention give Brian some perspective on human suffering. Anyway, I wanted to show him my hometown. I'd seen where he grew up, and even though a visit to my family home was out of the question, I wanted to show him my favourite places in London.

Although I hoped the concert would give Brian something to look forward to, I couldn't have known exactly how much the prospect would invigorate him. After I surprised him with the tickets, he came back to life. He got up early every morning again, started scanning the paper for jobs, and checked out books on the history of Ethiopia from the library. All he could talk about was the concert and how to help famine efforts in Ethiopia. I think it gave him purpose again to have a cause.

In July, we headed down to London—my first time back in the three years since I'd left for Sheffield—to attend the concert at Wembley Stadium.

We arrived in London a week ahead of the concert in order to spend some time in the city of my childhood and uni years. Brian was eager to see plays, visit bookstores, and drink at legendary gay-friendly bars. He made us an itinerary based on suggestions from his friends at the CHE.

Seeing London through Brian's eyes changed the way I saw the city. I'd always been fond of my home, but the events around my coming out had soured me to the place. Even after three years, I still felt nervous about running into my mum or dad while walking around the city. But they barely ever left Dagenham, so I knew my fear was irrational.

Brian had no trauma associated with London, and he loved it. Everywhere we went, he was wide-eyed with awe. He'd never been before, and the sheer size of the place, as well as the number of options at our fingertips for places to go and things to see, amazed him.

I, meanwhile, looked over my shoulder everywhere I went in case I ran into Debbie—or worse, my parents.

On our first night there, we went to the Coleherne, a gay pub in Earl's Court, which was well-known as a gay-friendly area. The pub was crowded and raucous, and it was hard to believe that the disease we'd heard so much about was really such a threat. People seemed happy, healthy, and overjoyed by the freedoms this decade had given them to live as their true selves.

We were sitting at a table at the Coleherne, drinking our fourth pints and getting quite tipsy, when a young man at the table next to us turned around and squinted at Brian.

"I'm sorry to butt in," he said, "but is that a Yorkshire accent I hear?"

"It is," Brian said, grinning at the man, who had ginger-brown hair and a gap between his two front teeth. "Sheffield, like."

"Ah, grand." The man raised a pint. "I was just up there myself. Bad break, with the strike."

"Thanks." Brian raised his pint as well. "I were a miner before I got injured."

The man's eyes lit up. "A gay miner?"

"Aye..." Brian glanced at me, and I shrugged. "Owt wrong with that?"

"Not at all!" The man stood and came around the table to ours, where he held out his hand. "I'm Mark Ashton. I was running an organisation called Lesbians and Gays Support the Miners until the end of the strike. We were trying to make inroads up in Sheffield but didn't get as much support as we would have liked."

Brian shook his hand enthusiastically. "Ay up, Brian Teller 'ere. Pleased to meet ya. And this is me boyfriend, Edward Turner."

Mark Ashton shook my hand as well. "I'd love to talk to you more sometime about your experience as a gay man in the trade unions," he said to Brian. "How long are you in town for?"

"Jus' till aftah t'Live Aid concert."

"Great, well maybe we can meet again later this week? Or after the concert, if you stick around? It'll be madness this week until it's over."

We made plans to meet Mark Ashton two days after the concert. After Mark had returned to his friends, Brian turned to me. He looked happier than I'd seen him since before the strike's defeat.

"Aye, I proper like London," he gushed as he grabbed my hands. "Seems like the place ya gotta be if ya wanna crack on wiv gettin' stuff done."

On Saturday, Brian and I joined 72,000 other people in Wembley Stadium for Live Aid. We heard later that when Joan Baez started her set in New York, she yelled out, "This is your Woodstock!" I can't think of any better way to describe what that day was like.

When I think of it now, the concert feels like a blur. I've seen so many pictures and recordings that friends made on their television sets that when I think about it, I often see it from the point of view of the cameras sweeping the stadium, not as I experienced it from the crowd.

Brian and I were in the middle of a mass of seventy-two thousand people, roaring and bouncing up and down to the music from the best bands our generation has ever seen. It's impossible to express what that energy was like. Being in such a crowd, you lose your individuality, but unlike with mob mentality, it felt more like being in a place of worship or attending church.

I'd never been religious. But as I stood in Wembley Stadium that day, I understood, at last, what it felt like to love God. To lose your flesh and blood body and pledge your immortal soul to Him. Except our God wasn't the Abrahamic one of the Bible, Torah, or Quran. He was Rock 'n' Roll.

There were so many life-altering performances that day that to pick one as my favourite felt like betraying the others. I've never had more fun dancing to anything than Dire Straits' "Sultans of Swing". And Brian nearly lost his mind at the drum solo in Phil Collins' "In the Air Tonight". But if I had to choose one performance that took me to the other side of this life and back, it would be Queen.

Brian and I loved Queen. Who didn't? They were the biggest rock and roll band in the world. We had all their records and played them constantly in our flat in Sheffield. Queen was, well... royalty. And as gay men... well, we didn't know Freddie was gay, but we knew. And if you didn't know after he strutted onstage at Live Aid in those tight, white-washed jeans and gyrated his way through his twenty-two-minute set, then you were just blind. Brian and I spent the set clutching each other, half-screaming, half-crying. And when he raised his hand over his head and let out the Aaaaaay-o that was heard around the world, I swear I saw God.

Queen closed their set with "We Are The Champions". Brian sobbed through the whole thing. I wrapped my arms around him, and after the song was over, we both clapped until our hands were numb.

After that was David Bowie, The Who, Elton John, Freddie Mercury again with Brian May, and then Paul McCartney. The mic cut out during his rendition of "Let It Be", but that didn't stop all of us from singing along to every word. Then Band-Aid finished the concert with "Do They Know It's Christmas?"

I wasn't fully aware of when we stopped cheering, or when we left, or even taking the Tube back into the city. The adrenaline coursed through me for hours after. All I knew was that I couldn't sleep. Brian and I wandered the streets that night, ducking in and out of pubs and kebab shops that were still open. But we barely drank. We wanted nothing to ruin the high of the concert.

We arrived at Hyde Park in the early hours of the morning. We just kept rehashing all the concert's best moments, laughing giddily and stealing kisses.

It was as the sun was coming up over the treetops of the park that Brian turned to me. "Let's make our 'ome 'ere," he whispered against my cheek, his voice full of hope and promise. "Sheffield's got nout more to offer us. We can make a diff'rence 'ere an' live a better life."

Chapter Twenty-One

Brian and I moved to London in September 1985 and purchased a flat on the top floor of a refurbished Victorian mansion in Earl's Court. A small residential neighbourhood nestled between Kensington and Chelsea, Earl's Court was an up-and-coming area characterised by leafy Victorians and quaint English pubs. It was also the centre of gay life in the mid-1980s. I've heard now that the gays are migrating to places like Vauxhall and Soho, but in 1985, it was all about Earl's Court.

Being close to Chelsea and Kensington, Earl's Court was more expensive than I had expected, but I could afford the flat on my doctor's salary, which rose significantly once I transferred to a private hospital in London. Brian thought the area was posh. "If me gran knew I owned a flat in West London…" he would often say, shaking his head. I wasn't sure if his gran, who had been dead for several years, would be proud or ashamed. I never asked him to clarify; I was afraid to know.

Unlike Brian, I found no shame in the upward mobility my career had given me. My memories of Dagenham—our small terraced house, the smoke of the Ford factory clouding the horizon and my lungs—were not exactly happy ones. I was glad to be away from the poverty of that area and in a place like Earl's Court, where the buildings were beautiful and well-maintained and where you were just a fifteen-minute walk from iconic areas such as Kensington and Chelsea.

And then there was Earl's Court itself. The moment we arrived there, I felt as if the place had cast a bubble of safety around us. We'd felt it on our first trip to the Coleherne, and we felt it even more strongly once Earl's Court was our home. The neighbourhood was teeming with lesbians and gay men. Young gay couples in chequered shirts, 501 jeans, and Doc Martens walked the streets hand in hand, seemingly without a care in the world; lesbian couples picnicked in the park; drag queens strolled around with glamorous hairstyles and extravagant clothes. It was unbelievable and thrilling to two sheltered gays who'd been living in Sheffield. At first, I was worried someone would attack these people. Soon, I learned this was the only place in London where they felt safe.

I also soon learned, to my displeasure, that my time in the North of England had made me hopelessly unfashionable, old, and behind the times.

Old... What did that mean to me then? In 1985, I was twenty-seven. That seemed old to me, then. Much too old. I'd fought in a war, had a profession, was practically married, and owned a flat. By any measurable standard, I was an adult. When my parents were my age, they were also settling into their long-term relationship and thinking of having a child.

But I didn't want to feel old. Not when I had so recently come alive. I'd only come out three years earlier, and now I was living in London, the gay capital of the world at the time—apart from New York. I wanted to be young and wild, live fully and dangerously, be risky and adventurous, and live—as the cliche goes—like there was no tomorrow.

Looking back now, only five years after I moved back to London, I can see that I wasn't old at all. My youth screams out at me as I picture the man who strode the streets of Earl's Court, hand in hand with the love of his life. I wish I could go back in time and tell that man to appreciate every second, to hold on to every moment, that living like there's no tomorrow is a waste. You lose nights to blackouts and days to hangovers; you abuse your body in ways that shave years off your life; and you get into stupid, drunk fights with the man you love and can't even remember the next day what you were fighting about. That's not really living. That's throwing your youth away.

I've learned a lot more about life in the five years since. I'm thirty-two today, and I feel younger than I ever have. Now that there is no tomorrow, now that I can hear death knocking on my door and smell it in the air when I open my window to let in a fresh breeze, I understand exactly how young I am. And I understand what this will mean for the next generation of gay men: they will not know how to appreciate their youth because there will be none of us left to tell them.

My impending death might be the reason I'm here on trial today, but it wasn't something I thought much about in 1985.

Despite the joy surrounding Earl's Court—the joy of people living as their authentic selves for the first time—I'd be lying if I said there wasn't a black cloud hanging over it all. Every week, it seemed, one of the blokes we had met, or a friend of a friend, would vanish without a word. Their disappearance was usually preceded by a short illness. Sometimes, the illness was severe; sometimes, it wasn't. A few who knew me well would ask for my professional advice, but I didn't have much to give them.

When I never saw them again, I tried to remain blissfully ignorant. My attention was elsewhere. After all, I was living my dream life in the city—there was partying, drugs, rock music, and plenty of men.

Countless, countless men.

Because even if I couldn't touch, I could look. And flirt. Brian always laughed at me about this. He didn't really understand the appeal of flirting.

"If I can't t'sleep with 'em after, it's jus' a waste," he'd say. "And there's no one ah wanna sleep with anyone other than you."

I would roll my eyes and return to making eyes at whoever was in my sights that day. Flirting, I always said, was an art form. "I can get as much pleasure from the feel of a man's desire as I can from actually fucking him," I told Brian one night at Copacabana. The main gay nightclub in the area, Copacabana, was the biggest of all the bars in Earl's Court and had the largest dance floor. This was my favourite place to end the night, where you could dance until all hours of the morning and take increasingly potent drugs. It reminded me of the discos, except less seedy, and now, Brian was with me.

"Aye, good to know," Brian teased. We were sitting at the bar, drinking gin and tonics instead of beer because we wanted to feel fancy, while strobe lights lit the crowded dance floor, turning the sea of men purple and green and blue. "So ah reckon we dun't need to shag as much, could jus' give yer some attention instead?"

I laughed and lightly jabbed him under the chin. "It's hard to be monogamous here," I said. "There are just so many sexy men, and all the couples we know…"

I didn't have to finish that sentence. Brian knew. Most of the gay couples we knew liked to play with other men, sometimes together, sometimes apart.

"Aye, I know." Brian laid a hand on my knee. "I'm not daft, and I'm not a proper prude. Can see there's a fair few fit blokes 'ere. Especially compared to Sheffield..."

We both laughed, then his expression grew serious. "Ah wouldn't mind 'avin' someone else in our bed, or tryin' a bit of experimentin' wi' other folk, as long as ah know tha's mine emotionally." He bit his lip. "But... ah'm a bit scared, like."

"Of what?" In the purple light of the club, I could see that he was distressed, so I leaned closer.

"O' this illness," he said. "The one tha's takin' t' lives of gay blokes."

"Oh..." I looked away. Brian and I rarely discussed the disease. We knew by then how it was transmitted, and since we were monogamous, we knew it couldn't affect us. Of course, there was some risk at my job, but most HIV patients were sent to the Broderip Clinic or other AIDS-focused hospitals. Anyway, my job was already so much about death, the last thing I wanted to think about was death when I got home or when I was out with my boyfriend.

"Ye must 'ave seen some fellas wi' it," he insisted.

"In an A&E doctor?" I raised my eyebrows. "Unlikely."

"Surely tha sees 'em abaht t'hospital."

"No, they hide themselves from people because they're worried people will treat them like lepers."

"That's terrible," Brian said, sighing and looking at his feet.

"Yeah, it is," I agreed.

Brian looked so dejected that I wanted to say something to cheer him up. I cupped his face, and he looked back up at me. Bringing my face close to his, I murmured, "Do you want to try it tonight?"

Brian's eyes grew big. "But t' disease—" he began, but I shook my head.

"Not that. The other thing we discussed."

Brian hesitated, then nodded. I grinned and pulled a bottle from my pocket, which I snapped open. From it, I took a pill, which I placed on my tongue. Then I leaned back into Brian.

"Kiss me," I murmured. The nervousness vanished from Brian's face, and he pressed his lips against mine. Slowly, we kissed, long and deep, my tongue swirling against his, our salivas mixing, and the acid melting into both of our mouths and bloodstreams.

An hour later, our fears and worries were a distant memory as we swayed to the music, feeling euphoric and unbridled joy coursing through our veins. I could see Brian's pupils dilated, just like mine probably were. Time seemed to slow down, and the beat of the music pulsed through our bodies, creating an indescribable sensation of pure bliss.

"Let's do 'at more often," Brian said on the walk home, many hours later.

"Finally like discos, do you?" I teased.

Brian laughed. "I dunna if I like discos, but I definitely like drugs."

This was in the spring of 1986. By the following year, 1987, Brian and I would be regulars in the new rave movement that had appeared in the UK.

Chapter Twenty-Two

"Eddy, wheer's the E?"

Even though Brian was shouting, it was still difficult to hear him over the incessant beat of the electronic music. It reverberated throughout the rave we were in, rattling my skull and filling me with adrenaline. The swirling strobe lights, which had turned the whole rave neon, only enhanced this. Bodies pushed against us, sweat pouring from them. Strawberry-scented fog floated past, pumped out from fog machines, making the air look thick and humid.

To less experienced ravers, it might have been overwhelming. To us, it was just a regular Saturday night.

Brian was digging through his bum bag, and I could tell from the clawing movements of his fingers that he was growing manic.

"Wheer is it then?" he shouted again. There was a definite tinge of desperation to his voice now, and when he looked at me, I nearly took a step back. His pupils were already huge.

"It's here!" I shouted back. I pulled the bag with the tablets out of my leather thong and watched Brian's terror and need turn to relief and amusement.

He snatched the baggie from me. "Ya were keepin' it in there?"

"This way, the straights won't ask for any of ours," I shouted back, grinning, as I watched him peel open the bag and pull out another tab. The look on Brian's face was now something closer to adoration. Blissed-out adoration. Despite the E making it difficult for my brain to experience anything other than euphoria, I felt a momentary tug of conscience as I watched him ogle the E like it was his firstborn.

"Are you sure you haven't had enough?" I called to him as he lifted the ecstasy to his lips.

He gave me an ironic look. "Can anyone ever 'ave enough o' this feelin'?"

As a doctor, I could have told him that, yes, a person could definitely have too much MDMA. But it was difficult to worry about the consequences of the drug when it was currently releasing so much serotonin into my bloodstream. Anyway, it's not like this was our first time taking multiple pills in one night. This was, again, just a regular Saturday for us.

Brian swallowed the E, and I turned away, letting the rhythm of the music carry me away from my worries. My body moved with the thump of the Acid House music, and dancing overtook me until I was no longer thinking about Brian or how many E's we had taken that night. The rave was good tonight. But then, the rave was always good.

Shoom was our favourite rave. It wasn't a gay club, but that didn't matter in the rave scene. Shoom was for everyone. Even enemies became friends there. Being gay wasn't taboo; being anything wasn't taboo. We'd made the exodus from the gay clubs to the better raves in the summer of 1987 when we'd realised that the best DJs were not limiting themselves to gay spots. By that point, we had expert opinions on raves, and we wanted the best DJs, the best clubs, and the best drugs. We'd found Shoom that summer. That was when it was still in an underground gym with a maximum capacity of three hundred people. It had since moved to Raw, deep in the bowels of a tower block on Tottenham Court Road. Raw was a better venue, but Brian and I took pride in having been going to Shoom since its humble beginnings.

There were other good clubs, like Future and Trip, but we were loyal to Shoom. The music never stopped at Shoom. All weekend, every weekend, Danny Rampling and the other DJs played morning and night, giving us the party that never ended, the party that let us forget the rest of the world—the dying boys, the sound of John Hurt's voice telling us not to die of ignorance, the worsening economy, and our own failures—before we had to return to our humdrum lives.

Returning to our lives was becoming increasingly difficult. It was easier for Brian, who worked as a barman at the Coleherne. If he showed up to work surly and hungover, the other barmen merely laughed at him and gave him a shot. Anyway, with all the boys dying right and left, there was already a lot of doom and gloom at the Coleherne. When I showed up to the hospital hungover and low on serotonin, I was potentially risking my patients' lives. And my coworkers had begun to notice. They made comments—some concerned, some annoyed—but I always assured them I was okay. But the situation was becoming untenable, and there were days—usually mid-week when my serotonin was finally returning, and I felt motivated to reform my ways—when I swore off the raves and the drugs and told Brian I was done. But come Friday evening, when the sun set over the city and Brian dangled a pill in front of me, his smile wicked, I would always give in again.

At least we weren't doing intravenous drugs, I told myself. That was where the risk of HIV came from.

For most of my life, I had hidden away from myself and my desires, and now, I didn't want to miss out on anything. Of course, the drugs also numbed me to my worries. But my primary motivation was to feel everything I'd denied myself for years.

As I danced next to Brian, my limbs otherworldly—almost robotic—under the strobe lights, I felt the opposite of numbed: I felt alive. What did it matter that I was ruining my body? That my career was on the line? That my partner, once an activist and trade unionist, was now more interested in doing drugs than saving the world?

It didn't matter. Only feeling this good mattered.

At that moment, someone in front of me stumbled. I reached out to grab and steady the man, and as my hand closed on his arms, I noticed he was very sweaty. This was normal enough. We were all sweaty. E did that, and we were also dancing in a hot, crowded place. But this man was very sweaty. His arm was actually slippery. And he was hot. Burning up. The man turned towards me. My stomach jolted. His face was completely slack. His pupils were even bigger than Brian's. He didn't seem to see me at all.

"Are you okay?" I shouted over the music. The man didn't respond. "Hello?" I leaned closer and snapped my fingers in front of his eyes. He didn't blink. "Can you hear me? I'm a doctor. Are you alright?"

The man opened his mouth as if to respond. Instead of speaking, he vomited all over me.

Around us, people shouted and gagged. Someone shouted, "Get him out of here!"

Seizing the man under the arm, I lifted him as best I could. I half-dragged, half-carried him out of the middle of the dance floor. Brian followed me. I waved for him to stay. "I got this!" I yelled at him. He hesitated.

"I waant to 'elp!" he shouted back.

I shook my head. He was too high to help in any meaningful way. "He just needs water," I lied. Brian still looked sceptical, but at last, he fell back. Closing his eyes, he raised his arms above his head and let the music sweep him away.

When the man and I reached the edge of the dance floor, I laid him down on his side. Ignoring the vomit on me, I crouched down and checked his breathing, then his heart rate. It was too fast. Unclipping my water bottle from where it hung on my harness, I lifted it to his lips.

"Here, drink this," I murmured. "You're dehydrated."

The man's eyes were closed, and I wasn't sure if he heard me or just felt the bottle in his mouth. Either way, he drank. For several seconds, I let him gulp it down. Then I pulled the bottle. Too much water would lower his sodium levels by a dangerous amount. I poured the water over him, letting it cool his sweaty body. Then I massaged his limbs, which were still jerking of their own accord. I had a muscle relaxant on me because I always worried that Brian might succumb to the same serotonin syndrome that this guy had, so when I next gave him more water, I also let him swallow a muscle relaxant.

It took at least fifteen minutes, but the man finally stopped sweating so much. Intermittent water helped. At one point, I even shouted to a barman to bring me ice. I rubbed this all over the man's body as his limbs began to relax and stop jerking. Finally, finally, he seemed to come back to himself.

Blinking up at me—his pupils had shrunk just a little, to my relief—his eyes swept over my chest, which had become crusted with his vomit. "Did I... throw up on you?"

"Don't worry about it," I said at once. "You were overdosing, but you're okay now."

The man looked confused. "That was you this whole time? Taking care of me?"

I nodded. "You have what's called serotonin syndrome. I've seen it before in clubs. It can lead to dehydration and muscle spasm." It could also lead to stroke and death, but I didn't say this part. "So I gave you water and a muscle relaxant."

When he looked mildly alarmed, I set a reassuring hand on his shoulder. "Don't worry, I'm a doctor. I know what I'm doing."

"A doctor, eh?" Now that he was regaining some of his strength, his voice had become louder, and I thought I detected the traces of a Dagenham accent. "Never met a doctor who also likes to rave."

Definitely Dagenham. My heart leapt at the warmth and familiarity of the accent, and I grinned. "Yes, well, having us around for incidents such as this is useful."

He squinted up at me, realisation etching his own face. "Are you from Dagenham?"

"I am, but I haven't lived there since I was eighteen. I've been in Sheffield and West London since."

"What's your name? Maybe we know each other."

I hesitated before responding. Although I didn't recognise this man, I couldn't be sure I hadn't been in school with him. There were lots of boys I didn't remember from school. And if we had gone to school together, there was no saying what memories my name might elicit. Maybe he'd known me as the nancy boy Tommy Burke beat up. Maybe he'd seen me save Shaun Windham's life and had bullied Shaun about being "gay".

But it had been years since I'd lived in Dagenham, years since boys like this had bullied and beaten me. I was an out and proud gay man now. So I held out my hand and said, "Edward Turner."

"Nice to meet you, Edward," he said, shaking my hand. "Lewis Barnes." Then he paused for a moment, looking me over. "Say... you aren't Lenny Turner's kid, are you?"

My stomach fell out of me. Of all the people I'd been prepared for him to mention, my dad was not among them. How did a kid younger than me know my dad! Hearing his name was like a slap to the face. It was abrupt and painful. But also, underneath that pain was a rush of love.

Confusing emotions raged inside of me, but I tried to keep my face neutral and still. What had Lewis heard? Had my father disowned me to everyone he knew after I'd come out to him? Had he told everyone I was gay? It was unlikely, but not impossible.

"Yeah, that's right," I said gruffly. "How do you know Lenny?"

"He's one of the older lot, ain't he?" Lewis laughed. "Been over West Ham since before I was born." Ahh, of course. They knew each other through football. Now jealousy joined the other emotions burning through me; Lewis shared my father's greatest passion, the one I could never reach. My father probably liked him more than he'd ever liked me. "I'm in the ICF," Lewis continued.

I froze. I wasn't sure if Lewis noticed. He was still high, after all, and the strobe lights in the club made everything look like it was moving. And he was grinning at me, clearly not at all apprehensive that I would have anything but support for the ICF and hooliganism. Goosebumps prickled up my spine and neck. I'd grown up around the Inter City Firm and older hooligan firms over West Ham, like the Mile End Mob. But I hadn't run into any in years, and not since coming out as gay.

The ICF was violent. In 1980, Cass Pennant received four years in prison for hooligan-related crimes. The firm was famous for the calling cards they left on their victims: Congratulations, you have just met the

ICF. I was terrified of the ICF. Terrified, horrified, and disgusted. But also fascinated.

The ICF was who my father had always wished for me to be part of. Nothing would have made him happier than for me to end up a hooligan with those boys. And I had just saved the life of one of them. Of all the people in the club... who could have overdosed... just feet from me... it was a member of the ICF. It felt like more than a coincidence; this felt like fate. A chance for me to redeem myself in my father's eyes, at least in theory.

My stomach fluttered again. I thought I had left behind the need to impress my father long ago. Brian had helped put that hopeless quest to rest. Or so I thought.

Why, then, was my heart soaring now at the thought of using Lewis to win back my father's love? To finally earn his approval? Why was I already imagining our tearful reunion when he saw me on the terraces at West Ham, arm thrown casually around the shoulders of one of the ICF?

I still hadn't responded to Lewis, but he hadn't seemed to notice. He was still grinning at me. "It's mad running into you like this," he said. "To think... Lenny Turner's boy! He used to talk of nothing but you; always made me wish I'd met you before you shipped out."

I gaped at Lewis. That didn't sound like my dad at all. "He-he did?" I stuttered.

"Yeah! How great a boxer you were, and then how you joined the Marines and fought in the Falklands. Now that I think of it, I haven't seen Lenny much since then. He hasn't been coming to the matches. But when he did, you were all he ever talked about."

So many emotions rattled through me: shock that my father had spoken of me with pride, hope that this meant he had forgiven me, and worry that he hadn't been attending matches. "He's not sick, is he?" I asked as I helped Lewis to his feet.

"I don't think so. Just old. You can't be a hooligan forever." Lewis laughed and slapped me on the back. "Look, I should let you get yourself cleaned up. You've still got my sick all over you. If you ever see me over West Ham, come over and say hello, and I'll buy you a few beers as a thank you. We'll be in the Brit, where your dad always used to drink."

I wanted to say that I had no interest in football and wouldn't be over there. That's what Brian would want me to say. That's what was good for me. But all that went through my mind was what my dad might say if he walked into the Brit and saw me drinking with the ICF.

"Yeah, I'll pop in for a few drinks," I said. "I'm over Upton Park in a few weeks."

Chapter Twenty-Three

"Tha's a bad idea, Eddy," Brian told me for the hundredth time as I prepared to set out for the West Ham game a few weeks later.

I didn't bother to respond. Brian was sitting on the sofa, cutting a line of cocaine ahead of his shift at the Coleherne. He wasn't exactly in a position to lecture me on what was right and what wasn't.

When I didn't answer, however, he looked up, scowling. "Those ICF nutters are gonna sniff out yer queer and bash ya proper. You think I wanna find you, lyin' there 'alf dead with one o' their sodding calling cards on ya?"

"They won't find out I'm gay," I snapped as I checked my image in the mirror. Today, I was dressed like a football casual. A Lacoste polo shirt, Sergio Tacchini tracksuit top, dark denim jeans and Stan Smith trainers. You see, across the country in the early 1980s, hooligans started to dress in expensive clothes so that police couldn't easily identify them. The police were looking for thugs in football shirts or those in bomber jackets and Dr Martens boots. I learned all this from my dad, of course. So the smart, expensive clothes acted as a disguise, and I knew I'd fit in down the Brit wearing similar clothing.

"Even if they dun't find out," Brian continued, turning back to the line of coke, "I don't reckon it's healthy to 'ang out wi' these blokes. They're proper scum o' the earth." He leaned over the table and inhaled the coke up one nostril. "An' you 'ave nowt in common wi' them!"

"Well, they like to rave, and we like to rave," I pointed out.

Brian glowered at me. "We both know why yer doin' this. It's fer yer dad's approval."

"My father isn't even going to know," I said huffily. Of course, Brian was right, but I would never admit it.

"Yer 'opin' they tell 'im. That they see 'im at a match and mention 'ow they've been drinkin' with 'is son, what a lad yer are."

I whirled around to face Brian, suddenly and irrationally irate. "And what's so wrong with that?" I demanded.

"Cos yer never gonna get 'is approval!" Brian slammed a fist down on the table, disrupting the next line of cocaine. "Not as long as yer gay. And as long as yer keep chasin' 'is love, yer'll nay be able to accept yourself."

"You're one to lecture me," I snarled.

"Wot's tha s'posed to mean?"

I stomped my foot on the ground. "It means that there was a time when you wanted to fight for a future of fair wages and gay liberation. Now you sit around doing drugs and complaining about your job!"

Brian flushed with anger. For a moment, I regretted my words. But before I could apologise, he spoke. "In case tha dun't remember, Thatcher crushed all me dreams o' t' future. Thatcher, n' t' bloody plod. I'm nowt now, Eddy. Or 'avent tha noticed? Not a miner; not a trade unionist; not an activist. Just a cripple!"

"You don't have to add drug addict to that list as well!" I yelled.

"It were you who got us inta' ravin'!" Brian was on his feet now, his face scrunched up with fury. "It were you who got us inta' drugs!"

"Well, it's you who's made them our whole lives!" I shouted back.

I didn't wait for Brian's response. Grabbing my keys, I wrenched open the door, slamming it hard on my way out.

The fight with Brian echoed in my head all the way to East London. We'd been having more and more fights like that recently. The arguments scared me, but I tried not to think about them often. It was better to ignore the pain, to push it away. Block out the noise. That's how I'd gotten through my teenage and uni years. That's how I'd gotten through a war. And that's how I would get through this rough patch with Brian now.

After taking the Tube across town, I arrived at the Britannia pub, which the ICF called "the Brit". It was the sort of place where you walked in, and everyone looked at you. And if they didn't recognise you, you'd get dirty looks, or worse.

Indeed, the moment I walked through the doors, silence descended, and heads swivelled in my direction. All the air seemed to have been sucked from the room at my entrance. I held my breath. Luckily, I saw a few of my father's friends sitting at the bar. It was a shock to see them again after so many years, their skin more weathered and their hair greyer than the last time I'd seen them. They stared at me for a moment, as if they couldn't believe their eyes. Then, chairs scraped as they got up and approached to shake my hand. "It's good to see you, Eddy," they murmured, and "Long time no see," and one even said he was sorry to hear about my dad. I assumed he must have told them what happened, but they didn't treat me differently. And I wanted it to stay like that, so I thanked them, told them that their kind words meant a lot, and headed over to where Lewis was sitting in the corner.

He'd been watching this interaction with squinted eyes, and as I approached the table, he smiled. I had a strange feeling that I'd passed some kind of test.

Lewis introduced me to his group and explained that I saved his life at a rave. It was the same when Brian had introduced me to his friends, but I suppose that's the perk of being a doctor. It's the best icebreaker. Lewis and his friends spent the rest of the time asking me about my experiences as a doctor: the worst injuries I had seen, how many deceased patients I had encountered, if I had ever made any mistakes that resulted in death, and more questions along those lines. They were genuinely interested, and I was happy to answer their questions.

Soon, it was time to head to the Boleyn Ground for the game. Lewis said I could go with him. There was little talking there; instead, Lewis and his pals abused the other team's players, shouted at the opposing fans, and sang multiple chants. When they sang, "You're going home in a London ambulance," they smiled at me. The boys occasionally threw coins at opposing fans, who responded with jeers and threw things back. Several times, I tensed, afraid a fight was about to break out.

But despite the hateful language and simmering animosity, there was no violence. I wasn't completely shocked, as Lewis had mentioned that trouble at games had decreased significantly in recent years. He explained that many of these firms had started families, had responsibilities, and were too preoccupied with weekend activities like raves to engage in fights. He even mentioned that friendships had formed between members of different firms because they would see each other at raves, where the drugs created a sense of love and camaraderie among everyone.

I was glad not to be involved in any violence. After all, I quit boxing because I didn't like people getting hurt. Lewis had heard stories from my dad and said, "If it does kick off, then it's handy we've got a boxer with us, eh?"

I nodded but said nothing, looking away over the heads of the crowd. I wasn't entirely sure what he was asking, so I waited for him to continue. Nor did I know how I would respond. If he wanted me to take part in a fight, I would be hard-pressed to choose between my lifelong abstention from violence and my new friends.

"Then after, you could patch us up if we get into any bovver," Lewis continued.

It wasn't as bad as it could have been. He didn't want me to fight. He just wanted me to care for those who did.

"I thought you said there wasn't much bovver anymore," I said slowly. "That you're all mates now."

Lewis laughed, and he patted my arm and winked. "Very funny, Eddy."

Still unsure exactly what this meant, I opened my mouth and said the first thing that came to my head: "Yeah, I don't really want to get in any trouble, Lewis. I don't think the misses would appreciate it." Guilt flooded me at once. I was a coward, a coward who had betrayed every single gay man in existence. But I didn't want to be part of any violence, and I was too scared to admit to Lewis that I was gay.

Lewis patted my back. "I understand, mate."

Another wave of guilt hit me. I had successfully passed as a straight man, and I felt terrible because it hadn't taken much acting.

If that first match was a test, I seemed to have passed because Lewis took my phone number and kept inviting me to the games. I was often the centre of conversation in the pub—questions about my time in the Falklands, what it was like to live up north, if I had met any of the miners involved in the strikes, and so on. Frankly, I liked the attention, especially from people my dad admired. It made me feel like the "real man" my dad wanted me to be.

I didn't go to as many raves during this time. I knew the ICF boys went to them, and I didn't want them finding out that I was gay and ruining the friendship that we had built up. So instead, I hid my true self. Brian still raved without me. Sometimes, this worried me, but I also thought the time apart would do us well. It was good for couples to have different interests.

No one would say I was a part of the ICF because I wasn't. But I ended up spending a lot of my time in their company. And if anyone got into a scrape at a match, they'd seek me out in the pub for first aid. When several showed up with broken fingers, I started bringing a medical bag stocked with supplies. The barman said I could leave it behind the bar.

While the injuries never got worse than some broken ribs and a few dislocated shoulders, there were several times when the old bill showed up and started grilling Lewis and the other lads about recent run-ins with other hooligans. Once, they grabbed Lewis by the front of his shirt and dragged him out of the pub to ask him questions outside.

Lewis had scrapes on his palms and knees from this encounter that I patched up for him while he spewed venom about the coppers.

A few weeks later, the police visited the Brit again, and this time, they started questioning me. Fortunately, I knew nothing about whatever tear-up had recently taken place, as Lewis always kept me in the dark. But the experience still rattled me. I came home that night ready to stop going to West Ham. But of course, the following weekend, I was back at it.

Brian disapproved. "If tha' got arrested, tha' could lose ya' job," he reminded me after the incident with the police.

"I know, but..." I couldn't think of a justification for my behaviour, so I trailed off. Brian raised an eyebrow.

"Tha's not like thi'."

True, it wasn't like the "me" Brian knew. I was averse to violence. But in a way, it was like the "me" I'd once been, the boy from Dagenham whose roots lay in violence and hooliganism. And while I'd never participated in the firms, they had always been a presence in my life, just as they were now.

Soon, Brian lost patience, and after I'd been drinking with the ICF for several months, he exploded.

"Ya 'ate violence," he lectured one night after I'd gotten a late-night call from Lewis requesting my aid.

"Yeah, and it ain't me doing any fighting, is it?" I argued back as I reached for my coat.

He crossed his arms. "Aye but by bein' around 'em y' endorse and legitimise their violence. Yer like a mascot. The firm's doctor."

I rolled my eyes. "They don't go out looking for fights. Just occasionally, trouble finds them." This wasn't, strictly speaking, true, but I didn't want Brian to know how often the ICF started fights. "And what am I supposed to do, let my friends get injured? I'm a doctor—it's my job!"

Brian shouted, his arms raised and his palms facing the sky. "Why are ya defendin' 'em? They're bleedin' football hooligans. They ruddy well take pride in that. They even made a bloody documentary about it. And they ain't yer mates, they're just fuckin' usin' ya."

I couldn't control myself and punched the wall. "You think I don't know that? I don't hang around with these people because I want to. I hang around with these people because I need to. They remind me of my dad, and being around them is the only thing that will ever make my dad talk to me again. Do you know how hard that is? Being around people you don't particularly like, but doing so through necessity? It kills me inside being around them, but needs must."

But Brian wasn't done. "Eh, ya see, this is exactly what I mean. Bein' around t'ICF is makin' ya an angry person!" he seethed, throwing himself down on the settee and burying his head in his hands. "Tha's turnin' inta one o' 'em. Ya're becomin' yer dad."

"Don't mention my dad," I snapped. "You don't know him."

"Ya dunt 'ave t'! Y' told me what 'e did t' ye. Yer dad—th' football hooligan!" Brian looked up from between his hands. "Or do ya not remember t' time 'e gave ya a good thrashing?"

It was as if a cold, sharp icicle had stabbed me, and for a moment, I couldn't breathe. "Of course I remember!" I finally gasped. The memory was as clear and as painful as if it had happened the day before. I didn't need Brian to rub it in my face for me to remember every detail. "I've thought about that moment every single day since it happened. Don't you think it upsets me that my dad hates me because of who I am? It's alright for you. You have a dad who loves you. That's all I want—a dad that loves me. And if hanging around with the ICF helps make that happen, then it's something I'm prepared to do."

"Y' don't need 'is love. Y' have mine." Tears laced Brian's voice, and as I watched, he began to cry. His eyes were red, both from the coke and crying, and he was trembling. It suddenly struck me how thin Brian had become. His skin looked pale and sickly, and there were hollows in his cheeks. How long had he been like this? I wondered. Was it the coke? The late nights at the raves? Or something worse? "I love y', Eddy," he wailed, "but yer becomin' someone I dowt recognise. We're both becomin' people I dowt recognise."

There was too much truth in this for me to face. I turned away, as much to hide my shame as to check the time on the clock above the door.

"I have to go," I muttered. "Lewis is expecting me."

"Please, dunt go!" Brian cried. "Please, Eddy, I'm beggin' you."

I left without a backward glance. His tears hurt too much, and his words cut through me, almost as painful as my father's fists had once been.

Barking was worse than I remembered, the epitome of poverty. It was located right next to Dagenham, and it was where I was born. But it was a place that poor people look down on and take comfort in knowing they don't live there. This is where the ICF boys were. After a nasty bust-up, they'd gone back to one of their houses, and I said I'd meet them. Of course, they wanted my medical skills, not my company, but that didn't bother me.

There were no fractures or sprains, just a few bruised eyes and cuts that needed cleaning and dressing. After finishing my task, I joined Lewis out in the garden. "We really appreciate you doing this for us. You know we can't turn up at the hospital like this—it would bring too many questions," Lewis said after a while. He was several cans deep, but he still spoke with no slur to his words. I nodded in thanks but said nothing. After what had happened with Brian, I wasn't in a talkative mood, and I thought nothing would change that.

Lewis put his hand on my shoulder. "I wish your dad were here with us right now. He would be proud of you, Eddy. You are an important part of the ICF. And I mean that."

As the night ended and everyone left, I didn't want to go home. And with Lewis's words echoing in my head, I got on the District line back to Dagenham. *He would be proud of you, Eddy. You're an important part of the ICF.* With the ICF considering me as one of their own, could my father forgive me? After all, he'd always wanted me to be one of the ICF lads. It had been years, and time was a great healer.

I decided I had to take my chances. I had nothing else to lose, and I'd regret it forever if I didn't make things right.

When I found myself outside of my old childhood home, I didn't let myself hesitate. I knew that if I did, I'd get scared that my dad might chase me down the road. So I knocked and prepared to hug my father when he answered the door.

Instead, it was my mum that answered. There were several moments when she stared vacantly at me, and I was afraid she didn't recognise me. Then she threw herself forward. I caught her just before she hit the ground. Crouching, I held her as she crumpled against me and wept in my arms.

"Oh, Eddy..." she kept repeating. The rest of it was blubber. "Oh, Eddy..."

"I came to see you and Dad," I murmured, stroking her hair as the tears continued to spill from her eyes. "I want to make things right."

Mum finally looked up. Her face was stricken, and I could see how old she looked in the front's light hall. In six short years, she seemed to have aged decades. Her hair was almost entirely grey, her face lined, and there was a haunted look in her eyes that made me shiver.

Interrupting her sobs, Mum uttered the words I never thought I'd hear. "I'm sorry, Eddy, but you can't see your dad. He killed himself."

Chapter Twenty-Four

The rain pelted relentlessly against the windows of Mum's quaint living room as she gently placed a warm cup of tea in my hands and settled beside me. My old dear's voice trembled as she revealed the heartbreaking tale of how my father had taken his own life. The lampshade above us acted like a floodlight, highlighting the sorrow etched on her face. The storm raging on the outside mirrored the turmoil within our hearts.

It had been a tumultuous few years for my dad. Not only had he severed ties with his only child, but he had also left behind his career at the Ford factory. While retirement should have been a time of celebration and relaxation for him, he had instead descended into a state of deep depression. The endless days stretching ahead without purpose or structure weighed heavily on him, and losing his career and son left him feeling lost and disconnected from the world.

Mum's words struck a chord within me, causing a wave of sadness to wash over my heart. "I don't think he knew who he was anymore." She sighed heavily. "As much as he disliked being told what to do, being a factory worker was who he was. It was part of his identity." Despite all that had gone on between me and my dad, a tear escaped my eye as I thought about how hard it must have been for him to have everything he knew and loved taken away.

"What about the Mile End Mob?" I asked. I hadn't touched my tea. It sat on the coffee table, getting cold, as I stared at my mother. "That was a bigger part of his identity, and he still had that."

Mum shook her head. "After... After the last time we saw you, your father stopped going to football. His friends tried hard to get him to go, but eventually, they stopped trying."

"Why?" I demanded. Mum just stared at me. I tried to read the answer in her eyes for several long moments. Then it hit me. "Because..." I began slowly. "Because he was afraid someone would ask after his war hero son, and he'd have to admit he was gay?" At the last word, my mother flinched. It hurt more than I cared to admit.

"I think he didn't know what to say to people," she whispered, her eyes filling with tears. "He was so proud of you for your part in the war. But then... he couldn't reconcile that pride with the..."

I briefly felt grateful that she was sparing me from knowing my father's exact feelings. Not that she needed to conceal them. I knew his feelings about me: disappointment, disgust, and betrayal.

"I was still the same person who fought in the Falklands," I said instead. "Being gay didn't change that."

"But your father didn't understand," she hurried to say. "You know what he was like. He had his views on the world and how people should be."

"Yes, I know what his views were all too well. What I don't understand, Mum, is why you didn't contact me?" I snarled, my temper rising. "If I had known how bad things were for him, I would have tried to make things right with Dad. If I'd known what he was going through, maybe he would still be here today."

Mum's eyes filled with tears, and I softened. She put her hand on mine and murmured, "You knew where we were, son. But we didn't know where you were. So how could we contact you? I'm not blaming you. I would have done the same in your shoes. It just would have been nice to hear from you. It's been horrible for me. I lost a son, and I lost a husband." With that, Mum got up and walked to the kitchen.

I knew what she said was right, so I got up and paced around the room. Stopping before the mantel, I picked up a small framed photo. It showed Dad and me. In it, I was just four or five years old, wearing a West Ham shirt, and my father and I were standing in front of the Boleyn Ground. I'm holding a football, and he has his hand on my head. We're both grinning broadly.

"He didn't throw out all the pictures of me," I shouted so Mum could hear me from the kitchen. Mum walked back into the room and saw me holding the photo. She opened her mouth as if to say something but stopped herself. I felt a pain in my heart and sickness in my stomach.

"He did, didn't he?" I asked. "You put this back up after he died."

Mum looked down again. Then, slowly, she nodded.

"Did he blame me?" I forced myself to ask.

There was a tense silence, and I knew she understood what I was asking: did he blame me for why he wanted to take his own life?

Still not looking at me, Mum nodded again.

I slammed the photo back on the mantle. The glass cracked, but I didn't care. "So it was my fault!" I shouted. Across the room, Mum began to cry. "I'm the great shame that killed Lenny! I'm the reason he couldn't go back to the Mile End Mob, the reason he lost his identity, the reason he had nothing to live for anymore."

My mother's sobs pierced through me, but I couldn't let myself break down. Desperate for answers, I darted over to where she was sitting and pulled her trembling hands from her face.

My tone was anxious and angry as I blurted out, "Did he leave any kind of note? What did it say? Did he say that his shame killed him?"

Mum shook her head. But it didn't matter. I knew the truth: Dad might not have left a note, but I knew he blamed me. If it weren't for me, he would have spent his retirement years happily getting drunk with his friends over West Ham. Instead, he'd spent it holed up in this house, slowly decaying, too afraid that someone might ask him about his fairy of a son.

I released Mum's hands and let her crumple back into the sofa where she sat. Standing, I made my way to the door. There, I paused. I returned to the mantel, ripped the broken glass from the frame, and took the picture. Folding it, I put it in my pocket.

"I was the one who found him, you know."

Mum's voice was quiet, but I still turned at the sound. She had stopped crying and was looking up at me with a terrified expression. "He hung himself in our bedroom. I was the one who found him."

Steeling myself against sympathy, I straightened my shoulders. "I'm a shit son. I get it."

I left the house much the same way I did the last time I was there. Full of shame, thinking that I'd never see my mother again.

I went straight to the off-licence and bought four cans of beer, which I drank wandering the streets until the trains started working in the morning. Dagenham at night was a rough place, and men followed me on more than one occasion. But I was so angry that I shouted at anyone who got too near, and they cleared off. Otherwise, the streets were silent and empty. Only the occasional dog barking broke the solitude of the night.

The sun had already risen by the time I arrived back in Earl's Court. Brian, I supposed, would be asleep. But when I let myself into our flat, I was surprised to find him sitting on the settee, waiting for me.

Brian looked different from how he'd been the past few months: more alert, more calm. He watched me without comment or censure as I closed the door and dragged myself to the sofa. I sat across from him, and he handed me his cup of coffee.

"Drink," he commanded. "Y' look like shit."

I doubt I would have stayed awake without it. Setting it down, I glanced around the flat, which was unusually clean. There were no empty cans or take-away containers. The counters looked like they'd been freshly bleached, and the floor had been vacuumed. Even the ashtray had been emptied of cigarette butts.

"Did you spend the whole night cleaning?" I asked, turning back to Brian.

"Yup."

I narrowed my eyes. "Something's different about you."

He smiled. "I'm sober now. Gonna give it all up, ya know? Drugs, booze, partyin'... the lot."

"Just like that?"

"Just like that." He sighed and shifted on the sofa. "Well, our row last night got me thinkin'. Weren't 'appy at first, o' course, so ah went fer a drink at Heaven. Thowt ah might get reet fucked up, forget t'row. But then ah bumped inta some regulars from t' Coleherne, an' tha knows what they told me?"

"What?" I was too exhausted to feign interest.

"Mark Ashton's dead."

I stared at Brian, uncomprehending. "Who?"

"Mark Ashton. That chap we met when we came daahn fer Live Aid. Who organised t' Gay an' Lesbians Support t' Miners."

"Oh... right. How did he die?" But I had a feeling I already knew the answer.

"AIDS. Snuffed it a couple o' months ago." Brian was quiet for a moment, his eyes unfocused. "Hearin' that, and thinkin' of t'legacy he left behind, it made me realise you were spot on. T'were me makin' our life about drugs. Been wastin' me life. Used to be so full of purpose with t'union and CHE. But after me accident and movin' down 'ere, I lost meself. Lost me sense o' direction. Drugs were a bit o' fun at first, escapin' me depression and whatnot... but then they became a way o' life. And that's not what I want outta life. Not when better men than me, men who never aba'ned their ideals, are dyin'." His eyes misted over, and he took my hand. "I'm a miner, Eddy. Even if I can't work in t'mines no more, I can still work for t'mining company. Still be part o' t'union. That's who I am. Don't belong 'ere livin' this life o' excess. Belong with me own people up north. Belong with t'miners."

His words hit like a hard thud to the head. My body felt heavy, and it was with some difficulty that my brain digested what this meant.

"What about me?" I asked finally. As much as it made me happy to think of Brian getting back to who he really was, there was no escaping the fact that I was not a miner from the north. And if those were the people Brian belonged with, then he didn't belong with me.

Brian's hesitation confirmed my fears. "Aye, o'course you're welcome to come back to Sheffield wi' me," he began carefully. "But, Eddy... I dun't reckon ya wanna be in this relationship neymore."

Rage filled me, and I wrenched my hands from his grasp. "I really don't fucking need this right now."

Brian spread his hands wide. "Yer still livin' ta make yer dad proud. Bein' wi' me, aye, bein' wi' a man, will ne'er make 'im proud. Sacrificin' yer happiness by spendin' time wi' t' ICF just so yer dad talks ta ya again. But mark my words, he'll ne'er talk ta ya whil'st yer wi' me. And I don't want ta wait around fer ya ta choose yer dad o'er me."

It all got a bit much for me: my dad, the lack of sleep, and now this. I bit the nail on my thumb and looked at the floor, staying silent for several minutes. I needed time to process everything. Brian sat there in silence, too, as if he sensed what I needed. Loss was filling me like helium in a balloon. To lose my dad and Brian on the same day was too much. Although maybe it was for the best. I couldn't continue living in the perpetual pain of trying to make things right with Brian. Things had just been too bad for too long.

Finally, I rubbed my eyes and raked my fingers through my hair.

"My dad is dead," I said. The words sounded dull and cold, my voice expressionless. I glanced up at Brian. His mouth had fallen open. "I went to see him last night. To... Well, yeah, to repair things with him now that I'm hanging around with the ICF. My mum answered the door, and she told me..."

"Bloody 'ell. I'm proper sorry, love," Brian said slowly. He grabbed my hands again, holding on tight this time. " 'Ow did it happen?"

"He killed himself, Brian. He killed himself because he couldn't handle the shame of having a gay son."

Brian squeezed my hands tighter. "It ain't yer fault, Eddy. I know ye think it is, but it ain't. Yer just livin' yer life true to yerself. 'E was the one who couldn't accept ye."

"I know..." I looked away. Did I know? "But it's my dad. And he died because I brought him so much shame. And now I have to live with his death on my conscience for the rest of my life. Which means..." I swallowed as I realised what it meant. That Brian was right: I was always going to choose my dad. "I think you're right. We should end things. I can't be openly gay anymore. I couldn't make my father proud whilst he was alive, so I will have to do so now."

"Y'can't just stop bein' gay, Eddy. It's not a tap tha' y'can switch on an' off…" Brian shook his head in disbelief. "A lot 'as gone on fer ye in t'past twenny fower hours. Y'just need some time ta process things an' get yer 'ead reet."

I didn't bother responding to that. Brian didn't understand. Brian had never understood. I stood, looked at Brian briefly, then turned around and headed for bed. As the door closed behind me, I thought I heard him let out a short, dry sob.

Two days later, with a heavy heart, I watched as Brian packed up his belongings to move back up north. Part of me was relieved that he was finally leaving, but the other part couldn't help but feel sadness and regret. Four years together, and it all came down to just a few days of packing amidst silence and anger. Another chapter in my life was over, and frankly, I didn't know what to do next.

Chapter Twenty-Five

Brian's words proved true—you can't simply switch off your sexuality. I fell back into my old coping mechanism: indulging in endless, nameless sexual encounters. It was 1988, and the fear of HIV loomed over everything. But in the rave scene where I met these men, safe sex wasn't a priority. All that mattered was living in the moment and seeking pleasure for the sake of pleasure. Despite being aware of the risks, I had little motivation to use protection. Anyway, it wasn't like there was any risk of pregnancy like there had been with Debbie.

I didn't want to contract HIV during this phase of my life, but I also didn't really care if I did. With nothing to live for, I understood my father's mindset when he took his own life. I had no family or significant other, very few friends outside of partying, and a job that surrounded me with further death. On top of all that, I carried the burden of believing that I had caused my father's death and would never have the chance to make him proud.

By the summer of 1989, little had changed. It had been a year since Brian and I had broken up. Brian had written me a letter with his forwarding address, and I'd given him his share of the money for the flat we bought together, but other than that, we hadn't spoken. Although I yearned to know what he was up to—if he'd rejoined the union and found purpose again—I was too afraid to reach out. It was too depressing and humiliating to think that he'd found happiness and joy only after leaving me. Meanwhile, I was still rotting away in London, sleeping with anyone who would have me.

Then came the pivotal night, one that brought both salvation and condemnation. It was a night when a young man, who I later found out was called Jesse, just barely twenty-one, took me to the squat where he and his friends were living.

Having been inside squats before, my expectations were low. I planned to have a quick encounter with him and leave as soon as possible. But everything about that night surprised me.

The squat wasn't the kip I'd been expecting. Jesse led me to a shabby but surprisingly clean and organised house in Dalston. Most of the rooms had been converted into bedrooms for multiple people. Despite the crowdedness, it was tidy. There was no scattered food debris or foul odours of urine, sweat, or drugs. The living room table wasn't littered with drug paraphernalia, and there was no stench of sewage. In fact, the bathroom was spotless.

The second surprise was that when Jesse brought me into his small room shared with two others (who were conveniently out for the afternoon), he refused to engage in sexual activity without a condom.

As I climbed on top of him, my naked lower half exposed, he turned to me with an accusatory and angry tone. "Do you even care about the risk of HIV?"

Out of all the men I shagged after Brian, this was the first person to bring it up.

I shrugged. "Not really," I admitted. "As a single gay man, I've come to terms with the fact that I'll get HIV eventually."

Jesse crossed his arms. His eyes were big, brown, and full of hurt. He really was exquisite. "What sort of response is that? You think just because you're gay that you're condemned, that you should just apathetically accept death? It's people like you who give us all a bad reputation. I get tested regularly. And I always use condoms." His round eyes narrowed slightly. "When was the last time you got tested?"

I didn't answer, shame twisting in my gut. In the silence that followed, Jesse seemed to realise what that meant.

"Not getting tested is even more selfish than not using a condom," he snapped. "You're risking every man's life that you sleep with. No offence, but someone your age should realise that."

He'd hit a nerve, and I growled back, "I'm a doctor. I can hardly go in for an HIV test. The other doctors would ask questions about my lifestyle choices. I could lose my job!" But of course, that wasn't the only reason. Getting tested would also mean acknowledging how recklessly I was living: admitting that Brian was gone, that my father was gone, and that I, too, might soon be gone.

Jesse just tutted. "It's scary getting tested; I understand that. I have lots of friends who are too worried about getting tested, too, in case someone they know sees them entering the clinic. But you have to get tested regularly. If you have HIV, you could pass it on to your patients. I tell you what, get dressed and follow me—if this doesn't make you want to get tested, then nothing will."

He led me down the hallway into a larger room where four young men lay in bunk beds, watching a small TV.

All of them were thin and pale—too pale. Two of them had sores on their faces. My heart hitched, and my stomach lurched at the sight of that ghostly paleness. Even though I'd seen AIDS before—even though I was an emergency doctor—it still frightened me beyond reason to see these boys. Perhaps because I could become one of them.

Or perhaps because they were in a squat when they should be in the hospital.

"What are they doing here?" I hissed at Jesse as the boys looked around incuriously at us. "They should be in hospital being taken care of!"

"Why?" Jesse snapped back. "There's nothing they can do for them in hospital. Why should they have to die surrounded by fluorescent lighting and homophobic doctors, with no friends in sight? These are our friends. And they have nowhere else to go. Their families don't want them. They chose this; they want to die here with us. And we want to care for them."

There was some sense to this. After all, we knew by then that AIDS didn't spread through the air. As long as everyone in the house was careful with any open wounds, there was no reason they couldn't care for friends with AIDS. Still, it felt wrong, somehow...

"The boy with the sores on the top bunk, that's my ex, Benjamin. I really love him, Eddy. I begged him to go to the hospital. But he wants to be here with me. With all of us. There are twenty of us that live here, and we take care of each other. The world has abandoned us. They've left us to die. The government isn't funding research or experimental trials. They just made it harder for us to get information about staying safe."

I frowned at him, confused. "What do you mean?"

The look he gave me was incredulous. "Umm... they just passed Section 28. You have heard of that, right?"

Guilt twisted in my stomach. Truthfully, ever since my father's death, I'd had my head in the sand.

"It makes it illegal to 'promote homosexuality', which a lot of people interpret as material explaining how to stay safe from HIV. They think that by educating gay men on how to practice safe sex, they're encouraging it." He shook his head. "Seriously, where have you been? How could you not have heard about this? There were protests throughout the country; some lesbians stormed the BBC during the six o'clock news and handcuffed themselves to the desks." His eyes sparkled with admiration, and I felt another tug at my gut: this time of jealousy. Protesting for what mattered was the old me, the me who had loved and been loved by Brian. Even through my mask of shame and grief, I missed that part of me.

"Anyway," Jesse continued, "it's clear that Thatcher and her goons want us to die. They'd probably be relieved if we all just disappeared, and they didn't have to pour money or energy into talking about us. So we're helping each other survive and thrive. And for those who can't survive, we're helping them die with dignity."

I looked Jesse over slowly, guilt and jealousy turning to admiration inside of me. "That's why the house is so clean..." I said, glancing around again. "You want this to be a refuge. A safe place."

Jesse nodded. "We have a chore chart, and we all do our part. We take turns cooking as well. And caring for those of us who are sick. We keep the house stocked with condoms. And we all get tested regularly. Once a month, at least." He glared at me defiantly. "I know it's unusual, but we all chose this. To live communally. To support each other when the outside world won't."

As I looked around, I felt as if fate had brought me here. Jesse led me back into the hallway, and I realised what I had to do; what, it felt, every decision in my life thus far had led me to.

Everywhere I'd gone, I'd craved community. And everywhere I'd gone, it had eluded me. Probably because everywhere I went, I was the odd one out. My dad had never accepted me; I never had it inside of me to be a boxer; I couldn't be out and gay in the Royal Marines; I was too bourgeois for Brian; and the ICF... well, I'd never be one of them, thank God.

But what Jesse was describing was something different: a clean, safe place where gay men could live freely, where we took care of ourselves and each other, where we respected medical knowledge and adhered to it.

Jesse was still watching me nervously, so I touched his shoulder to reassure him.

"I think it's great what you're doing here," I murmured. Something was shifting in me: a determination and a sense of purpose that made the world around us tumble away. You might call it tunnel vision. My hand tightened on Jesse's shoulder. "And I want to help. Take me back in. I'm a doctor. I'm going to see what I can do to help them."

Chapter Twenty-Six

Several days later, Jesse and I held a meeting at his flat at No. 14 Lillie Road. This was ostensibly a chance for me to meet his flatmates and lay out my plan for helping to care for those with AIDS. But I also knew it was an opportunity for them to decide if they wanted my help.

As I'd observed last time I visited, No. 14 was shabby but comfortable. It was furnished eclectically with furniture that looked like it had been scavenged from various historical periods. The wallpaper was faded and curling in some places, and the curtains were sun-bleached. But everything was clean, and when I sat down on the centre sofa and Jesse handed me a (chipped) mug of steaming hot tea, I felt right at home.

The rest of the sofas were crowded with young men with fashionable haircuts and trendy outfits. None looked older than twenty-five, and each stared at me with curiosity and wariness. I knew that wariness well; the look of people whose families and authority figures had all failed them.

Many boys also exhibited the telltale signs of AIDS. While a decent number looked robust and healthy, far too many were pale and thin, their lips white and chapped, hair missing in clumps on their heads, and the sores typical of Kaposi's sarcoma blistering across their skin. I was too experienced a doctor to flinch at these sores, but the sight of them on such young men did make my heart ache.

When quiet had descended over the room, Jesse cleared his throat. "This is Doctor Turner," he said, gesturing at me with a flamboyance that reminded me of the theatre. "He's come to talk to us about helping out in the house."

All the eyes in the room came to settle on me, and my stomach squirmed with nerves. These boys were dying of AIDS, and I might be the only hope they had.

"I'm Eddy," I said, my voice wavering slightly. "You don't have to call me Dr Turner."

"But you are a doctor, aren't ya?" a boy with a cockney accent called out.

"Yes. I'm an urgent care doctor at the Wellington Hospital."

"And you want to help us?" another boy asked. He sounded incredulous.

I focused on the boy's thin, pale face. "Yes. I've never worked with HIV-positive patients before, but I'm familiar with the disease."

"Because you're a fag?" It was Jesse's ex, Benjamin, who asked this. He was sitting directly opposite me on an ugly green sofa, smirking. It was clear he was sceptical. Jesse had warned me that Benjamin was the person whose trust I would have to win, so I took a steadying breath and nodded.

"Yes," I said. "Because I'm gay." The flatmates seemed to exhale simultaneously, and I thought I saw several shoulders relax. Jesse had told them I was gay, but hearing it from me still reassured them.

"I never seen a queen like you before," one of the boys beside Benjamin said. He was studying my face, his arms crossed. "You look proper... well, proper." The boys laughed.

I chuckled as well. "Well, I have to look a certain way because of my job."

"Like a wanker?" More laughs.

I folded my arms, feigning offence. "Yes," I agreed, my tone acerbic. "Like a posh cunt."

This brought on a louder howl of laughter from the boys. Even Benjamin grinned. The atmosphere in the room relaxed, and I plunged forward. "As a doctor and a gay man, I am in a unique position to help. I understand both the disease and the sensitive social issues that affect our community. The world hasn't taken HIV/AIDS seriously. Thatcher's government especially hasn't. I know from personal experience that physicians care, but without the resources to fund research, they're scared of getting it wrong and making the situation worse. Now, Jesse has already explained the situation in the flat to me." I glanced at him, and he gave me an encouraging smile. "I'm not trying to convince anyone to go into hospital. I know many of you have already been there, only to be treated like lepers and denied basic human rights. Some of you were even outed to your families. Hospitals aren't always safe for people like us." There were nods around the room and murmured agreement.

"With the AIDS prognosis is what it is," I continued, "it makes sense that you don't want to be in an uncomfortable, unfamiliar place as you near the end of your lives." The room had grown very still. All the eyes were fixed on me. "However, as AIDS progresses, many of you will face health situations that will make it challenging to live in this house without proper medical care. That's where I come in. I want to provide the care a hospital staff would but in the safety and comfort of your home."

The boys shifted, glancing at each other as if silently asking what the others thought. There was some soft muttering as they processed what I was saying.

"How would you do that?" one boy asked nervously.

I had prepared for this question. "Well, I would treat sores, help with bathing, control seizures, and manage your pain. Jesse tells me that no one here takes morphine because of the risk of spreading HIV through needles. As a doctor, I could provide morphine injections while minimising the risk of transmission." This was met with nods and cautious enthusiasm, so I kept going. "Can I ask... how many of you are HIV-positive?"

Thirteen of the twenty flatmates raised their hands. More than half. My stomach dropped as I looked around at all the fresh, unlined faces, which shouldn't have known the spectre of death. "And how many of you have AIDS? As in, you know that your HIV has progressed to AIDS."

Most of the boys put their hands down. Only about five remained in the air.

Thirteen HIV-positive cases. Five AIDS cases. My whole body felt cold. Half the boys in this house would be dead in the next few years.

I forced myself to continue. "What do you think you need most, outside medical care? Is there something I can provide or arrange for you?"

Silence greeted this, and a few more exchanged glances. Then Benjamin spoke. "For me—for a lot of us—the hardest part is comin' to terms with death. I mean, we're young. I'm only twenty-four. I shouldn't be dyin'. It'd be decent if you could help us... process it."

I nodded, even though I wasn't entirely sure what to do about that. How did someone so young face death? Should I bring in a shrink? Spiritual leaders?

"I can do my best," I said. Deep down, I resolved to do more than just that; I was also determined to bring back a cure.

I wouldn't give them false hope by saying it aloud, but I was a doctor who had honed my craft on the battlefield, and my instincts were to save. To kill and cut out this disease before it took these boys in their prime.

I had the next day off from work, so after breakfast, I took the Tube to Middlesex Hospital in Fitzrovia to visit the Broderip Ward.

The HIV/AIDS clinic at Broderip Ward had opened the year previously. Famously, Princess Diana presided over the opening and shook the hands of several patients—without gloves. This was newsworthy because even by 1987, the general public still thought you could contract AIDS from just touch or saliva.

I'd arranged the visit through professional contacts, and when I arrived, a young doctor who introduced himself as Alfred Hinshelwood met me at the entrance.

"We're excited to have you here today, Dr Turner," Dr Hinshelwood said as we shook hands. "It's not often we get visitors from other hospitals."

"I'm glad to be here." I'd told the director of the Broderip Ward that I was visiting to compile information that could help us treat patients at the Wellington. There was no need to mention my side project at Jesse's flat. "As I told Sister Elliot, I often deal with a lot of blood. In the past, we never had to worry about infection, but with the new research on the transmission of HIV, we want to implement proper measures to keep our doctors and patients safe."

Dr Hinshelwood nodded, but I could tell he was only half listening. He didn't seem to care about my reasons for visiting; he was just happy anyone was paying attention.

"You'll notice that our ward is a bit different from others," he said as he unlocked the outside door. "We find that flexibility allows us to better serve the unique needs of the HIV-positive community."

I didn't need him to point out what was different about this clinic. When I entered, my jaw dropped as I took in patients in street clothes, meandering around the ward as if it weren't a hospital but a shopping centre. There were lots of visitors, too, many of them sitting around beds eating lavish meals that had been set out on foldable tables. The smells of food and sounds of laughter drifted through the corridor, raising my spirits.

Hinshelwood grinned at me. "You should see your face."

"Is it always this... upbeat?" I asked as we began to walk down the ward.

"We deal with a lot of doom and gloom around here. But we work hard to make the ward as comfortable and cheerful as possible."

"By letting families bring in food," I said, nodding at the picnic we were currently passing. "And letting your patients wear their own clothes."

"We need to be flexible," Hinshelwood repeated. "We aren't dealing with typical patients."

"Because they're gay?" I asked, my voice more aggressive than I intended.

Hinshelwood raised his eyebrows. "No... because they're in their twenties and facing terminal diagnoses." We stopped near the end of the ward, and the doctor's eyes moved restlessly over the nearest patients. His brow was wrinkled, and there was a tightness around his eyes.

"I just qualified as a doctor, you know," he murmured. "When you go into a palliative care ward, you expect old people, you know? Patients who accept their time has come. These lads... they're my age. We go to see the same films at the cinema. Listen to the same music. It's not easy telling them they're going to die. That's why we need to make exceptions. This disease has taken so much from them, including their youths. We can't let it take their pride. We all work around the clock to make life easier for them. It's hard work, but we want to do it. If not for us, most of these boys would have no one."

I was quiet for a moment, thinking about all this. "Palliative care..." I said at last, my mind snagging on the word he'd used. "You think of Broderip as a palliative care ward?"

Hinshelwood seemed surprised by the question. "Well, of course. There's no known cure for AIDS. The patients who come here... they come to die."

"But you must be running some experimental trials," I insisted.

"We're always trying out new antiviral medications," he said, nodding. "Many of these patients are on zidovudine, although it's too early to tell the results. But Dr Turner... if you're going to work with AIDS patients, there's something you need to remember: most of them will die. Quickly. At very young ages. And there's nothing you can do to stop it. Palliative care isn't about finding a cure. For most patients, the hardest part is feeling they've lost all control over their lives. We help them regain control by providing choices about their end-of-life care and respecting their decisions. Of course, we also try to make them comfortable and keep their loved ones safe. But we are here to make their deaths as dignified and joyful as possible, not to work miracles."

On the Tube home, Dr Hinshelwood's words echoed in my head. As a doctor, it had never crossed my mind that we shouldn't try to cure. Palliative care felt like a bad word; it meant you'd given up on your patient and the treatment you'd assigned. But everyone died, didn't they? Sometimes, there was nothing you could do to prevent it. And in that case, wasn't it better to do as Hinshelwood said and make their lives as dignified and joyful as possible?

Glancing out the window at the darkness of the London Underground, I thought of my dad. Did he have it easier by ending his own life? Was that the "taking back control" that Dr Hinshelwood had spoken of? Or had the pain of his shame been as heavy and fearful as the pain of a terminal diagnosis? There was no way to know. I wished I could have asked him; I wished I could have been there to provide whatever kind of palliative care he needed. What were his last thoughts? I wondered. Were they filled with shame? Regret? Or a sense of peace that he had decided his own destiny?

I had no answers to any of these questions. The only thing I knew for sure was that to provide the highest quality end-of-life care to boys at No. 14, I would have to move in with them.

"Living here will help, but there are still a lot of medical supplies and medications I need," I told Jesse that night as I helped him wash the dishes. I'd come over to No. 14 for dinner, during which I'd shared my insights from the visit to the Broderip Ward. "Even on my salary, they will be difficult to afford."

Jesse quivered the bottom of his lip as he thought this over. "You've already done so much; I don't want you going into debt for us, too. I'll find a way; there's always a way." I could see the determination in his eyes as he spoke, and it only made me more grateful to have him by my side on this difficult journey we were facing together.

"We could ask ACT UP for help, or maybe I could do a charity event, or maybe I could go around the local gay pubs and bars every night asking for financial help," Jesse continued as he patted the plate dry and set it on the counter.

I turned to Jesse, desperation creeping into my voice. "Look, we need supplies, and we need them quickly," I exclaimed, hoping he would understand the gravity of the situation.

I shook my head, sighed, and continued. "Let's ask ACT UP if they can help. But in the meantime, I'll see what I can take from work that they won't miss too much."

For a moment, Jesse didn't seem to understand. Then comprehension clicked into place, and he stuttered a little "erm". His eyes widened in disbelief as he spoke. "You would really risk losing your job for us?" I could see the fear and hesitation in his expression, knowing that my decision could have dire consequences. But my heart was torn between following protocol and doing what felt right.

I leaned in close until our bodies brushed against each other. The hairs on my arms stood at attention, sensing the heat emanating from him. In a low voice, I whispered, "There's nothing I wouldn't do to make a difference here." His eyes glinted with admiration and understanding. "You have given up your whole life to help the people here," I continued. "What I'm doing doesn't even compare to your sacrifice."

Shortly after, I began taking medical supplies from my employer. It wasn't an easy choice, but I never regretted it. Private hospitals earn huge profits, and the boys I was helping had nothing. What were some missing supplies if it could help ease their passing? Anyway, Jesse was right—the government, the NHS, and the world had all abandoned us. Taking from the Wellington was my small act of rebellion. A way of taking back control, as Dr Hinshelwood would say.

He was right about control. Giving people choices about how they want to die helps ease the pain of why and when. I learned this when I sat down with each of the HIV-positive boys in the flat and asked their preference for the end of their life. Most had never been asked this before, and they stared at me with barely concealed shock. When they mumbled they weren't sure, I reminded them that they had already chosen not to die in hospital.

"You've already thought about what's best for you," I would say gently. "That was the first step. Now we just have to think about the other steps." Things like DNRs, pain management, and your will. Most of the boys wanted small, private funerals. Many didn't want their families invited.

"Don't let my old man take my body back to Durham," Benjamin told me one frosty December morning in 1988. He was near the end of his life. I had moved him into my room and was sleeping on the floor so that I could care for him full time. Cool winter light slanted into the room that morning, making his pale skin even whiter. His breathing was shallow and quiet, and his voice was a raspy whisper.

"He won't let anyone come to the funeral." His eyes travelled over the room, and I knew he meant anyone gay. "It will kill Jesse if he's not able to attend. He needs to go through it, to process it. He's sensitive like that." Benjamin's bloodshot eyes, usually restless, settled on mine, where I bent over him. "Tell my parents after it's done. After Jesse's had a chance to say goodbye."

A single hot tear landed on Benjamin's chest, and he smiled. His lips cracked as he did. "Don't cry, Dr Turner. This is good for you. You'll have Jesse all to yourself now."

I laughed and placed my hand on his chest, over the tear. With whatever strength he had left, he placed his own over mine. "Thanks for helpin'. It's nice to know that there are some people out there that care about us."

Benjamin died two weeks later, on Christmas Day, 1988. He was twenty-six years old.

We held a small service three days later. Jesse, who'd been inconsolable for days before, was calm at the funeral. He didn't cry, even as he read the eulogy, and when he placed flowers on the casket at the end, his expression was serene.

After the funeral, I told the boys there was something I had to do and took the Tube out to Dagenham East. From there, I walked to Eastbrookend Cemetery. I hadn't yet visited my father's grave, but the woman at the cemetery office was able to direct me to it. When I arrived, it grew dark, and long shadows stretched across the wet grass.

Dad's grave was still new-looking. Fresh flowers had been placed in the vase at its base. Mum's work, no doubt.

I crouched in front of the tombstone, and my breath caught as I read the words etched into it: Leonard Turner, Loving Husband and Father.

"Dad..." I whispered. Stretching my hand out, I touched the word Father. It felt strange to speak out loud to a gravestone, but I forced myself to continue. This needed to be said. "I think I may have found my life's purpose. I know you never understood it, but all I've ever wanted is to have a positive impact on the world. To help people. Being able to help gay men dying of AIDS feels like the reason I was put on this earth. And who knows, maybe someday I'll help find a cure." A short laugh escaped me. It echoed around the silent graveyard, bouncing off the stones. "I wasn't living a good life, Dad. I was being selfish and self-destructive. Your death changed everything. It woke me up and reminded me of my true purpose. Now that I've found it, your death won't have been in vain. I promise you that. You may never have been proud of me—and you probably wouldn't be proud of my work now—but that's okay." I stood. A breeze stirred the tips of the grass, and I shivered. It felt like a spirit passing through me. "Because I'm finally proud of myself."

Then, I turned and returned home to No. 14, where my new family awaited.

Things would have continued this way—peaceful and content to do my best in the face of the AIDS crisis, with no desire to make my late father proud—if not for the Thatcher government's introduction of the poll tax in early 1990.

Chapter Twenty-Seven

As you jurors know, fury over the poll tax had been building for some time. First in Scotland, then down here in England. Protests had broken out all over the country. The tax, which would raise rates significantly for poor and working-class families, especially large ones in relatively small houses, had reinvigorated left-wing ideologies. Things would have calmed down if the Labour Party had come out against it, as we could have made our voices heard through the ballot box. But they didn't, and in doing so, they betrayed their core voters: the working class. My father, a staunch Labour supporter, would have been spinning in his grave.

After Labour announced that they wouldn't oppose the tax, the All-Britain Anti-Poll Tax Federation called for a demonstration on 31 March, the day before the tax was supposed to come into effect. All the boys in the flat—the ones that weren't sick—were going to the rally, which meant I was also going. I wouldn't have missed it for the world. The struggle against the poll tax reminded me of my mum's struggle against the Ford factory, my father's life as a working-class union man, and, of course, Brian's struggle against the closures of the mines. My parents had ingrained in me the value of fighting against unjust treatment. I knew my father would have joined in the protests against the unfair poll tax had he still been alive. In his memory, I felt compelled to take a stand and join the protest.

Maybe part of me was still trying to make him proud, too. And he would have been, to know his son was sticking it to the man. But of all the things I'd ever done to make my father proud, this seemed to be the least self-destructive—which would also make Brian proud, I knew.

I thought about writing to Brian during this time to see how the union was doing and if they supported the poll tax protests, but I decided against it. Although I was finally proud of my life and wouldn't have been ashamed to tell him about it, fear still held me back. I couldn't bear the thought of hearing he was dating someone new, that he had forgotten about me, that he didn't love me anymore.

On 31 March 1990, my flatmates and I left the house together and headed to Kennington Park. It was late morning, and the day was cold and drizzling. Me and the boys from the house knew we might not see the benefits of our protests, especially those who already had HIV. But we had to do our part for the poor, even if there was nothing we could do to help ourselves from illness and death.

And on a personal level, I knew that going to the protests would have made my father proud.

We arrived at Kennington Park a little after noon. The event organisers had initially predicted 30,000 people, but even I, who had little experience with large-scale protests, could tell it would be much bigger. The park was already so crowded that it was difficult to move. Soon, it was overflowing. Everywhere I could see, people held aloft signs with slogans such as No Poll Tax; Don't Collect, Don't Pay; and Break the Tory Tax. People were shouting and laughing, chatting excitedly, and I felt my energy surge in response to the surrounding energy. I had never seen so many people united for a single cause. It felt powerful. Individually, each of us might be powerless against the Tory government. But together, we had enough power to make a difference.

Looking around at the crowd, I couldn't help but wonder what it would be like to be surrounded by this many people protesting the government's lack of response to the AIDS crisis. What would 50,000—100,000!—gay men and our allies marching the streets and demanding help look like? How many lives would it save?

My friends also felt the energy of the protest. By the time we started marching at around 13:30, they were chanting along with the other protestors. The crowd moved quickly, which kicked up our excitement even more. Soon, we were out of Kennington Park and onto the road, where protestors split up on either side of the street to march.

Our route took us north across the Thames to Trafalgar Square. The whole way, I felt lighter and happier than I had in a long time. People were chanting, singing, hugging, and laughing all around me. Even though we were there to protest injustice, the mood was jubilant. Kids swung from their parents' arms, couples walked hand in hand, and excited chattering filled the air. Seeing that so many people cared about this issue and were doing something about it was inspiring. People had come from all walks of life. There were banners identifying groups as librarians, teachers, bus drivers, students, unemployed miners—my heart hitched thinking of Brian—and even rugby players. Entire teams had come to the protest, and it made my heart swell with hope to think of these young athletes showing up to fight against injustice.

The energy persisted for several more hours until the march seemed to have ground to a halt. Around 16:00, we were standing in Trafalgar Square, just outside the South African Embassy. We hadn't moved in some time. There were probably speeches going on somewhere, but it was hard to make them out over the noise and crush of the crowd. By this point, I was getting tired. I'd had a late shift at the hospital the night before, and I'd now been on my feet for hours. Of course, the younger boys I lived with didn't seem tired.

"Do you want to go home soon?" I said to Jesse, who was standing next to me, holding a sign and chanting loudly.

"Go home?" He laughed and swung an arm around my shoulder. "Is it past your bedtime, Granddad?"

"We've been marching for hours. And someone has to be the responsible one in our house," I grumbled. Jesse responded by kissing my cheek.

"You're not my dad," he said, giggling.

"I could be if you wanted me to be," I said with a wink.

"You couldn't be my dad," he mused. "You don't hate gays, after all." I looked at him in alarm, but his eyes were twinkling. Today wasn't a day to dwell on the disappointments of our blood families; it was one to celebrate our chosen family.

I was never sure what was going on between Jesse and me. Strictly speaking, nothing was going on. We hadn't kissed since the night he'd first brought me home to the squat. Neither Jesse nor I had ever made a move again. And yet, the tension between us was palpable. I couldn't decide if I wanted something to happen or if I preferred just to be friends. It was probably easier to just be friends, considering we lived together. And while Jesse was attractive, he was young, flighty, and flirtatious. If Jesse and I got together, I knew I'd want him exclusively, and he would never be okay with that. Jesse liked his freedom, and I respected that.

Still, I was very fond of him. Not only did I admire how he had created the community he'd never had, but I felt protective of him.

He was only twenty-one years old. Despite all he'd accomplished in creating the cooperative, he was still a child.

Now, as I felt his kiss on my cheek, my face flushed with warmth and pleasure, and I entwined my fingers in his hair and nibbled at his ear. Jesse laughed, and I released him. His bright blue eyes sparkled in the cold light of the afternoon sun, and he leaned close to me. I wasn't sure if it was from the cold or the pleasure of kissing my cheek, but his cheeks were pink, and his lips were bright red. He licked his chapped lips, glistening the ruby flesh, before murmuring, "You know, Eddy, I've been thinking... Maybe we should—"

Wham. The sound of something large and metal hitting fragile human bodies filled my ears, accompanied by the screech of tyres on pavement. Almost simultaneously, guttural screams filled the air.

Whirling around, I scanned the crowd for the source of the commotion. It didn't take long to locate it. About a hundred feet from us, a police van seemed to have barrelled into the crowd of protestors close to the entrance to the South African Embassy. People were strewn on the ground in front of the van. Several of them looked unconscious, and there was blood on the ground and on the front of the van.

Immediately, my instincts to heal and save lives kicked in.

"Let me through!" I shouted as I fought my way through the crowd. "I'm a doctor! Let me help!"

The crowd parted, and I rushed forward to the nearest person, a middle-aged woman who was struggling into an upright position. Her sign lay broken on the ground next to her, and she looked dizzy and disoriented as I crouched in front of her.

"Stay still," I said, placing a hand on her shoulder. "I'm a doctor. How many fingers am I holding up?"

But I'd barely raised my hand when strong hands lifted me away. I writhed against my captor, tearing myself away, and turned to see a police officer in riot gear bearing down on me.

"Get away from them!" he yelled gruffly. "These anarchists are under arrest!"

The surrounding protestors echoed, then drowned out my shout of fury. The crowd surged forward, engulfing me. Turning, I saw an unbroken line of riot police emerging from the van. Some of them were handcuffing the protestors on the ground, while others were holding up shields and raising truncheons at the crowd. Some people they were handcuffing were bleeding freely from wounds.

"You can't arrest them!" I screamed. "They're injured! I'm a doctor—let me help them!"

At my shout, people in the crowd rallied around me.

"He's a doctor!" several of them shouted. "Let him take care of the injured!"

People linked arms, and, with me at the centre, we advanced en masse toward the officers.

"Stay back!" one shouted, and several raised their truncheons. Behind them, more continued to handcuff the protestors. Those who resisted were thrown to the ground without mercy. Several cried out in pain. One tried to grab at an officer's truncheon, and the officer raised it high and brought it down on the man's back with a sickening crunch.

The crowd screamed their fury and surged forward again. The police grouped closer together. They yelled threats at us, warning us not to come any closer, but we didn't stop. For at least a minute, the crowd and police seemed to play a game of chicken. Both crept closer to each other, but neither would strike first. It was as if we were waiting to see who would start the violence.

The fact of the violence felt inevitable. Now, it mattered who would be reckless enough to start it.

All at once, the tension snapped. A young man darted towards the injured people, and an officer swung forward with his truncheon, clocking him on the shoulder. Then all hell broke loose.

From the very beginning, it wasn't a fair fight. They had shields and truncheons. We had nothing but our fists and signs. But that didn't stop the crowd from rushing at the officers with all the force of a tidal wave. The current caught me in it, pushing me forward. I didn't want to fight, but I wanted to help as many injured protestors as possible.

As the protestors fought with the old bill, I slipped through the line and began attending to the injured. Several who weren't in handcuffs yet—and didn't look too badly hurt—I helped to their feet, then hurried them back into the crowd and to safety.

"I'm a doctor," I told them as I deposited them as far as I could get from the fighting. "Stay here. I'm going to go back for more."

But getting back was more complicated than I'd thought it would be. Everything felt confused, and I kept getting turned around. I had to use the South African Embassy as a reference point to find my way back, but it was hard to see over the heads of the crowd with all the signs in the air.

Finally, I made it back to the front. The fighting was more spread out by now. A fire seemed to have started, and smoke was clouding the air. There were no more injured people on the ground. I wasn't sure if the police had arrested them or if they'd escaped. For a moment, I stood still, unsure of what to do or where to go. Then I heard someone yelling furiously behind me, and I turned to see Jesse hurling himself at a police officer close to me.

The officer was holding a young woman in a headlock, and it was clear from her agonised screams she was in tremendous pain. The officer tightened his grip, and she stopped screaming. He seemed to have cut off her oxygen supply because her face turned red, and her eyes bulged out of her head.

Seconds later, Jesse leapt onto the officer's back. The copper roared in protest and released the woman. The copper writhed for a moment or two, trying to throw Jesse off. Then he fell backwards, crushing Jesse.

"Jesse!" I bellowed. Without thinking, I darted forward. The officer was back on his feet. Below him, Jesse lay crumpled on the ground. His eyes were closed, and a small trickle of blood was flowing out from behind his head.

Fear filled my gut and lungs. Fear and hatred. Pure, furious hatred.

The officer turned towards me and, for no reason, hit me repeatedly with his truncheon. I raised my arms to defend myself, but it was useless. As the blows rained down on me, I felt, for the first time in years, the instinct to fight, to take my fists and show him the boxer I had been, to hurt him.

But it was also more than instinct. It was training. I was a boxer. I was a fighter. More than that, I was my father's son. This was what he had encouraged me to do from an early age.

Words I hadn't thought of in years filled my ears:

Dad screaming at Mum when he found out Tommy Burke had broken my nose: *They broke my son's nose, and he did nothing!*

His fury when I quit boxing: *It's who every man is. From day one, men have been fighting. It's natural.*

His soft murmur, full of pride, after I'd given Tommy the beating he deserved: *That's my boy... That's my boy.*

This, I knew then, was what I had been born to do; this was how I was going to live up to my father's mantle; this was how I was finally going to earn his approval: I was going to do what I was best at—save people—and what he was best at—fighting. I was going to be a man and no longer let others walk all over me—whether that was the police, the gay-hating world, or even my father.

Adrenaline, fury, and certainty coursing through me, I threw myself into the fray.

The officer brought his truncheon down again, but I dodged it easily this time. My feet felt light and airy. My fists came up to protect my face. My body was responding as the boxer I'd once been. It astonished me that these instincts had been lying dormant in me all these years. But I barely had time to register my awe before the policeman came at me again.

I was ready. I dodged him for a second time, then punched him hard in the face. He stumbled back, and I pressed my advantage. I hit him again right on the cheek. The copper grunted, then fell to one knee. Next to him, Jesse was still lying motionless on the ground. The sight of him fuelled my anger and strength. I stood over the officer and hit him again. Then again. Then again. The truncheon fell from his hand as he collapsed onto the ground. I quickly positioned myself above him, straddling his body. My fist moved in a steady, calculated motion. It all felt so effortless and instinctual as if this were my true purpose. I needed to defend my own and prove my dominance over this man with my strength, to assert myself as the alpha.

In that moment, I felt like a wild animal, untouched by human laws or morals. I was fighting for something bigger than myself. This was justice. Gay or straight, this was what my dad meant when he talked about being a real man.

The memory of my father's disappointment—and my rage at myself, him and the world—brought me another surge of strength, and I pummelled the policeman even harder. Dimly, I knew that my hand

and arm were bloody. The man's face was bloody. People were screaming. I was screaming.

And then hands were lifting me away. I was being forced to the ground, face-first. Boots collided with my sides, back, arms, and legs. Cold metal wrapped around my wrists. People were shouting. And then I was being dragged across the ground and loaded into the back of a police van.

Chapter Twenty-Eight

The police station where they kept me that night was crowded, mostly with other protestors. I didn't recognise any of the voices that I heard from other cells, which was a slight relief: at least none of my flatmates had been arrested. Unless they were being held somewhere else... But I just had to believe that they were alright.

It was cold in the cell, and my injuries only compounded my discomfort. My whole body hurt. The police had hit and kicked me for a long time before dragging me to the van, and I had bruises all over my stomach, back, arms, and legs. I was pretty sure that I had a broken rib. My hand was also killing me. From my tentative exploration of the bones, I'd ascertained that none of them were broken, but it still ached. I'd cut my knuckles pretty deeply while punching the police officer, and I had to rip up shreds of my shirt to stem the bleeding.

Despite the severity of my injuries, a doctor wasn't called, and no one tended to my wounds. During my police interview, the cops didn't even comment on my injuries. I did what I could for myself, but I knew I'd have to see a doctor later. Not that I really cared about my own injuries. The person I was really worried about was Jesse. But I hadn't seen him since I'd been dragged away by the old bill. I had no way of knowing if he'd received treatment for his head injury, if he was safe, or if he was even alive.

I was so worried about Jesse that I found it difficult to sleep. My stomach was in knots with worry. Every time I closed my eyes, I saw my friend lying on the ground, the blood trickling from underneath his blonde hair. The stream of blood had been relatively small, and the wound might have been superficial. But head injuries were often serious, and my fear was consuming.

To make matters worse, I had no way of contacting the outside world. We were supposed to each get one phone call, but I hadn't received mine yet. Arrested protestors overran the police station, and I doubted the old bill had the staff to make sure we all got our phone calls that night. I also doubted they were inclined to let us. And deprived of the standard-issue blue mattress, I spent the night on the unforgiving concrete floor.

In the morning, the hatch on my cell door opened, and an officer called my name.

Slowly, I pushed myself to my feet. A policeman unlocked the cell and led me out into the reception, where I stood in front of a custody sergeant who was sitting on the other side of a desk and reading from a sheet.

"Edward Turner?" the sergeant grunted at me.

I unstuck my throat. "That's right."

"You're being charged with aggravated assault, assaulting an officer of the peace, resisting arrest, and disturbance of the peace." The sound of the crumpling paper filled my ears. Otherwise, my mind was blank. It didn't seem possible that this was happening.

The sergeant continued: "This is your charge sheet. You're being released on bail and will receive a letter shortly with a court date. Do you have any questions?"

The charge sheet was oddly blurry. I couldn't understand a single thing on it. Glancing up, I saw the policeman waiting for an answer. "Nope, all understood."

And with that, they released me, awaiting my first court case.

When I left the police station, I knew the charges were serious, and at that moment, all I wanted was my mum. I found a payphone across the road from the police station, and lifting the receiver, I punched in the almost-forgotten numbers and waited as it rang. It was still early in the morning, perhaps too early for her to answer.

After the fourth ring, I heard a click and a quiet, sleepy voice. "Hello?"

"Mum," I breathed as my heart pounded painfully. "It's Eddy. I need to see you."

Within an hour, I was home, and Mum sat opposite me. "You could go to prison for this, Edward." Mum's eyes were wide as she stared at me, her cigarette held limply between her fingers. With her voice trembling with worry, she continued. "You do know that, don't you?"

"Of course I know," I snapped, fidgeting under the intensity of her gaze. Even after all these years—even after how she'd failed me—she still had the power to make me feel like a child again. "I'm going to hire an excellent solicitor. The best I can afford."

"Do you need money?" she asked quickly. It was nice of her to offer, but from the way her hand shook—the ash from her cigarette falling in clumps onto the table—I could tell that she feared the answer.

I leaned forward and placed a hand over her free one. "I'm okay, Mum. I have money saved."

Mum nodded, took a drag on the cigarette, and glanced around. Her look was disapproving. "I suppose this flat can't cost much."

We were at the former squat-turned-cooperative that I almost exclusively paid for. I hadn't, however, told Mum that last part. She would only worry and say I was being taken advantage of. But she couldn't know how this flat—and the people in it—had saved my life, that paying most of the rent was a small price compared to what they'd given me. I could have told her this, but that would have meant bringing up Dad's suicide and the guilt I still felt. Doing that benefitted no one.

"The rent is cheap, yeah," I said, shrugging. "I'm fine for money, Mum. I'm a doctor at a good hospital. They pay me well."

Mum's face fell, and her hand shook again. "Eddy... you're going to lose your job."

"What?" I stared at her, sure I'd misheard. "Why would I lose my job?"

"You assaulted a police officer." Her eyes were wide with horror. "The police will inform the hospital."

Heaviness hit me in the stomach like a bowling ball. She was right, of course. There was no way the hospital would let me stay on after this. I was supposed to be in a healing profession, and I'd gone and hurt someone. I'd be sacked and have to leave in disgrace.

"Why did you do this?" she whispered. "Didn't you think through the consequences?"

"The policeman attacked me first! I was defending myself."

"You sound like your father," she said, her eyes filling with tears. "Always making excuses for why he had to beat someone up."

"Good," I said, crossing my arms. "I'm glad I sound like Dad. Because if he were here, he wouldn't be asking me stupid questions like if I'd thought through the consequences. He'd be telling me he was proud of me for standing up for myself and doing what had to be done. He'd tell me that's what being a man is: fighting against authority when you have to and always having your friends' backs."

"Your father wouldn't approve of you beating up old bill," Mum began, and I actually scoffed.

"Are you taking the piss? He was a hooligan and a factory worker, Mum—he hated the police. This tax would have incensed him. And he would have been proud that his son—finally!—wasn't afraid to fight back. But it's too late, isn't it? It's too late to win his approval. He'll never know his son finally made him proud."

The bitterness in my voice soured the air. I didn't look at my mother. I didn't want to see her disapproval and disappointment.

But when I finally glanced up at my mother, it wasn't anger and disgust that I saw arrested on her face. It was guilt.

My stomach jolted. Despite everything she'd done, I still didn't want to make her feel bad. I reached for her hand again. "Mum...?"

She started and blinked. Then, her eyes filled with tears.

"Eddy..." She flipped her hand over and squeezed mine. "I owe you an apology. I know it isn't enough and that I owe you so much more, but the last time we spoke, I was in such shock that I didn't know what to say. Eddy, my beautiful, darling boy... I'm so sorry for letting your father hurt you like that." The tears were leaking from her eyes, but she held my gaze steadily.

"And I'm sorry for not trying to find you. If I were a good mum, I would have tried every avenue to contact you. I've thought about you every single day since your father first threw you out. You deserve better. Your father's death was my fault. I should have found you and made your father work things out with you. I knew it was killing him, losing you. He missed you so much. But I was too afraid. And I'll regret that for the rest of my days." Her grip tightened on my hand, and her tone became desperate. "Believe me, Eddy. I'll never live without this regret. It's my penance. And I know there's nothing I can do to make up for all the years we lost, for what your father did, and for his absence now. But I want to try. I want to repair things. Because I love you, Eddy. No matter what."

I burst into tears. As sobs racked me, she stood and came around the table. Still standing, she wrapped her arms around me. And then my mother held me for the first time in years.

"It's going to be okay, Eddy," she murmured. "We're going to fight this. Things will get hard for a while, but then they'll get better." Her grip on me tightened. "But you can't do this kind of thing again. You can't keep trying to win your father's approval because even if he weren't gone—you wouldn't want it. He wasn't a good man, Edward. He was violent, mean, and disappointed by everyone and everything because, deep down, the person who disappointed him most was himself. Trying to please him will only lead you down a similarly self-destructive path."

I nodded into her shoulder, tears still slipping down my face. How many times was I going to learn this lesson? What would it take before I stopped trying to win Dad's posthumous approval? I'd already lost Brian over it; now I'd lost my job and possibly my freedom. I had to stop before it claimed my very life.

Little did I know it was too late for that.

The next few months proceeded much as I expected them to. The first thing I did was hire a renowned barrister, who, despite the grimness of my charges, convinced me we could get them reduced.

"You're an exemplary member of society," he explained in his office during our first meeting. "A war hero. A doctor. That will help a lot. The jury will be sympathetic."

"I'm also gay," I said. Mum and I were sitting on the sofa opposite him, and I almost laughed at how quickly his jaw dropped.

"But... you don't look gay!" he sputtered.

Again, I almost laughed. Instead, I grimaced. "Well, I am. And if that means you won't represent me, so be it. But I'm not denying that part of myself."

"If you choose not to deny it, then it will come out in the trial's course," he said slowly. "It could bias the jury against you. I don't care one way or another, but as your barrister, I have to recommend that you—"

"I'm not denying myself." My tone was so final that he closed his mouth and nodded.

"Very well."

Soon after, the Wellington Hospital fired me. Vaguely, I wondered what my colleagues were saying about me. But it didn't matter. I had to block out the noise. Which included the opinions of people who didn't understand.

The next week, I had my first trial in the magistrates' court, at which they remanded my case up to the Crown Court, since assaulting a police officer was a serious offence.

"It'll be okay," my barrister reassured me after. "I'm sure we can get you a reduced sentence or a plea. Especially if we prove the police attacked you first, and you were simply defending yourself."

Three months after the poll tax riots, as we were waiting and preparing for the trial to begin, everything changed. It was morning, and I was cutting up fruit for breakfast when the house phone rang. Jesse was sitting across from me at the kitchen table, drinking coffee and reading the paper.

It was my barrister. The moment I heard his voice, I could tell something was wrong.

"The officer you assaulted is dead," he said without preamble. His voice shook, and I felt the quaver go through me and rattle my bones. "The police have asked to change your charges to manslaughter."

My body went cold. The room spun. I had to grip the table to keep myself upright.

"What?" I whispered. "He died from his injuries? How is that possible? He would have died there and then if he was going to die from them..."

Jesse looked up, and his brow furrowed with concern.

"It wasn't from his injuries. They did the autopsy today, and..." His voice caught, and he had to clear his throat. "He died of AIDS. He was a married man, Eddy. With a wife and kids. They're insisting that the only way he could have gotten it is if you gave it to him when you attacked him. There were cuts on your hand and on his face. Lots of blood. They have photographic evidence."

Sound turned off, then back on. Colour faded, and it never fully returned. "But... I don't have HIV."

Across from me, Jesse's mouth fell open. He stood, scraping the floor with his chair in his haste. *What's going on?* he mouthed at me.

My barrister was still speaking. "They found out you're gay, so they have put two and two together. They want you to get tested. The CPS has agreed to upgrade your charges should you test positive."

"What the fuck! That has to be illegal!" I couldn't quite believe what I was hearing, but it seemed too awful to be real, like something from a nightmare. A strange metallic taste filled my mouth, and my heart hammered violently. "I don't have HIV, but even if I did, our fight was only a few months ago! HIV has to turn into AIDS, and that takes time. He would have had to have had it long before our fight. It just can't have been me. It's totally outrageous to even suggest it!"

"That will be for the prosecution to prove in court, Eddy," my barrister explained. "But look at it from their perspective: you're an openly gay man who lives in a house full of men dying of AIDS. The officer, meanwhile, was a family man, and no one is going to believe he got it from homosexual activity."

"But—" I didn't know how to explain to my barrister how common it was for a nice-seeming "family man" to have a secret, second life screwing around with men.

"You need to get yourself tested right away, Eddy," he continued. "If the results are negative, and I hope they are, then the prosecution will have no case. But if they're positive, well..."

"If they're positive," I argued, "then the officer might have given HIV to me, and therefore, I'd be the victim here!"

"Perhaps... But we don't really know that, do we?" He sighed, and as he did, I realised he was right: there was very little research on how HIV spread. I supposed it was possible—although highly unlikely—to have spread through the cuts. And although it usually took years to become AIDS, I knew of some cases where it progressed quickly. Still, the chances that I'd given HIV to the police officer were minuscule...

"Look," my barrister was saying, and I forced myself to focus. "We're dealing with a court system that knows very little about HIV. We will try to educate them, of course, when we plead your case, but the courts have deeply entrenched biases about HIV being an incurable 'gay disease'. Everyone does! And it isn't just anyone you're accused of transmitting it to; it's a police officer. The Met doesn't want it being said that one of their own was gay. They want a scapegoat. And so does the family."

"So they have no problem beating up peaceful protestors, but they draw the line at having a poof in their ranks?" I snapped.

My barrister coughed uncomfortably. "It's also possible they truly believe you gave him HIV and want to punish you for handing him a death sentence."

"Allegedly," I corrected. "Allegedly handing him a death sentence."

"Right..."

From the sound of my attorney's voice, I had a bad feeling that he didn't believe me any more than the courts would. "I wish you good luck," he said. "Please keep me updated on the outcome."

Everyone in the house got tested regularly, and they thought I did, too, but I'd been lying to all of them. I was a doctor, and I knew my body. If I had HIV, I'd know. Or so I thought.

Several weeks later, my test results came back.

I was positive for HIV.

Chapter Twenty-Nine

I didn't know how to get in touch with most of my sexual partners from the past year. With many of them, I hadn't even gotten their names, let alone their phone numbers. I called the ones whose numbers I had. Most no longer lived at those residences, and usually, the new occupants didn't know how to reach them. But I got in touch with a few. They were each silent as I delivered the news. They already knew. Even if they hadn't gotten tested yet, they knew. We all carried the spectre everywhere we went, the feeling that we were next.

The hardest call I had to make was to Brian.

It had been more than a year since we'd last spoken, but the moment I heard his voice, nostalgia flooded me. Brian sounded exactly the same, and for a moment, I couldn't speak. Emotion clogged my throat, and tears burned in my eyes.

"Ey up?" He continued. "Ey, is thi' onnyone theer?"

"Brian," I finally murmured. "It's me."

Silence. Then, "Eddy?" He sounded astonished. "I never thought I'd 'ear from ya again."

"You didn't?"

"Well…it'd been that long. An' tha were inta all them drugs last time ah saw thi'. Sometimes ah wor worried…"

Several years before, the accusation that I could have died from a drug overdose would have offended me. But now I knew Brian was right to have been worried: I had lived recklessly and put myself in harm's way; I was dying because of the bad choices I had made.

"I've been meaning to call for a while," I said. "I know I was in a bad place back then. But I got myself clean and moved into a house with a bunch of other gay lads. It's kind of like a cooperative. They were squatting until I came in, and I got everything square with the landlord. About twenty of us live here, but it's clean and comfortable, and we cook for each other, take care of each other…"

I wanted to mention that we looked after several HIV-positive men, but that would mean turning the conversation to AIDS, and I wanted a few more moments with him before that.

Brian was laughing at my description. "Sounds like tha' 'as become the daddy, and I don't mean that in a sexual way."

"That's most certainly my role," I agreed, laughing as well. "How are you?"

"I'm doin' right well!" From the way his voice brightened, I knew he was telling the truth. "I'm workin' wi' t'union on t'management and admin side o' things. It's not as satisfying as bein' in t'mine, but it's probably better for me health. And it feels reet good to be doin' what I'm meant to do, to be part o' t'community I grew up wi'. Sheffield's changed, though. It's gettin' more right-wing. I reck'n that's 'ow these things go. They ebb an' flow."

"The only constant is change," I agreed, and I felt, rather than heard, Brian nod through the phone. I took a deep breath. "Actually… there's something I wanted to talk to you about."

"Ah?" I couldn't tell if I imagined the hopefulness in his voice or not.

I braced myself. "It's... not good."

"Oh..." I knew then that he knew. This was the phone call we were all getting. The one we lived in fear of. In some ways, he might have been expecting it.

"Brian, I'm—" The words couldn't get out. They stayed in my throat, like unchewed food blocking my windpipe. And then suddenly, I was crying, hacking sobs that shook my whole body and turned into screams.

"Oh, Eddy," Brian whispered, repeating my name as if it were a prayer. I slid down the wall as I continued to sob. The phone dropped from my hands, and I put my head in them. For a long time, I sat there, my body shaking as sobs tore through me. There was so much anguish inside of me that I thought the tears would never stop, even when my eyes ached from crying. Every thirty seconds, Brian would murmur my name. He wasn't trying to get my attention. He was simply repeating my name as if trying to mark it into the air, into the universe, before I was gone forever. In his mouth, my name was proof that I had existed and that my memory would continue, even after my all-too-brief life was cut short.

Ten minutes must have passed before my tears ran out, and I picked up the telephone. Snot and tears covered my face, and I wiped it on the back of my sleeve.

"Brian?" My voice was as foggy as a window on a rainy night.

"Aye, I'm still 'ere." His breathing was slow and steady, and it comforted me. "I'm so sorry, Eddy. I'm so, so sorry." His voice hitched, and he cleared his throat. "I don't mean t'sound insensitive, but should I get meself tested?"

"That's not insensitive," I assured him. "That's one reason I called. I'm pretty sure I got it after we broke up, but yeah, you should get tested. Just in case."

"Y'never... wi' anyone else... when we were t'gether?"

"Absolutely not." I hoped the force and swiftness of my refutation reassured him. "I loved you so much, Brian. I never would have done that to you. But... I suppose it could have been there since before we met. I doubt it, but it's possible."

"Aye, I'll get tested. Prob'ly should've done it by now, anyway."

"Me too. I only found out because my barrister said I should get tested."

And then I told Brian the whole story: the year I'd lost to sleeping with strangers, pursuing the numbness of sex; meeting Jesse and moving into the cooperative; the poll tax protest; assaulting the police officer; the night in a cell; my reconciliation with my mum; and finally, the policeman finding out he had HIV and my subsequent test.

When I was done, Brian sounded dazed. "Blimey, Eddy. You've been through the ruddy wars. But I'm chuffed, at t'very least, that you and your mum have found some peace."

"Me too. She's been helping me with this court case. But the HIV diagnosis... I think she might lose it."

"It must be reet 'ard for her," he murmured. "So soon after losin' yer father."

"I don't... I don't want to leave her alone again." I swallowed the lump in my throat. The kitchen went in and out of focus as fear seized me and then abated. "Now that we have reconciled, that's my worst fear: that she'll waste away without Dad or me to take care of her."

"Ah'll keep an eye on 'er," Brian said at once. "Bloody 'ell, Eddy, no need to fret about that. I'll pop round and check on Linda. Do whatever she... or thee... needs me to do."

I rubbed my eyes and cleared my throat, trying to fight the tears that threatened to reemerge. "This feels surreal, having this conversation with you."

"It's the same fer me, too." He chuckled. "I were 'opin' to 'ear from ya, but not like this."

"You were?"

"Aye, o' course. I've been missin' ya, Eddy."

"I've missed you too." We both fell silent. It felt companionable, and in the peaceful silence, memories of our four years together rushed back to me: meeting in Sheffield, cosy nights watching films in my small flat near the hospital, the Live Aid concert, buying our home together in London, even the beginning of our rave days. Before we got too heavy into the drugs, that was a good time.

"Did you ever think… that we might get back together?" I hadn't expected to ask it, but now I had to know.

Brian let out a small "oh" of surprise. "I don' know…"

"I know it can't happen now because of the HIV…" I rushed to say.

"Don't be daft, Eddy," Brian interrupted. "It's not about t' HIV. We could sort summat out."

"What is it about, then?" I demanded.

"It's yer dad," Brian said simply.

"What?" I clutched the phone harder. "But my dad is dead."

"Aye, I know. But I need to know tha' you're not still chasing after 'is approval, even in death."

"I'm not!" But my response was too quick, and I knew he didn't believe me. "Believe me, Brian, I'm not. Mum has said the same things as you, and I'm serious about it this time."

Brian breathed in sharply. "Ah, tha's doin' good, Eddy. Sounds like tha's makin' strides to get out from under his influence. Ah'm proper chuffed yer mum's helpin' ya. An' this cooperative seems reyt grand.

Ah'm so proud o' ya for bein' part of it an' standin' up fer them protestors. Them bobbies deserve a right thumpin' fer what they did to ya, when all ya were tryna do was save folks' lives. An' course ah'm scared shiteless about yer diagnosis. But…well, ah'll always be yer mate, Eddy. Always. Ah'll take care o' ya in any way ya need. But t' get back together, I'd need t' know fer sure tha this were goin' t' stick, tha weren't gonna do summat mental like 'ang around wi' hooligans."

"I understand," I muttered. What else could I say? I couldn't promise it would stick after all the times it didn't.

"I'm right sorry." He truly sounded it, and I wished I could reach out and hold him, at least just for a moment. "But I reckin' ya should keep in touch, aye?"

"Okay." Realising how sullen I sounded, I forced myself to sound more cheerful. "Yes, of course. I'll keep you updated."

"Maybe… maybe I can pop down and see ya in a few months? Then we could 'ave another chat…"

"I might be in prison in a few months."

Another long silence, this one much heavier.

"Cheers for ringin', love," Brian said at last. "It's grand to 'ear yer voice. I'm missin' ya somethin' terrible."

I hung up, then rested the phone in my hand so Brian couldn't call back. His rejection hurt more than I had thought it would. I might only have months left to live, but he still didn't want me back. I could only conclude that I had caused him immeasurable pain from my constant obsession with impressing my father.

There had to be a way to prove that I had changed. Even if I never got Brian back, it could serve as an apology, as a way of making up for all the ways I'd hurt him by chasing a dead man's approval.

I didn't know how to do this but I was determined to try.

The next week, I went to Chelsea to shop for a present for Brian. I wanted to get him something nice to go along with the letter from my solicitor, in which I detailed that a portion of my estate would go to him after my death. This wasn't a bribe to make him get back together with me. Brian was the most significant relationship of my life. He'd been like a husband to me, and he deserved to inherit a substantial portion of my wealth. I might have left all of it to him were I not also leaving some to the cooperative, Jesse, and my mum. Also included in my will was the charity ACT UP. This organisation was dear to my heart. It was one of the few charities helping gay men with HIV and AIDS. It also funded badly needed research on the disease.

I had just come out of a menswear shop, having purchased him a beautiful silk pocket square, and was about to cross the street to a record store when someone called my name. The day was warm and bright, shoppers filling the pavement, and for a moment, I thought I had imagined it. Then I heard it again, my name being called even through the crowd of people:

"Eddy! Eddy Turner! Wait up!"

I turned, surprised by the sound of my name, and saw a woman striding towards me, beaming. In the sunshine, her auburn hair glittered.

It was Debbie.

Chapter Thirty

"Debbie!" I gasped, my breath catching in my throat at the sight of my ex-girlfriend standing before me. My body froze for a moment, stunned by the unexpected encounter. Slowly, I gathered my composure and made my way towards her, unsure how to greet her after all this time. Would it be a polite handshake or an intimate embrace? In the end, she decided for us, pulling me into a warm and familiar hug that sent a rush of memories flooding through me. It was both awkward and comforting, like trying on a favourite pair of jeans that still fit just right.

"Eddy," she breathed into the lapels of my jacket. "It's so wonderful to see you."

She released me, her hands falling from my grip as she stepped back, her face illuminated by a radiant smile. Her eyes shimmered with unshed tears, and I couldn't help but feel a twinge of emotion in response to her joy. Debbie looked much like I remembered her, although the years had left their mark on her face. The freckles that dotted her nose were more pronounced now, and there were fine lines etched around the corners of her eyes from a lifetime of laughter. Silver strands mingled among the auburn waves of her hair, evidence of the passage of time. "It's good to see you, too," I said. "What are you doing here?"

She tossed her head. "Oh, just getting some quick shopping in before I pick up my boys."

My heart skipped a beat. "You have kids?"

Her smile slipped, and she nodded. "Yes. I have three sons. I'm married now. My husband and I live in Kensington."

"Kensington?" I whistled. "I assume you are working as a consultant now to afford that?"

"Oh god, no." She laughed. "I gave up on that dream years ago. Didn't you hear I'd dropped out of medical school?"

"You did? I thought you'd just transferred." I gaped. "You were so passionate about becoming a doctor. Was it...?" I was unsure if I should mention the abortion.

"I know, but I was young," she said, "and I didn't know what I wanted. Instead, I took a few years off, travelled, and then returned to university to study international relations. I work for a charity now that does development work in Latin America."

"Wow, Debbie..." I shook my head. "I always knew you'd do amazing things."

She waved away my compliment. "What about you?" she asked. "Are you married? Kids...?"

It was the moment to tell her I was gay and about Brian, but somehow, I couldn't bring myself to do it. If Debbie was anything like how I remembered her, she wouldn't have any problem with me being gay. But a deep, twisted instinct to survive—to prevent more disapproval and disgust—kicked in before I could find my courage. I didn't want her to reject me or think I'd never cared about her. That wasn't true at all; I had loved Debbie in my way. It differed from my love for Brian, but it was still real. Of course, I could have explained all that, but fear kept me silent.

"I'm not married," I said. "Not yet, at least. I'd like to settle down eventually, but I'm very busy with work. I'm an urgent care doctor at the Wellington Hospital." Conveniently, I failed to mention that my employment had been terminated after I was charged with assault. "I own a flat in Marylebone. I live alone, so it can get a bit lonely, but it's a great investment." Obviously, I was lying about the last bit, but I didn't want Debbie to think badly of me.

"Wow, so you actually made it happen." She looked impressed. "And I heard you were in the Falklands War."

"You heard that?" It took me aback—and unnerved me—to think that she knew anything about my life.

"It was in the papers," she explained. Then she smiled. "Your old man must have been proud of you. I know he gave you a hard time when you were young, but he must have mellowed out now that his son is a war hero!"

"Yes." I allowed myself a few glorious moments to imagine my father alive and well and proud of me. That's how life might have really turned out had I just never come out to him, I thought bitterly. "He's very proud," I lied. "We patched things up after the war, and our relationship has been good ever since."

"I'm so happy for you." She squeezed my arm. "It's funny running into you like this. I was just thinking about you and everything we went through... wishing we had stayed in touch. We were the only ones who understood what we went through, weren't we? No one else could get it except you. And I cut you out..."

"It's okay," I said as her hand tightened on my arm. "I understood then, and I understand now. It was too difficult to be around me or any reminders of the abortion."

Debbie blinked, and for a moment, her face clouded. I held my breath, afraid that mentioning the abortion would upset her, but then her face cleared, and she nodded. "Yeah. Still... I wish I'd handled things better."

"Well, it's like you said. We were young. We didn't know what we wanted. And it's not your fault. I should have kept in touch with you, too, checked in to see how you were doing."

She was looking away, and for several moments, we stood in silence, the weight of the past and the choices we'd made then filling the air between us. Finally, she turned back to me. "Well, I suppose we're both doing well now, so maybe it was better we went our own ways. Maybe we wouldn't have turned out so happy if we'd stayed in each other's lives."

"I doubt that," I murmured.

Debbie grimaced. "It's hard not to wonder, I suppose... about the paths not taken." Her eyes swept over me, and she looked sad for the first time during our conversation. "Do you ever wonder about that?"

Truthfully, the answer was yes. Many times over the last few months, I had thought about a path where I hadn't assaulted a policeman. I wouldn't be facing prison on that path, but I also wouldn't know about my HIV status. It was better it had happened in some ways because it had forced me to take stock of my life and health. But then there was Brian... I sometimes thought about the paths I could have taken that still had Brian in them. But would he have been happy in those scenarios? Or did being with me mean forcing himself to give up a part of himself?

"Maybe there are no paths not taken," I said slowly. "Maybe we're always going to make the same decisions when given the same options because that's who we are. And there's no changing who we are."

Debbie looked thoughtful. "I never thought of it that way."

I shrugged, suddenly self-conscious to wax philosophical when I didn't know what I was talking about. And it wasn't good to linger too long on regret. I'd spent years regretting everything that had happened with my dad, and it had never done me any good.

"Well, it was nice to see you," Debbie said, and we shook hands. "Maybe we can go for lunch sometime. You could meet my kids!"

"Yes," I said. "I'd like that." But I knew I would never meet her kids. Not when they would remind me of the child we never had. And not when she might catch me in my lies and discover that I hadn't lived the happy life of my dreams.

I felt a faint tug of painful uncertainty as she darted across the street toward the Underground. If Debbie had kept the baby and we'd raised it together, maybe I never would have come out. I'd have been unhappy all my life, but I wouldn't now have HIV. And I'd be a father.

Then again, maybe what I said was right: maybe there was no way we could have chosen that path because that would require us to be different people.

Talking to Debbie got me thinking a lot about the past decade and the choices I'd made, and I realised, a few days after seeing her, how much I wished I'd lived the life I'd described to her. If I'd never come out, then perhaps I would have. I could have been secretly gay and made my father proud. We really might have patched things up after the war.

These thoughts brought up old, painful feelings. I spent the next few days locked in my room, not speaking to anyone, even Jesse. I couldn't get Brian out of my mind. His words still echoed in my ears: *But I need to know tha' you're not still chasing after 'is approval, even in death.*

I'd been so sure he was wrong—that I had no desire to still impress my dad. But it wasn't true. Because now, all I could think about was the life I'd outlined to Debbie, in which he was still alive, and we were closer than ever.

As I watched the news coverage of the Desert Storm campaign, I realised there was still a way for me to make him proud.

I'd been out of the Royal Marines for four years by then. But hearing about the necessity of liberating Kuwait from Iraq, I had a strong and undeniable urge to see combat again.

Of course, part of me was worried that this instinct to serve overseas in a conflict area was the same instinct that had led me to have unsafe sex with strangers: an urge to self-destruct. My father had had this urge, and I clearly did as well. But I convinced myself that the reason I wanted to rejoin the Royal Marines was a selfless one: that I wanted to spend whatever time remained to me serving my country. Maybe part of me also thought it would be better to die while saving lives overseas than in a hospital from AIDS.

I'm not stupid. I realised I couldn't treat men directly whilst having HIV, but I'd seen conflict before, and that made me the perfect person to oversee a team of medics in this war.

However, the recruitment officer at the centre I visited the next day had other ideas.

The officer scanned through my questionnaire and then looked up at me seriously. "According to this, you have an upcoming court case, Mr Turner. Unfortunately, that would disqualify you from enlisting." I couldn't help but feel a twinge of anger and embarrassment as the much younger officer spoke to me in a condescending tone.

"My barrister rates my chances. Assuming I get off, can I reenlist?" I mumbled.

The recruitment officer snorted. "Please stop wasting my time, Mr Turner. I thank you for your previous service, but you'll never reenlist. It says here you have HIV, which means you are gay or very unlucky.

And we do not allow gay people into the Army. What you wish to get up to in your free time is your business, but we will not have you soiling our good name. Honestly..." His eyes glittered maliciously. "You should be ashamed of yourself for trying to reenlist. If you cared about your country, you wouldn't waste my time." The officer rose from his chair with a stern expression, his hand reaching out to grasp the door handle. He swung the heavy wooden door open, gesturing with his palm for me to exit the room. As I walked past him, he shook his head.

I left feeling almost as bad as I had when I'd received my HIV diagnosis. The officer's rejection brought up deep feelings of grief, resentment, self-loathing, loneliness, and anger. The military had been my home, my brotherhood, and to be rejected by them felt like my family turning its back on me. Again.

It felt like my dad kicking me out of the house. Again.

When I arrived home, my stomach was churning, and I was sure I would be sick. Unsure if this was the trauma of another rejection or my HIV finally manifesting as AIDS, I went to the kitchen to make myself some ginger tea. That always calmed me down.

No one was in the kitchen. It was still early, before dinnertime. I had just poured the hot water from the kettle into a mug of freshly cut ginger when the telephone rang.

I answered absentmindedly and was surprised to hear Debbie's voice on the other end.

"Hello?" She sounded nervous. "Is Edward Turner there?"

"This is Eddy," I said. "Debbie?"

"Oh! Yes, it's me." She laughed awkwardly. "Sorry to bother you."

"It's no bother." I took a sip of my tea and leaned back against the counter. "It's always good to hear your voice. How did you get my number?"

"I looked your mum up in the phone book, and she gave me this number. She said you live with a group of boys in Earl's Court and that you might be hard to get a hold of?"

"Oh..." My stomach lurched as I realised she had caught me in my lies. "Right... Look, Debbie, I know I said I live alone, but—"

"You also said you live in Marylebone." She didn't sound angry, just confused.

"Right..." Sweat beaded on my forehead. "I'm sorry for lying. It's only me being ashamed of the truth."

Debbie took a deep breath on the other end of the line. "I am too, Eddy."

For a moment, her words didn't compute. "What do you mean? You're ashamed of me?"

"No, I'm ashamed of myself."

"What do you—"

"Eddy, there's something I must tell you," she interrupted. "Something I've been lying about, too."

"Okay..."

When she spoke again, her words rushed together as if she were forcing herself to speak before she lost her nerve. "I didn't have the abortion. All those years ago. I kept the baby. That's why I dropped out of uni." The phone felt slick in my hands, and I knew that I had stopped breathing. She took a deep, rattling breath. "Eddy... you have a fifteen-year-old son."

Chapter Thirty-One

Debbie and I agreed to meet at the Natural History Museum the following weekend. She would bring Carson with her so he and I could get to know each other. Debbie would be there the whole time in case anything went wrong, but she promised to give us space.

"He wants to meet you," she told me on the phone the afternoon she informed me I had a son. "He's wanted to meet you for years."

"Why didn't you tell me sooner?" I blurted out. My shock was so great that it had squeezed out most of my anger, but I could feel it there, flickering on the edge of my consciousness. Debbie had kept my son from me. It was unforgivable, really.

"I didn't want to cause more problems between you and your dad," she said. Her voice was small, evidence of the guilt she felt. "He didn't want us to have the baby, and he seemed to think you'd thrown your future away."

"There was nothing I could do that would make my dad proud of me," I said automatically. "At least his disapproval would have been worth it for my son."

"I'm s-so s-sorry, Eddy." In her nervousness, her stammer had returned, and I felt a flare of empathy. "I was so s-scared back then," she continued. "Overwhelmed. Unsure of what was right and w-what was wrong. I know I didn't make the right choices."

"So that day you went to the abortion clinic..." My mind drifted back to that day, to the hours I'd spent in nervous anticipation. "Did you just not go through with it?"

And then she told me the whole story: how she'd gone to the clinic but, once there, had changed her mind. She realised she'd gone to medical school for all the wrong reasons and didn't know what she really wanted from life. It would have been easier to figure it out without a baby, but she just couldn't do it.

"I ended up leaving," she explained. "After that, I knew I couldn't go back to the house. You were there, and I thought you would want me to get the abortion. So, I had my brothers pick up my stuff. My parents wanted me to stay at university, and I tried transferring, but I eventually dropped out. After Carson was born, I lived with my parents for a while and got a job in a pub. When I returned to uni, my parents helped me out, but it was hard... When all my friends were living in flats with their friends and partying, I was pulling pints, going to university, and taking care of a baby. Those were dark years. I was afraid I'd made the wrong choice."

"I would have helped you out," I said. "I wish you'd told me, Debbie. It would have been easier for you with me sharing the load."

"I know, but the more time passed, the more ashamed I was that I hadn't told you, and the harder it became to reach out. Then I heard you were in the Falklands, and I thought you were probably happy you didn't have a kid holding you back from pursuing what you wanted. I was sure you wouldn't want to give up your young adult life the way I'd given up mine."

My young adult life. Had that really been so wonderful? Looking back, it seems like all I did was make one mistake after another. Whether it was to gain my father's approval or in response to his rejection, I couldn't seem to get things right.

Brian was the one good thing that had happened to me in my young adult life. Would I have been able to fall in love with Brian and live with him if I'd had a young child to care for?

The thought left me cold. It seemed impossible to have come out as gay and pursued relationships with men while sharing custody of a child. Not to mention that I would never have moved to Sheffield if my son had been in London. The thought of a life without ever knowing Brian filled me with fear. On the other hand, I felt deep-seated rage and despair at the knowledge that I'd missed out on fifteen years of my son's life. And what could be a more worthwhile pursuit in life than raising my son? Wasn't knowing my son more important than loving a man I'd lost?

The thought made my heart ache. My own father hadn't seemed to care about being a father or about knowing his son. But I wouldn't have been like him; I would have been an exceptional father. I will be an exceptional father, I corrected myself.

Euphoria bloomed in my chest, and I gripped the phone harder.

"I want to meet him," I said, and tears came to my eyes. "I want to meet my son."

I got to the Natural History Museum early and waited anxiously on a bench near the entrance. My eyes kept scanning the crowd for Debbie, even though I knew she wasn't due for another ten minutes. Time slid by at an interminable speed, but at last, I glimpsed her walking towards the museum, a tall ginger-haired gangly boy by her side.

It was my first glimpse of my son. Immediately, my heart sped up, and my palms started to sweat. I stood and waved, and Debbie caught sight of me. She smiled and waved back, then glanced at her son. He was staring at me, his expression guarded. The two of them approached, and Carson slid his hands into his pockets. Disappointment curdled in my stomach, but I pushed it away. I couldn't expect him to throw himself into my arms. Even if that was what I wanted more than anything else.

They stopped in front of me, and Debbie put a hand on her son's shoulder. Our son's shoulder. "Carson, this is Edward Turner." She smiled at me. "Your father."

Carson blinked, then held out his hand. "It's nice to meet you," he mumbled, his voice shaking slightly.

I gripped his hand and shook it. His palms were sweating. Quickly, we both let go. Carson was staring at anything but me. Part of me wished I could do the same. But I had to be strong now; I had to show him there was no reason to be afraid or embarrassed.

Debbie cleared her throat, breaking the awkward silence. "Why don't we go get tickets?" she suggested.

Once inside, Debbie said she fancied a cup of tea and would wait for us in the cafe while we explored the exhibits. After she left, there was another awkward moment when Carson still couldn't look directly at me. He was watching his feet, his brow furrowed in concentration. I steeled myself and placed a hand on his shoulder. At once, he looked up at me, eyes wide.

"What do you want to see first?" I asked. "The dinosaurs?" We were standing in the towering entrance hall of the museum, with a huge diplodocus skeleton in front of us, so it was the first thing that came to my mind. The pure size of the entrance hall made my voice echo. The place looked more like a train station or cathedral than a museum. It was exquisite. The architecture would have mesmerised me if I hadn't been so focused on Carson.

Carson shook his head. "Did you know there are a hundred and fifteen real skeletons here?"

"Really?"

"Yeah, and the rest are just made to look real." He seemed to brighten, flushed by the pleasure of being so knowledgeable. "We used to come here on school trips," he added as a way of explanation.

I shook my head in wonder. "So, if you've seen the dinosaurs before, maybe we should start somewhere else?" Carson hesitated as if uncertain whether I would approve of his choice. So I added gently, "I want to see your favourite exhibit."

He bit his lip, still looking doubtful. "It's a bit weird, but I like the spirit collection—it's named after the alcohol that preserves the items."

Five minutes later, Carson led me through the museum, past impressive skeletal remains and recreations of some of the earth's most majestic and beautiful creatures, to the spirit room. It was large and lined with shelves. Various-sized jars were stacked neatly on these shelves, each containing a fully preserved animal floating in yellowing alcohol.

Carson was right: the room was weird. There were jars containing octopi, squid, strange-looking fish, and even mammals. In the putrid-yellow liquid, they looked almost otherworldly. Along with the smaller jars along the walls, there were also large containers on the floor, which held some of the bigger specimens.

Carson watched me furtively as we walked around the room. "Everyone at school thought this room was boring. They preferred the dinosaur exhibits. But I find this stuff interesting. Especially the bodily organs."

I raised an eyebrow. "Carson, do you know what I do for a living?"

He bit his lip again. "Mum said you're a doctor…?" Many of his sentences, I realised, were questions, and I wondered if he was bullied at school for being different if it had made him doubtful of himself. The thought tugged at my heartstrings, and I wished I could have pulled him into a hug.

"That's right," I said, smiling. "I work in A & E. And I used to be a doctor in the Army. So, I've seen most human body organs at some point. This"—I gestured to the room—"this is nothing."

"Really?" Carson looked impressed. "What kind of stuff have you seen?"

I hesitated, sure that Debbie would disapprove of me telling Carson about some of the more horrific injuries I'd seen. But my son looked at me with such eager curiosity that I couldn't resist.

"Well, one time someone came in with their shin bone sticking all the way out of their leg," I began, and Carson's eyes grew wider.

"Eurgh!" he whisper-shrieked. "I bet that wasn't pretty?"

"Yeah, I wanted to rectify that one as quickly as possible."

"Did you gag when you saw it?"

I shook my head. "You can't when you're the doctor who has to treat it. But it was gnarly."

"What else?" he asked eagerly. "What else did you see?"

I thought for a moment. "Well… there was this guy who'd had an accident with a chainsaw. He'd cut his hand almost clean off. It was hanging on by a tendon."

"Uggggghhhh." But even with his face twisted with disgust, I could tell that Carson enjoyed this story.

"He technically died on the table," I continued. "From shock. But I brought him back with CPR and reattached the hand. He made a full recovery."

"You brought someone back to life!" Now Carson looked doubly impressed. "That's... incredible." He stared around at the jars of dead creatures. "I wish you could bring some of these animals back to life..."

Together, we strolled around the room until we stopped in front of the largest case of all. Inside was a giant squid. A card beside the display explained that the squid's name was Archie and that a fishing trawler had accidentally caught him when he was swimming at a depth of two hundred and twenty metres.

"Giant squid are so rare that people used to think they were a myth," Carson said as he stared down at the tank.

"I didn't know that," I admitted to Carson. Although I could easily believe it was true. If I wasn't looking at this giant squid in front of me, I might not have believed it was real.

"The first time I saw the squid," Carson went on, "I thought, what if it wasn't really dead but just in hibernation, like in *Alien* when Ripley hibernates in her pod or all the people that HAL kills in *2001: A Space Odyssey*? I mean, I know these animals are dead, but sometimes they just feel like creatures out of a sci-fi movie."

"Do you like space?" I asked, and Carson nodded vigorously.

"I like science fiction, really. Especially sci-fi comic books. I'd really like..."

I nudged him. "You'd like what?"

"I'd like to write a comic book someday." He smiled shyly. "Sometimes at home, I sketch the animals in the jars I see here. When we see aliens in movies, we always think they're so strange-looking. But truthfully, none of those aliens are that much weirder-looking than anything that already exists in the world. It's just that most of the really bizarre-looking animals are under the water. So, sketching the animals here gives me ideas for how I'll design the aliens in my comic book. Archie is actually a big inspiration." He nodded at the giant squid.

"The main race of aliens in the comic book I'm writing kind of look like giant squids. And they use their tails to move through space like squids move through water."

I was so impressed and astonished by what Carson said that, for a moment, I didn't know how to respond. My hesitation, however, seemed to make him nervous because he blushed and looked back down at his feet.

"It's probably s-stupid…" he stammered, and I heard an echo of his mother's stutter.

"No, Carson, it's not stupid." I touched his shoulder again, and he looked back up at me. He was hardly any shorter than me, and I knew that he would surpass me in height in a few years. But it still felt like comforting a small child, to feel his body relax under my gentle touch. "It's brilliant, in fact."

"It is?"

"It is. In fact, I'd love to see your comic book sometime if you're interested in showing me."

"It's not done yet," he rushed to say, but I just shook my head.

"That's alright. I'd love to see it in progress. But if you'd rather wait until you're done, that's fine, too."

I didn't say that I might not be around when he finished his comic book. It was possible I'd be in prison or, worse, dead.

For the first time since my HIV diagnosis, it hit me exactly how much I didn't want to die. I wanted to live, and not for myself. Certainly not so that I earn my father's posthumous approval. No, I wanted to live for my son. So that I could see him grow up and see all he accomplished. Because no matter what he did with his life, I knew I would be proud of him.

"I'd like to show you," he said, and my heart soared. "Maybe we can get together again, and I can bring it with me?"

"I'd love that."

After leaving the spirit room, we wandered through the rest of the Natural History Museum, and Carson told me more about himself. He liked school, especially science and maths, and had a close group of friends who all read comic books. He wasn't a big talker, but the longer we spent together, the more I realised that his shyness wasn't just because of my presence. Carson was a quiet, contemplative young man who got lost in his thoughts. If I was being honest, he reminded me a little of myself at that age, how I had been more interested in the internal landscape of my mind than in the external world. The difference, however, was that he had a tight-knit group of friends. Hearing him describe them, I wanted to weep. With a good group of friends, a mother who loved him, and a stepfather who treated him as his own, Carson would never be alone like I had been.

At last, after we'd walked through all the exhibits, I couldn't think of a reason we shouldn't collect Debbie. She was still in the cafe reading, and she looked happy as she greeted us.

"Did you have a fun day?" she asked Carson as we made our way to the exit.

He nodded and blushed, and she laughed and tried to ruffle his hair. He was so tall that this was difficult, and he dodged her easily with a half-whispered "Muuuuum" of protest.

"It was a very nice day," I agreed. Carson smiled at me, and I grinned back.

Outside of the museum, I went for a hug. Carson seemed surprised, but he hugged me back. "We should do this again," he muttered as we broke apart, not making eye contact.

"I'd love that," I said. "Then you can show me your comic book."

I hugged Debbie goodbye, then watched as the two of them walked away together until they were lost in the crowd of people.

My chest felt painful and constricted, and breathing was difficult. A fire had erupted in my mind, an urgent and all-consuming conflagration, and it was burning through me now. It was the will to live, see my son grow up, and be the father I hadn't had. That didn't just mean trying to find any experimental trial I could that might cure my disease. It also meant fighting like hell against the charge of manslaughter so that no matter how long I had left to live, I could spend those years in freedom with my son.

That day, as a fire raged through me, I finally burned the part of me that had, for so long, sought the approval of my father. That day, I was reborn. I no longer cared about my father's approval, and I never would again.

Chapter Thirty-Two

"So that's what brings me to today. Here, in this courtroom, where I have told you the story of my life."

I look up from the bench where I'm sitting, and my eyes briefly land on Mum's. They are wide with astonishment. This is the first time she has heard my full story. She has asked questions before but never wanted to know the full truth. I think she suspected it would hurt her too much. But now, I have told it in front of her and everyone else who is listening. And I don't regret telling my truth. Mum needs to know all the pain I went through because of who I am. I'm not trying to punish her; I don't want my mother to feel any more pain than she already has in this life. But she has to know so that maybe, someday, the world can change.

This is the most crucial point, so I look at the jurors and speak it out loud to them.

"This is my story," I reiterate. "You know now what events led me to the poll tax protests and why I assaulted the plaintiff. You can understand, hopefully, the pain and despair that drove me to that moment. That isn't an excuse for my actions. I'm not asking you to find me not guilty or say it wasn't my fault. I, and I alone, beat the plaintiff. It was wrong, and I shouldn't have done it. But my hope in telling you my story is that you can see that I didn't act in a vacuum: that I deserve leniency in my sentencing, that I acted in self-defence, and that the plaintiff not only attacked me but my friends beforehand, too. I have spent my life fighting injustice, but I'm not a violent man. In fact, I've spent my life trying to heal and save others, even when I was told the only way to be a man is to be violent. On this one occasion when I was violent, I did so because my father conditioned me to do so—to fight back."

I take a deep breath. The jurors are watching me, their expressions still neutral. But I think I detect some sympathy in the slow blink of several eyes. The judge also hasn't stopped me from speaking, which is promising. After all, if the jury convicts me, it is she who will decide my sentence.

"So much in my life has been preventable," I continue, to the room at large. "If my father hadn't raised me to value violence over compassion, then I think I wouldn't have made most—if not all—of the bad choices I made. I know I wouldn't be standing before you now, begging you to give me a second chance. Not because I didn't do wrong, but because I have finally learned my lesson: that to live for my father's approval was a mistake. It only ever ruined my life, repeatedly. Meeting my son taught me this. It would kill me if he lived his entire life trying to impress me. I want him to know that he has my love, support, and admiration, no matter what he does; that my love is unconditional." I take a deep, rattling breath. "That's why I'm asking for a second chance, for the minimum sentencing required of my charges. So that I can help raise my son better than my father raised me. So that I can break the cycle of violence, of fathers abandoning their sons, of leaving them feeling like disappointments. Please..."

I look the judge deep in the eyes. She holds my gaze, and I think I see the conflict raging in them. "Please let me be the father to my son that I never had. Please give me a chance to redeem myself. Isn't it enough that I only have a few years left to live? Isn't that punishment for my crimes? I will die long before I can watch my son grow old. Please, give me these few years with him at least so that I can heal what's broken and ensure that he doesn't live with the same regrets and mistakes I lived with."

I fall silent at last, and whispers fill the courtroom. I know the onlookers are discussing my worthiness of being given a reprieve. There's no way to know if their opinions are friendly or not. However, when I glance at the audience, I think I see sympathy in their eyes.

"Order in the court!" the judge calls out, banging her gavel, and the whispers cease. I turn back to her. She is gazing at me steadily.

"Thank you for your statement, Mr Turner," she says. "You have given us all much to think about. The court will adjourn now, and the prosecution will begin their cross-examination tomorrow."

The following two days are filled with cross-examinations and witness statements, including from the widow of the policeman I attacked, who tearfully insists her husband was faithfully heterosexual, and which is countered by testimony from the preeminent Scottish physician in AIDS diagnoses, Dr Roy Robertson, who insists the officer's HIV could not have become AIDS in such a short timeframe. Then the trial is over, and all that's left is the final verdict. Although the evidence against me is circumstantial, the prosecution is arguing that I behaved recklessly, that as a doctor, I shouldn't have been living in a house with HIV-positive men, where I could easily contract it and spread it to my patients, and that as a gay man, I should have been getting tested regularly. Although none of this is enough to convict me on its own, my barrister says they're trying to paint me as a man of low moral character to the jury. It will be easier to believe circumstantial evidence if they already think I'm a dangerously irresponsible person.

With no sleep the night before, I look harried and ill, and I wonder if the jurors will think my HIV has finally become full-blown AIDS and take pity on me.

The trial starts at 09:00. When I arrive, the courtroom is already packed. I can't look at anyone as I file inside, although I know my flatmates are there. Even though they are hungover—and possibly still drunk from last night's antics—I can hear them cheering for me over the hubbub inside the courtroom. A handful of reporters yell at me for a comment as I pass.

When the judge enters, we all rise. I feel numb and anxious all at once. My body doesn't feel real; it is as if I am floating above it, watching myself from above. The jury files in. Their foreman is holding an envelope, and he looks very serious as he clutches it to his chest.

"Will the defendant please rise?" the judge says once she's settled behind the bench. Again, I stand.

The court clerk faces the jury. "Mr Foreman," he begins, "will you please rise?" The foreman stands, and my heart leaps into my throat. "Have you reached a verdict upon which you are all agreed? Please answer Yes or No."

The foreman's eyes flicker. "Yes," he says, his voice thin and reedy.

"On the first count of assaulting a police officer, do you find the defendant guilty or not guilty?"

"We find him guilty," the foreman responds. Air rushes into my lungs, and I think I might faint from the sudden oxygenation.

"On the second count of disturbing the peace," the clerk continues, "do you find the defendant guilty or not?"

"We find him guilty," the foreman says. I swallow. That isn't so bad. Just disturbing the peace...

"And on the third count of manslaughter," the clerk says, and the room seems to grow even more tense with anticipation, "do you find the defendant guilty or not guilty?"

For a fraction of a second, I think the foreman glances at me, but I could be wrong. He clears his throat.

"We find him guilty."

There are gasps in the courtroom behind me and even a few outraged shouts—I'm pretty sure I hear Jesse's incensed cry. My guilt has been a foregone conclusion. It is the sentencing that will decide my fate. Meanwhile, I seem to float higher above myself, staring apathetically down at my body.

The foreman sits, and the courtroom fills with commotion: onlookers whispering to each other and my mum's stifled, despairing moans.

"The sentencing will happen now," I hear my barrister say, as if from far away. "Since manslaughter constitutes inevitable custody requirements."

I nod. I'm still floating somewhere above, not fully present in what's happening. Dimly, I hear the judge thanking the jury for fulfilling their public duty and warning them against discussing their deliberations with anyone outside of the jury.

I tune out after that, only to return to reality when my barrister puts his hand on my shoulder and tells me it's time for my sentencing. Again, I stand and face the judge. "Mr Turner," she begins. Her eyes are intelligent and soft, and seeing the gentleness of her expression, hope once again flares in my breast. "I want you to know that I have been considering your case long and hard, taking into consideration everything you told us about your upbringing. I will not pretend that your story did not move me. You have, indeed, suffered from the prejudice levied against gay men. It is abominable to me that in the twentieth century in Great Britain, people of an underrepresented group should still face such egregious persecution. Your relationship with your father also explains why you became the man you are today. And, of course, I feel for you and your hope of reconnecting with your son and breaking, as you say, the cycle of fatherly abandonment." She shuffles the papers in front of her, and I hold my breath.

"When deciding your sentencing, I am taking into consideration your background, your service to this country in the Falklands, your character, your years of helping people as a doctor, and the fact you acted in self-defence. It is also relevant that you are a father and that you have a terminal illness and may need medical attention sooner rather than later, which would be a drain on public resources should you need to receive it in prison. Added to this, that the evidence supporting the manslaughter charge is circumstantial at best..." Here, she threw a disdainful look at the prosecution. "Considering this all, I sentence you to five years in prison."

Five years. I slam back into my body with all the force of an avalanche, and my knees buckle. Then I collapse back into my seat. Someone is crying. Probably my mum. People are yelling. Probably my flatmates. My life is flashing before my eyes: the years playing doctor with my friends, getting bullied at school, winning the boxing match, saving Shaun's life, the night I thought Debbie was getting an abortion, the fight with Teddy in the Falklands, meeting Brian, losing Brian, and meeting my son. Carson's shy smile as he explained how the alien species in his comic book look like squids.

It is as if I am already dead because I might as well be: I will die in prison. Very few people last longer than a few years with HIV.

I close my eyes as the tears pour.

Chapter Thirty-Three

I am thirty-three years old in the spring of 1991, and I have been in prison for nine months when I begin to feel my body dying.

A funny thing, feeling yourself nearing death. It isn't just the weakness, or the constant cough, or the sores that give you away: it's the taste in your mouth, like rotting flesh; it's the smell of death, like that of a decayed animal in your house that you can't seem to find; it's the feeling of disintegration, like your body is decomposing in front of you before you've even been able to enjoy your last few moments on this earth.

The one good thing about having AIDS in prison is that I'm kept isolated from the rest of the inmates. The state doesn't want other prisoners to become infected, as this will increase their medical expenses. With the number of fights that happen in prison, it would be all too easy for me to infect some of my fellow inmates. I think they're also worried about the disease being sexually transmitted since prisoners use sex for power and protection.

Of course, many things are difficult about being isolated in the prison. The hardest part is that I don't have many people to talk to. A few other prisoners are kept in isolation near me, but they're not the most talkative. Even if they were, these are the most violent and dangerous inmates—the type they can't trust around the general population—so I'm not exactly eager to become well acquainted.

My closest companions are my guards. They're not bad people, it turns out. Although a little wary of me at first—probably because of my AIDS and knowing I'm a homosexual—they warm up to me when they see how polite I am. I always say please and thank you and never yell at them. I remember to ask after their wives and kids. They're used to being screamed at and threatened all day, and my kindness goes a long way. Soon, we're friendly, and they even sometimes bring me treats, like a book or a crossword puzzle.

The loneliness, however, is the price I gladly pay for the relative freedom of my isolation. I'm not in solitary confinement; I just have my own room on a separate block. Of course, I spend lots of time outside of prison for hospital visits under the supervision of a guard. I know this amount of time will grow, but for a while, at least, I will be mostly in my cell. I never have to worry about any of the violence that other men face in prison. This is a relief. After a lifetime of reconciling my violent nature with my desire to help people, I'm glad to no longer have to worry about the temptation to fight.

I spend my days working out, reading, and writing letters. Many of these are to my mum, Carson, Brian, and Jesse, but even more are to newspapers, news stations, editors, and publishers. I am convinced that my story needs to be told. Although HIV/AIDS has finally gotten some of the attention it was due, there is still more work that needs to be done to raise awareness about the disease. I don't care about telling my story for fame or fortune; I'm motivated by the desire to help others feel less alone. To show the world the destructive power of homophobia and familial rejection. And to change hearts and minds about both being gay and about AIDS.

The crazy thing is, it is working.

My barrister was the first person to tell me this. He visited me in prison after my first three months, and he was excited as he told me that radio and television stations had requested interviews with me.

"It all started because several gay rights organisations started camping outside of the court," he said through the Plexiglas in the visitation room. "They claim it's homophobic that the courts convicted you of giving the officer HIV when there's no definitive evidence."

Soon, scores of more gay rights activists were protesting outside of the courtroom and even the prison. Newspapers began writing about my case and the protests; television stations covered the story. Several channels have interviewed me. Inside the prison, the other inmates learned about how I got there, and one of my guard friends told me I was being celebrated as a minor celebrity because I effectively killed a policeman.

"I didn't kill him," I told him, scowling. "At least, we don't know if I did. And I certainly didn't mean for it to happen if I did."

"I know," the guard reassured me. "I just thought it'd be interesting to know how positively the other prisoners view you."

I didn't want to be celebrated for being violent, and I asked the guard not to tell me anything else about this.

Being a gay man who stood up for the poll tax protestors and then eloquently told my story—all the good and all the bad—in a courtroom full of witnesses feels like a much better reason to be famous. All the newspaper articles have called me brave. Gay rights organisations have given me awards that I'm not able to accept until my prison term is over. A legal action fund for inmates has looked into how I can be granted parole early on compassionate release grounds. And, best of all, as Jesse and Brian tell me when they visit, people are talking about AIDS more than ever now.

"Donations are flooding into ACT UP," Jesse told me enthusiastically on his last visit. "And a lot of the donations are in your name."

I tried, and failed, to hide my emotion, and Brian held my hand before the prison guards told us to stop.

"Y'ar a hero to so many, Eddy," he murmured, and the admiration on his face was the best thing I had seen in a long time. "So many folks are comin' forward abaht their HIV statuses at their workplaces, inspired by ya courage. It's normalisin' what were once a taboo topic."

"And I know more than a few people who have said you've changed their relationships with their parents," Jesse continued. "Gay men have been writing letters to the house, saying that you are the reason they've finally cut ties with their mums and dads, rather than trying to win their love and approval. They've realised they can't change their parents' minds about being gay and that they don't want to sacrifice their own happiness anymore."

"Wow." I couldn't manage anything else, and both men seemed to understand. Brian opened his mouth, and I suddenly knew he was about to tell me he loved me. But I shook my head, and he nodded and said nothing.

I can't let Brian love me—not like that, not anymore. Not when we'll never be able to be together. He has to move on and be happy with someone healthy and free. He can't waste his one precious life loving a man who will die in prison. If having AIDS has taught me anything, it's this: that life is short, and we need to spend it living fully and happily, not chasing after the affection of someone who can't properly give it.

The one person who doesn't seem to think I'm a hero, however, is Debbie. I've also written her multiple letters explaining the situation, apologising repeatedly, and asking her to come see me, to let Carson come see me. I know prison isn't pleasant, but I also think he's old enough to deal with its challenges. And I want to see him before my time runs out. In his letters, Carson says he wants to visit, but Debbie isn't sure it's a good idea. She, of course, hasn't responded to any of my letters.

Which is why today, nine months into my prison sentence, when I'm told I have a visitor when I wasn't expecting one, I assume that it's my mother, surprising me.

I'm shocked when I walk into the visitation room and see my son sitting on the other side of a table.

Carson looks resolute, determined. He has also grown taller, and the muscles in his arms and shoulders are more developed. He's becoming a man, and the realisation makes me stop dead.

When he sees me, he stands, and I walk slowly over to the table that he is on. My heart is hammering in my throat. I wish I'd made myself look a little more presentable. My hair is greasy, and I know I look gaunt and sickly. At least there are no sores on my face right now. Some are on other parts of my body, but nothing is visible. I don't want Carson seeing how sick I am; I'm not even sure if he knows.

"You're here," I say, and he nods.

"I wanted to see you." He doesn't look scared, which impresses me. "I wanted to come sooner, but Mum wouldn't let me. She thought it might be dangerous for me."

"Does she know you're here?"

"Yes. She had to sign me in because I'm underage. But it took me nine months to convince her."

"I've been writing to her," I say. "Asking her to let you come see me. But I understand that she's been worried."

Carson shakes his head, and for a second, his eyes flash with anger. "It's perfectly safe for me. I'm not a child anymore; I can handle this. She just doesn't think I'm strong enough. She acts like I'm still a little boy."

"Mums always try to protect their children," I say softly, even as my heart wrenches. "When I was a child, my mum tried her best to protect me. That might change when you grow up and become a man, but you can't blame your mum for that. She's only looking out for you because she loves you."

"If she'd really wanted to protect me, she wouldn't have kept you from me for so many years," Carson snaps. "And now it's too late! You're in prison for five years. And you have… AIDS."

He hesitates before this last word, and it's the first time I see a flash of fear across his face. My stomach churns.

"So you know?" I ask quietly. "You know everything?"

"You mean about you being gay?" He nods. "It was in the papers. You're kind of famous, you know." He looks proud as he says this, and I want to weep. "I don't care. It changes nothing. You're still my dad. Anyway, some of the coolest people are gay. David Bowie, George Michael, and I think Prince is—not sure though."

I barely have time to marvel at the difference between my generation and my sons', where he has grown up with gay icons, before he continues, "I've been to some protests to support your release. It's true what they are protesting about. The police have no proof you gave that policeman AIDS."

I lick my lips. I don't want Carson getting into any dangerous situations because of me, but I'm also honoured that he would attend protests in my name. "Does your mother know you've been at protests?" I ask, and he blushes.

"No." He looks stubborn. "You're not gonna lecture me, are you? You were doing crazier stuff than that when you were my age."

I laugh, and this relaxes him a bit. "At fifteen? No, I wasn't. I didn't start making huge life mistakes until my twenties."

"Like me?" Carson quizzes.

I smile and tell Carson that I hadn't been aware he was a decision I was making.

"Well, I'm sixteen now anyway," Carson corrects, and I feel another tug at my heartstrings. I missed his birthday.

"Well, happy belated birthday," I say, then clear my throat. "Look, Carson... I'm not going to lecture you. I know you're going to have fun in life and do wild things. Everyone does. And it's important to have convictions and stand up for them. But I made the mistakes I did because I didn't have loving parents who made me feel whole inside. I spent my twenties partying because I wanted to fill that void. So many of the mistakes I made were because I hoped it would make my father love me." I look at him seriously. "No matter what happens in your life, I want you to know that you don't have that lack. I love you very much. I'm amazed by the things you say and do. And I would give anything to see the man you become."

Carson is quiet for a minute. His eyes are shiny, and his voice is husky when he speaks. "But you barely know me..."

"I know enough," I insist. "Anyway, I wouldn't need to know anything. You're my son, and I love you unconditionally. I was angry with your mother, too, for keeping you from me. But she's a great mum, and she only did what she did to protect you. She couldn't have known that I'd get AIDS or that I'd end up in prison. I know she wishes we had more time together."

He opens his mouth to speak, then pauses. His eyes flicker over my body as if searching for something. "Are you... really ill?" he asks finally, and I can tell it takes a great deal of effort. "As in, do you know yet how long...?"

I don't want him to finish that sentence for his own sake. So I smile sadly. "I'm becoming very ill, yes. The doctors don't know exactly how long I have, but it won't be more than a year or two. It's okay, Carson," I add when the colour drains from his cheeks. "I mean, it's not. I'm obviously devastated that I won't get more time with you. But I want you to know: meeting you, knowing you exist, is the best thing that's ever happened to me. My life has been short, but it's been full. I've lived. I've loved. I've fought for what I believed in. I've saved lives. I've seen distant lands and taken part in events that changed the course of history. But of it all, you're the best, most amazing, most extraordinary, most life-changing thing to happen to me. And if I were to change one thing in my life, it would be to be there for you your entire life, ever since you were born." Carson is crying now, and he's not even pretending not to. For once, I'm not crying. My voice feels steady, sure. Maybe because this is the most important thing I've ever said, and I need him to understand every word. "I'm so grateful to have known you, Carson, even briefly. And I will always be with you. No matter what."

We cry and hug across the table before a guard comes over and tells us not to.

"I'm proud to be your son," he says, and the tears catch in my throat. "I won't let the world forget you or ignore AIDS any longer. You'll see, Dad. I'm going to make you proud."

"You'll always make me proud," I say, and his eyes flicker with understanding. "No matter what you do. No matter the path you choose in life. No matter what you do or don't accomplish. I'll always be proud of you."

They are the words I've always needed to hear, and now I've passed them on to my son. Like a totem. A legacy. And I know they will stay with him, that they will sustain him through all the darkest hours of his life, through all the failures and self-doubt, of which there will be many because there always are; but that they will bolster him and give him confidence, give him strength and endurance to keep going, and show him the way forward, even long after I'm gone.

Epilogue

Edward "Eddy" Leonard Turner passed away on September 14 1992, at King's College Hospital from complications related to AIDS after being granted compassionate leave from HM Prison Wormwood Scrubs. He died peacefully in his sleep, surrounded by his family, friends, and former partners. He was thirty-four years old.

Eddy grew up in Dagenham, London, the son of Leonard and Linda Turner. In his youth, Eddy was best known as a precocious boxer and for saving his classmate's life at the age of fifteen. This experience inspired him to pursue a medical degree, and he graduated from St George's, University of London, with a BMBS in 1981. As a physician, Eddy served as a medical officer in the Royal Marines during the Falklands War of 1982. Those who served with him in 42 Commando remember him as a wartime hero who always practised medicine fairly and justly. After his time in the military, Eddy moved to Sheffield, where he worked as an accident and emergency doctor at Northern General Hospital. While living in Sheffield, Eddy met his longtime partner, Brian Teller. They lived together for four years, including three in London, where they owned a flat in Earl's Court. During their relationship, Eddy and Brian were regulars in the rave scene and enjoyed the vibrant and accepting social life they found available for gay men in London.

Near the end of his life, Eddy became active in political activism and advocacy. He lived in a cooperative where he gave free medical advice and care to young men dying of HIV/AIDS, and he was active in protesting the poll tax. Throughout his life, he was motivated by a deep desire to Do No Harm and to help those in need. His personal life mirrored his career as a healer, in which he always stood up for those less fortunate than himself.

In a final act of courageous truth-telling, Eddy used his arrest and conviction for assaulting a police officer at the poll tax protests to raise awareness around issues of police brutality, HIV/AIDS transmission, and gay rights. His trial became a notorious example of the United Kingdom justice system's bias and discrimination against gay men. During his trial, which was protested by many gay rights advocates, Eddy shed light on the many persecutions gay men face, both interpersonally and politically. In the aftermath of his conviction and imprisonment, he continued his activism from prison, where he raised money for gay rights and prison reform organisations. In lieu of a public funeral, he asked that all funeral costs go to the Broderip Ward and ACT UP to fund AIDS research.

Eddy was preceded in death by his father, Leonard Turner, and is survived by his mother, Linda Turner, and his son, Carson Whittaker. He is remembered fondly by all his friends, including his former partners, Brian Teller and Deborah Whittaker. He was buried privately in Eastbrookend Cemetery, Dagenham, next to his father.

THE END

Reviews

If you enjoyed this book, would you please take a moment to share your thoughts with others? Your review on Amazon, Goodreads, or social media could be the key to reaching new readers. Knowing that my work has resonated with you makes the prospect of writing another book all the more worthwhile.

Thank you for championing literature!

Printed in Great Britain
by Amazon